Captain Christopher Pike—
in his own words!

"Anything, Spock?" I asked.

"I can detect the eggs," he replied. "Anything smaller would be beyond the sensitivity of a hand-held tricorder through this much rock."

"Smaller I'm not worried about," I said. "I just don't want to surprise a kraken sitting on the nest."

My own shadow preceded me, cast by the others' headlamps as I led the way deeper into the aster-oid. I shifted my phaser from hand to hand so I could push off from whichever side of the tunnel I was close to, and I peered around each bend as cautiously as I could, but anything in there had to know we were coming.

It flashed toward us without warning. Spock barely had time to say "Captain, I read—" when two silvery forms burst out of the darkness and came straight for us . . .

STAR TREK®

THE CAPTAIN'S TABLE

BOOK SIX OF SIX

WHERE SEA MEETS SKY

CHRISTOPHER PIKE

AS RECORDED BY JERRY OLTION

THE CAPTAIN'S TABLE CONCEPT BY
JOHN J. ORDOVER AND DEAN WESLEY SMITH

POCKET BOOKS
New York London Toronto Sydney Tokyo Singapore

An *Original* Publication of POCKET BOOKS

POCKET BOOKS, a division of Simon & Schuster Inc.
1230 Avenue of the Americas, New York, NY 10020

This book is published by Pocket Books, a division of Simon & Schuster Inc., under exclusive license from Paramount Pictures.

ISBN: 0-671-02400-0

First Pocket Books printing October 1998

10 9 8 7 6 5 4 3 2 1

POCKET and colophon are registered trademarks of Simon & Schuster Inc.

Printed in the U.S.A.

For my brother, Ray,
who introduced me to *Star Trek*
and helped tune it in
by leaning out the basement window
to turn the beam antenna
while I fiddled with the knobs
on the black-and-white TV.
We did this even when it was 20 degrees below zero.
That's dedication.

Acknowledgments

The idea for the titans came from a convention panel a long time ago in Billings, Montana. We were trying to come up with plausible creatures that might live in space, and we designed something pretty close to what I describe here, but for whatever reason I never could find the right story to feature them in until now. They somehow seemed perfect for Captain Pike to discover, buried deep in a file cabinet in my study.

So for everyone in the audience that afternoon at Treasurecon III, and for Phil Foglio, who drew sketches during the panel (I still have those!)—a great big *Thank You!* Our crazy space whales have finally found their ocean.

WHERE SEA MEETS SKY

Chapter One

EVENING PAINTED the sky orange, and a chill wind off the bay made Christopher Pike shiver as he walked along San Francisco's waterfront. Red and yellow leaves swirled in the air and danced around the other pedestrians on the street. Coming toward him, a young couple struggled to keep control of both their hovercart full of baggage and their exuberant four- or five-year-old son, who called out happily as he passed, "We're going to Affa Centauri!"

"That's nice," said Pike, who had often traveled to Alpha Centauri and beyond. During his ten years as captain of the *Enterprise* he had gone many places indeed, most of them far more distant—and far more exotic—than Sol's nearest neighbor.

History moves in cycles, he thought as the family swept past. The street on which he walked had once been named the Embarcadero because it ran along the wharves, and it was from the wharves that people embarked on sailing ships in their travels around the world. When the age of ships had given way to the age of the airplane, the street had become a commercial center, full of warehouses at one end and tourist shops at the other, but nobody had set out on long journeys from there. Then had come space travel and the need for a good place to launch and land passenger ships. The airport was already too busy, and acreage elsewhere was at a premium for living space, so the fledgling industry had turned to the last open space near the sprawling city: the Bay. Now, four centuries after the Embarcadero's genesis, the same street was once again busy with travelers. They were boarding shuttles to take them into orbit rather than wooden ships that plied the ocean, but the spectacle of families struggling with overpacked bags looked the same no matter where they were headed.

Pike wished them all well, but he was glad to be on solid ground again. He'd done his time in space, and now he was putting that experience to use as fleet captain, assigned to Starfleet Headquarters right here on good old Mother Earth. He had the best of both worlds: an adventurous past and a position of responsibility on his own home planet.

So why did he feel so unfulfilled?

He'd been telling himself for the last year or so that he was just growing restless. It had been five years since he'd brought the *Enterprise* back home for refitting and renovation. He'd originally thought he would resume the conn when the ship was ready to fly again, but it had taken two years to replace all the worn and outdated machinery on board and to increase the crew compliment from 203 to 430, and by then Starfleet had already promoted him out of the job and given it to James Kirk. Pike didn't begrudge him the post; Kirk was a good officer, if a bit impulsive. He would do well if he didn't get himself killed in some defiant act of bravado. And Pike had come to enjoy his new position, but he had to admit he sometimes missed the thrill of facing the unknown.

Not very often, though. That thrill usually came hand in hand with mortal danger, and even when Pike survived it, other members of his crew often didn't. He had lost more friends than he cared to count during his decade on the *Enterprise,* and he had no desire to experience that again. Maybe some captains could go on after a crew fatality without blaming themselves, but he had never been able to. Every time it happened he went through days of anguish and self-recrimination. And every time he took the ship into danger again he worried that his actions would lead to more deaths.

No, he didn't envy Kirk the job.

Another gust of wind bit through his light topcoat. He had underdressed for the weather. Mark Twain had often said that the coldest winter he ever spent was a summer in San Francisco—well, he should have tried it in autumn. The western horizon was clear enough to allow a sunset, but the sky directly overhead threatened rain and the air was humid enough that it felt like mist already. Pike looked at the buildings along the waterfront, seeking a store he could duck into to warm up for a moment, and his eyes came upon a sign he hadn't seen before.

It was an old-style wooden sign, with letters carved deep into planks held together with black iron bands. It projected out over a windowless doorway and swung gently in the wind, its iron chain squeaking softly. The orange light of sunset made the words THE CAPTAIN'S TABLE stand out in bold relief on its rough surface.

Something about the place seemed inviting, yet Pike hesitated before the door. He couldn't very well just duck into a bar for a minute. He would have to order something, and it was a bit early in the evening to start drinking. That wasn't what he had come down here for anyway. He had merely wanted to get some exercise and some fresh air.

On the other hand, he didn't have any place special he had to be.

The first few drops of rain on his face decided him. He was willing to put up with cold, but cold and wet wasn't part of the plan. He reached for the wrought-iron handle on the solid door and tugged it open, noting a faint tingling sensation as he touched it. A security field of some sort? Or . . . a transporter? He turned and looked behind him. The Embarcadero was still there. Not a transport beam, then. It sure had felt like it, though.

"Close the door!" someone shouted from inside.

Pike nearly let it swing back into place without entering, but the rain was picking up so he ducked in and pulled the massive wooden slab closed behind him.

He couldn't tell who had spoken. Everyone in the bar was looking at him. There were a dozen or so people, mostly human, seated in twos and threes at tables between him and the bar itself, where a Klingon woman held down a stool and a tall, heavyset man stood on the other side, polishing a beer glass. The glasses were either very small, Pike thought, or the bartender had huge hands to go with the rest of his bulky frame.

Fortunately he also wore a smile to match. "Don't pay no mind to Jolley, there," he said. "That's just his way of saying 'Hello.'"

Pike nodded. He wouldn't. All his attention was on the Klingon woman. Not because of the unusual bony ridges on her forehead, nor her exotic face with wide, full lips and an enigmatic grin, nor even the ample cleavage revealed by her traditional open-chested battle garb, though Pike found the latter alluring enough for a second look. What drew his attention was the fact that she was there at all. The Klingon Empire and the Federation had been in conflict for nearly fifty years. All-out war seemed imminent, yet here sat a Klingon in a bar on the waterfront not a kilometer from Starfleet Headquarters.

She had to be a member of a peace delegation. She had probably snuck away from their hotel to check out Earth without a chaperone breathing down her neck. Maybe she thought she could seduce someone here in the bar and learn military secrets from them.

She had undoubtedly recognized Pike the moment he walked in. A fleet captain would be well known to the enemy. Well, Pike would keep his eye on her, too. One of the other patrons was no doubt a Secret Service agent assigned to tail her, but it wouldn't hurt to back him up.

He looked for a good place to sit. There was a piano to his immediate left, and a single small table wedged in next to the piano. A lizardlike alien with slits for eyes and talon-sharp fingers was sitting at the table, sipping at a glass full of something red. Pike didn't look too closely; he just nodded and stepped past, unbuttoning his jacket.

Most of the tables were to his left, clustered in a semicircle around a large stone fireplace that popped and flared as if it were burning real wood. The ones nearest the fire were obviously the popular places to sit. Pike didn't see any vacant tables there as he approached the bar.

"What'll you have, Captain?" the bartender asked.

Pike wasn't wearing a uniform, but he assumed the bartender called everyone "captain," after the name of the place. He looked to the mirrored shelves on the back wall to see what kind of stock they kept here, and was surprised to see several bottles of rare and expensive alien liqueurs in among the more common bourbons and gins. He was tempted to ask for Maraltian Seev-ale just to see if they had it, but he wasn't in the mood for the green stuff tonight. "Saurian brandy," he said instead. He had picked up the taste for that on the *Enterprise,* and it was still his favorite drink.

The bartender poured a snifter full from a curved, amber-colored bottle. Pike took a sip and smiled as the volatile spirits warmed their way down, then turned away to look for a quiet table. He didn't want to sit at the bar; he would either have to sit right next to the Klingon woman or close to a scruffy-looking fisherman who had taken a stool halfway between her and the wall.

There was a stairway to the right of the bar and two tables in an alcove between that stair and the front door. Neither table was occupied. Pike went over to the smaller of the two and sat facing the rear of the bar at an angle, neither turning his back on the others nor staring at them. He sipped his brandy and examined the decor while conversations started up again at the other tables.

There was plenty to look at. Artifacts from dozens of worlds hung on the walls. Pike saw drinking mugs with handles for nonhuman hands, wooden carvings of unrecognizable creatures, and metallic hardware that might have been anything from engine parts to alien sex toys. A Klingon *bat'leth* stuck out just overhead, its curved blade buried so deeply into the wood that Pike doubted anyone could remove it without a pry bar. A thick layer of dust on it provided evidence that few people even tried. A Vulcan harp hanging from a peg next to it apparently came down more often; there was no dust on it, and the strings were discolored near the fingerboard from use.

That was a good sign. Pike liked music better than fighting, too.

The fisherman belched loudly, then said to the bartender, "Another tankard o' grog." He looked over at Pike while the bartender refilled his stoneware mug. Pike looked away—the guy had a drunk and despondent air about him—but when the fisherman got his drink he stood up and walked over to Pike's table anyway.

"You look like a man who's got a lot on his mind," he

6

said as he pulled out a chair and sat down uninvited. Pike could smell the salt and fish and seaweed on him.

"I suppose I might have," Pike admitted, "but I didn't really come here to talk."

The fisherman didn't take the hint. He leaned back in his chair—the wooden frame and leather seat squeaking under his weight even though he was lightly built—and said, "What then? To drink yourself into oblivion? I've tried that. It doesn't work."

Pike laughed softly. "I came in because it was cold outside and starting to rain."

"An admirable reason for a drink," said the fisherman. He took a gulp of his grog—Pike could smell the rum from across the table—and belched again.

How could he make this guy go away? "Get lost" would probably do it, but for all Pike knew this was the bar's owner. Or the Secret Service agent. "I'd really rather not—" he began, but the fisherman waved a hand in dismissal.

"Now me, I drink because my wife and son were killed on a prison colony."

His statement hung in the air between them like a ghost. The short, brutal intensity of those few words and the deep sadness with which they were spoken left Pike gasping for breath even as he tried to think of a response to them.

"I—I'm sorry to hear that" was all he could manage.

"Tortured to death," the man went on. "Right in front of me. A place called Rura Penthe."

What had Pike gotten himself into now? He looked up toward the bar, saw the Klingon woman flinch as she heard the name of the place, but he had no idea why. It meant nothing to him.

"They damned near killed me, too," his unwelcome companion went on. "Forced me to work in the mines, digging nitrates and phosphates for gunpowder while I held the secret that would make their puny chemicals

7

obsolete overnight! I held it, too. Never told a soul. Saved the world, I did."

"I'm sure you must have," Pike said. "But perhaps you shouldn't be talking about it now, if it's such a dangerous secret."

The man laughed, a single, quick exhalation. "Ha! What do I care now? It's apparently old news. Nuclear power! Splitting the atom! The most elemental force of the universe—only two hours ago in this very bar someone told me it was nothing compared to antimatter annihilation. And that's apparently nothing compared to zero-point energy, whatever that is." He looked at Pike with eyes red as cooked shrimp. "I held my tongue for *nothing.*"

Who *was* this guy? Talking as if the secret of nuclear fission was something new. Pike looked at him more closely. His clothing was rough, coarse cotton and wool dyed in drab brown and blue, and he wore a red bandanna around his neck. He had a high forehead and wide-set eyes, and he sported a two- or three-week beard that hadn't been trimmed since he'd started it, but his features underneath it were fair. And young. His general appearance had made him look older, but his hair was still coal black and his skin smooth. He couldn't be much over thirty-five, if that.

"Who are you?" Pike asked him.

"A fool, apparently," he replied. "One who's seen and suffered more than should be required of any man." He slurped noisily at his grog, then said softly, "At first I tried to serve humanity, then when I realized what I had discovered I tried to protect it, but now I find that I despise humanity and all it stands for." He looked Pike directly in the eyes and said, "And a man who despises humanity must needs despise himself as well. Many's the day I've wondered if I should put an end to it all."

Pike heard the sincerity in the man's voice, and his experience as a ship's captain raised the hackles on the back of his neck. Just his luck. He'd come out this evening to dwell on his own problems, and now it looked like he might have to talk someone out of suicide.

"Come now," he said. "Whatever your past, you're safe now. You're a free man, warm and dry with a drink in your hand and a roof over your head. Your future can be whatever you make of it." *Especially with a little psychiatric help,* he thought, but he left that unsaid.

"Oh, aye, I'm aware of that," said his unwelcome visitor. "I'm clever enough to make a go of it if I choose. I *have* made a go of it, come to that."

"Oh?" asked Pike. That sounded promising.

The fisherman took the bait. "Well, sir, not to brag, but I masterminded an escape from the prison island. I and twenty men stowed away in empty powder casks and let the stevedores load us on board a warship. It was cramped, but no worse than what we suffered in our barracks at night. And there was no worry of being mistreated in a powder cask!" He grinned, then took a drink. "We waited until the ship was at sea, then rose up in the night and took her. The men pronounced me 'captain,' and we became pirates of a sort, preying on our former captors until they brought in too many ships for us to match. We eventually took damage too heavy to repair ourselves, so we withdrew and set sail here for refitting." The glint faded from his eyes and he shook his head sadly. "It may not be worth the effort. Even if we return to Rura Penthe, no amount of battle has yet managed to vanquish the memory of what I have suffered."

The man told his story with the air of someone who believed every word. Yet how could any of it be true? A prison colony, in the twenty-third century? Mining nitrates for gunpowder? And transporting it by sailing ship? This guy was about four hundred years out of phase with the rest of the world.

Yet he was so convincing that Captain Pike actually looked around the bar again for confirmation that *he* wasn't somehow in the wrong time. He found it in abundance: the Klingon woman on her stool, the Vulcan harp overhead, the Saurian brandy in his glass. He took a sip of it and savored the tart, smoky explosion of flavor.

His gaze fell on the alien by the door. He had seen a few lizardlike humanoids in his travels, but never one like that. It was from an entirely new species. And its kind had to be fairly common for one to be here on Earth, unescorted, in a hole-in-the-wall bar in San Francisco. Pike wondered how he had missed hearing about them before this.

The fisherman—if that's what he was—noticed where Pike was looking. He shook himself out of his reverie and said, "Yes, strange things are about. But I've seen stranger."

"Have you now?" Pike asked, interested despite himself.

"Aye, that I have. Under the sea. Even a single fathom below the surface, everything is different."

"So I've heard," Pike said. He had grown up in Mojave, and even after he'd moved away he'd never felt comfortable in the water.

"So I've *seen*," the seaman said. "Manta rays bigger than sails, fish with lanterns dangling before their noses so they can see in the black depths, pods of whales all the way to the horizon, making the sea boil as they breached and dove."

Now Pike knew the man was having him on. There hadn't been a whale on Earth for two centuries.

Well, if he was just telling tales then Pike had a few of his own to share. And maybe he could get this guy's mind off his troubles for a while. "I saw some whales once," he said. "But these weren't in the ocean."

His companion considered that a moment. "I've heard there are lakes in China where—"

"Not a lake, either. These were in space."

The man snorted, but when he spoke there was an air of sophistication that hadn't been there before. "Sir, you force me to express doubt."

Pike laughed out loud. "I didn't believe them myself when I first saw them, but they were real enough." He took a sip of brandy and settled back in his chair. "It was back when I was captain of the *Enterprise*. We were out in the Carrollia sector, mapping subspace anomalies and looking for new sources of dilithium, when we received a distress call from a planet called Aronnia. They had a problem with their interstellar fleet. Seems all their starships had run away. . . ."

Chapter Two

I WAS ON the bridge (said Pike) when the call came in. I had Communications Officer Dabisch put it on the main screen. A floor-to-ceiling image of Commander Brady, from Starbase 7, looked out of the screen at me and said, "Hello, Captain. How far are you from the Aronnia system?"

I looked over at my first officer, Lieutenant Commander Lefler, whom I generally called "Number One." She had been running the navigation console during our mapping sweep; she would know the figure or be able to retrieve it in seconds.

But Spock, my science officer, beat her to it. Without even consulting the computer he said, "Fourteen point two seven light-years."

Number One gave him a look that said plainly, "Thanks for nothing," but Spock's Vulcan upbringing practically guaranteed he wouldn't understand.

Brady merely smiled at what he no doubt thought was a simple case of one-upmanship among my bridge crew and said, "Close enough. We've just gotten an urgent request for assistance from the Aronnians. They were admitted to the Federation a few years ago under peculiar circumstances; their spaceflight capability is entirely biological. Now they've got some kind of problem with it, and they can't cross interstellar distances. They've asked for the loan of a starship until they can get things straightened out."

"Loan them a starship?" I asked, hardly believing my ears. "Not the *Enterprise?*" We were the pinnacle of Starfleet, a veritable city on the move. They wouldn't just loan us out as a taxi service, would they?

Commander Brady saw the concern on my face. "I want you to find out what their problem is and see if you can help them solve it. Failing that you can request a cargo transport or whatever's appropriate for them to use while they work on it themselves."

"Understood," I said.

"Very good. Brady out." His face blinked out, and the viewscreen switched back to the starfield we had been mapping.

Number One said, "Biotech? Sounds like a job for Dr. Boyce."

I laughed at the thought of our ship's chief medical officer waving his diagnostic scanners over a spaceship, but I wondered how far off that image would turn out to be. None of us had much experience with biotech. We would soon have quite a bit more, I imagined.

"Set course for Aronnia," I said. "Time warp, factor seven."

"Aye, sir," said Number One. She worked at her controls for a moment, then said, "Course locked in."

"Engage," I said. She fed power to the engines and we leaped away.

At warp seven we would get there in eight days. I hoped that would be soon enough, but I wasn't willing to overload the engines unless I knew for certain we needed to get there sooner, and this situation didn't seem that desperate.

Spock turned to his computer console and busied himself studying what we knew of Aronnia. I gave him a few minutes, listening to the busy bleeps and pings of the ship's instruments while I waited, then asked, "So, what's this place like, Mr. Spock?"

"Aronnia is a class-M planet," he replied. "Surface gravity point nine three standard gees, atmosphere twenty percent oxygen, seventy-eight percent nitrogen, and the rest trace gases. Three major landmasses, mostly desert in their interiors. There are twenty-three cities with populations greater than one million, seven hundred and—"

"How about the biotech?" I asked. Spock could get a bit didactic if you let him. "How do these spaceships of theirs work?"

Spock frowned. "The record is incomplete. The Aronnians were able to demonstrate interstellar flight capability to the scout team who discovered them, and they were invited to join the Federation on the basis of that ability, but apparently they consider the actual workings of their technology to be classified information. Later investigators were not allowed to board the ships, nor witness their construction."

"Do we have any visuals of them?" I asked.

"We do."

"Put it onscreen."

Spock did so, and I found myself looking at an oblong blob with fins sticking out the sides. It looked like an old-fashioned rocket ship, except it had a blunt nose with an enormous mouth, and the fins ended in tentacles. The fins were big, like the wind vanes on a blimp. In fact, that's what the whole starship looked like: a living blimp. There were eyes about a third of the way back; from the two on the side I could see I guessed there were four of them spaced ninety degrees apart around its circumference. The body tapered down to a narrow tail with two side-by-side bulges. From the bell-shaped nozzle one was clearly a rocket engine, but the other had no openings.

This wasn't just biotech, using self-replicating and self-healing organisms for various ship functions; this was one complete organism. "Their spaceships are living creatures!" I whispered.

"That is correct," Spock replied unnecessarily.

Its skin was gray-black, hard to spot against the darkness of space. A tiny silver bubble looked completely out of place on its back, like a single barnacle marring the smooth line of a ship's hull. Just at the limit of discernibility, I thought I could see faint markings on the silver dome.

"What's the scale on this?" I asked.

Spock turned to his computer console and said, "Here is the *Enterprise* for comparison."

The familiar saucer and warp nacelles of a Constitution-class starship appeared above the Aronnian "ship." We were larger, but only by a quarter of our length. That meant the "space whale," as I was already beginning to think of it, was at least two hundred meters long. I had never seen anything like it.

"Expand the silver dome on top," I said. Spock did so, and we could tell now that the markings I had seen were windows and an airlock. The Aronnians had tied a sealed habitat module to the creature's back. If their doors were of average size for most humanoid races, then the entire living space was only ten meters high and twenty across at the base.

"This is what they call a spaceship?" I asked incredulously.

"They do have more conventional craft for interplanetary travel," Spock replied, putting on the screen an image of a winged metal spaceplane. It looked boxy and primitive, with stubby wings for atmospheric flight and oversize reaction control rockets for spaceflight, but it looked like it should work well enough. It had no warp nacelles, though, and without them it would never leave its own solar system.

"But the space whale can travel from star to star?" I asked, just to be sure I was interpreting things correctly.

"That is what the record states," Spock replied. "I theorize that one of the two bulges at the tail of the creature—the one without a rocket nozzle—must be a warp engine."

Number One laughed. "How could a living creature develop a warp engine? Or a regular rocket for that matter? It's ridiculous."

"Yet it exists," said Spock.

There was no denying that.

"It must be the result of genetic engineering," said Dabisch. He scratched his left ear just under his transparent cranium. To someone who hadn't seen how many humanoid species filled the galaxy he would no doubt look like a genetics experiment himself, but the Galamites had evolved on their own, just like humans had.

"We don't know that," I told him. The clunky look of their interplanetary ships made me doubt that the Aronnians were capable of something that sophisticated. And if they were, why didn't they just breed smaller versions of the creatures for in-system use? It didn't add up, and we didn't have the information we needed to understand it. "Let's not jump to conclusions," I said. "If we do that we'll arrive with preconceived notions that we'll probably just have to unlearn. We're better off simply asking the Aronnians how it works when we get there."

"They were not forthcoming with information before this," Spock reminded me.

"They weren't asking for help before, either," I reminded him right back. But he had a point. They weren't likely to tell us any more than they had to, even if we were there to help.

When we arrived, I immediately had Spock scan for signs of the immense biological spaceships, but he reported none within sensor range. That meant none in the entire planetary system, since the *Enterprise*'s sensors

16

would certainly have been able to pick up a life-form that large if one had been there.

There weren't many of the boxy in-system ships, either. Nor were there any satellites. Normally there are at least a few defense satellites around any inhabited planet, but Number One brought the *Enterprise* into a surprisingly empty orbit around Aronnia, and from all appearances nobody there even knew we had arrived until Communications Officer Dabisch hailed them.

His hail was answered immediately by a slender humanoid with large green eyes, silvery hair, and smooth brown skin with dark stripes on the forehead and cheeks. Its wide smile revealed even, white teeth, and its voice was softly melodious.

"I am Consil Perri, director of spaceflight," said the Aronnian. "Thank you for coming to our assistance."

"I'm Christopher Pike, captain of the *Enterprise*," I said, wondering if I was talking to a male or a female. It probably shouldn't have mattered, but it always made me more comfortable to know, especially when I was talking with someone as close to the human phenotype as this. It made for fewer misunderstandings. Trouble was, you couldn't just ask an alien—no matter how humanoid it looked—what its gender was. Some societies would consider it too personal for discussion with an outsider, and others might consider it an insult. A Klingon would probably try to kill someone who asked that question. I had no idea what an Aronnian would do, so I merely kept my eyes and ears open for clues while I said, "We're told you have a problem with your starships."

"That's right," said Perri. "They haven't returned from their annual migration."

"Migration?" I asked. I glanced over at Spock, whose poker face revealed none of the intense interest I was sure he felt. Biotech was different enough, but we did at least have some experience with that on a limited scale. Starships that migrated were something entirely new.

The Aronnian hesitated, evidently unwilling to divulge more than was necessary about their technology, but after a moment's consideration said, "Every year the titans leave for a neighboring star system called Devernia, where they mate and raise their young. They return here to feed in the atmospheres of our gas-giants planets. For the last few years their numbers have been dwindling, but this year the migration stopped completely. We sent messages to the Devernians asking if they knew what had happened, but we got no response, so we sent the few tame titans we had kept with us to go see for ourselves, but they never returned. We are now out of starships, so we are asking you to help us investigate."

"I see," I said, feeling the hair on the back of my neck start to tingle. I hated going into situations where other ships were known to have disappeared, even if those others appeared much less capable than we were of defending themselves from attack. *Something* had happened to them, and we would no doubt have to face that something as well. It had apparently silenced the Devernians, too. If it was anything like what we had seen already, it would be completely different from anything we had faced before.

Headlong into the unknown, with danger waiting when we got there. I knew what I was getting into when I signed up with Starfleet, but at times like these I wondered if it had been a mistake. Nevertheless, that was what we were here for, so I said to Perri, "Very well, let us beam you aboard and we'll go have a look."

Chapter Three

CAPTAIN PIKE paused in his story. The fisherman, or escaped prisoner or sea captain or whoever he was, had a puzzled expression on his face. "Something wrong?" asked Pike.

The seaman shrugged slightly. "Have you ever experienced the feeling that someone is using English but they're nonetheless speaking a foreign tongue?"

"Ah," said Pike. "Sorry. I sometimes forget that not everybody has been in space."

The seaman drained his near-empty mug. "I am still struggling with the idea that *anybody* has. But you tell a convincing tale, Captain. I am willing to believe in your *Enterprise,* and in these 'titans' you speak of as well. I want to hear what you discovered at Devernia, but I fear I must replenish my beverage before we continue. May I get one for you?"

This would be the opportunity to say, "My, look at the time; sorry, but I have to be somewhere at seven." Pike considered it, but he had been enjoying his reminiscence despite the somewhat unusual company. And besides,

19

the Klingon woman was still at the bar. She had stopped talking with the bartender and was listening to Pike now, drinking from a pewter tankard of Warnog as she eavesdropped. When she saw him hesitate, she smiled at him, her pointed teeth making it both an invitation and a challenge. Typical Klingon. Pike glanced at her openly displayed cleavage again before he looked away; if that was typical as well, Klingon men were happier at home than they seemed in public.

Pike felt a bit surprised to realize that he enjoyed her attention. He even enjoyed the seaman's attention. What had started out as a gloomy walk on a rainy day had turned into an interesting, if unusual, evening, one that he was in no hurry to end.

"Yes, thank you," he said to his drinking companion. "I'm having Saurian brandy." Pike drained his snifter and handed it over.

"Very good. I shall return." The seaman stood and walked to the bar, narrowly missing someone who had just come down the stairway. He did a theatrical double take when he saw that he had nearly run down a peach-colored felinoid woman, but when she smiled and said, "Hi there, sailor," in an exaggerated drawl, he merely shook his head and continued on his way.

Pike watched her cross the bar and sit at a table with two young human men. Her graceful body was covered in short fur, but in deference to human custom—or maybe just to enhance her natural charms—she also wore a tight bodysuit of iridescent material that flashed between white and pale violet when she moved. She laughed at something one of the men said, and Pike smiled at the sound of her voice. He had always been a cat person.

When he looked over to the bar again he saw that the Klingon woman was scowling. That, too, was typical. Klingons hated anything soft or delicate or beautiful. No, that wasn't fair. It wasn't hate they felt, but disdain.

Klingons valued strength and honor above all else, and had little respect for anyone who didn't feel likewise.

Pike glanced at the cat-woman again, then back at the Klingon, glad he could appreciate both kinds of beauty. But he wondered what had happened to the Klingon's forehead. Some kind of accident? If so, it looked pretty serious. That looked like ridges of bone just under the surface.

Beside the Klingon at the bar, the seaman reached into a pocket and withdrew a metal coin, which he held out to the bartender. It shone bright gold in the light. The bartender held out his hands and shook his head, smiling as he did so, and the seaman shrugged and pocketed the coin. Pike wondered once again just who this person was, but his first attempt to ask had been turned aside, and as with the Aronnian director of spaceflight, he didn't want to risk trouble by pushing too hard for an answer. He would learn it in time.

The seaman returned with Pike's brandy and a second snifter of it for himself instead of the grog he was drinking earlier. "I decided to broaden my horizons," he said as he handed one to Pike. "It smells intriguing."

"It is that," Pike replied. "Potent, too. Go easy on it." He held up his glass. "Cheers."

"Cheers," the seaman replied. They drank, and his eyes widened. "Whoo!" he said when he could breathe again. "Whoever the Saurians are, they know a thing or two about brandy."

"True enough," Pike said.

"I did, too, at one time." The seaman's expression faltered, but he settled into his chair and said, "So then, where were we? You were about to face certain death at Devernia, I believe. . . ."

21

Chapter Four

So I FEARED, ANYWAY (said Pike). The Aronnian seemed a bit nervous as well, especially after beaming aboard, but I couldn't tell if that was from being reduced to elementary particles and rebuilt in our ship's transporter, or from the prospect of what faced us at our destination. Or perhaps it was the ship itself. I had gone down to the transporter room to welcome our new passenger and offer him a guided tour of the *Enterprise*, but we had just boarded the turbolift for the bridge when I noticed that his normally wide eyes were even wider than usual and he was clutching the handgrip for dear life.

After seeing him in person, I had decided that Perri was male. I still couldn't see any obvious secondary sexual characteristics, but that very lack argued for masculinity. Plus there was something in the way he carried himself, an indefinable combination of attitude and bearing that spoke to me even across the species barrier.

His apprehension in the turbolift didn't change that. I didn't ask what was the matter; that, too, could be a mortal offense in some cultures. I merely said to the computer, "Cancel bridge. Take us to deck six." To Perri I said, "Let me show you to your quarters first. There'll be plenty of time to tour the ship when you've settled in."

Perri laughed softly. "You are most kind, Captain, but I will be fine. It merely struck me how large your vessel must be, in order to need a transportation system just to move about within it."

"It's pretty big," I admitted. "But these beasts you ride—'titans,' you call them?—are nearly the same size. I would think you'd be used to spaceships of this scale."

"Our ships may be large overall, but the passenger space is small. Titans do not like to carry large structures." Perri looked at the marker lights flashing past just beyond the turbolift's translucent window. "As for me personally, this is my first time in space, though I must admit it hardly seems like I've gone anywhere."

"Oh, we're definitely in space," I said. "Your stateroom has a nice view directly out the starboard side. We're still in orbit; you'll probably be able to see Aronnia from there."

"I will?" He really *hadn't* been in space before. You can always tell a dirtsider by the twinkle in their eyes at the idea of seeing their planet from above.

The turbolift stopped at deck six and the doors slid open on the circular corridor that ran around the perimeter of the *Enterprise*'s saucer section. "Here we are," I said, stepping off and gesturing for Perri to follow. As we walked along toward the guest quarters, Perri staring at everything and peeking into every nook and cranny we passed, I said, "I would have thought the director of spaceflight would get into orbit quite regularly. Maybe even live there."

He laughed again. "Oh no, Captain. It's much too dangerous for that. Space is for the adventurous."

"That's true enough," I agreed, remembering all the dangers I had encountered during my years in Starfleet.

And I had seen what the Aronnians used for ships, both interplanetary and interstellar. I wouldn't want to trust my life to them either. But I didn't really know that much about them, did I? I had been too busy trying to decide whether my passenger was male or female to learn more about the ships.

That, at least, I could simply ask about. I might not get much response, but it was worth a try. "So tell me more about these titans," I said. "Who does ride them? And how do you control them?"

Perri said nothing. I turned to see if I had given offense, but I couldn't detect any difference in his expression. "It's . . . complicated," the Aronnian said at last. "You see—"

Just then Yeoman Colt came around the bend in the corridor, holding a datapad in one hand while she tugged her strawberry blond hair into a ponytail and tried to tie it in place. She abandoned the effort when she saw me, letting her hair fall down around her oval face to her shoulders as she said, "Captain, I was just heading to the bridge to see you. I have those inventory figures you wanted."

I had been concerned about perishable supplies, since it had been some time since we had put in at a starbase. "Thank you, Yeoman," I said, taking the datapad from her. Nodding to each of them in turn, I said, "Yeoman Colt, Director of Spaceflight Perri of Aronnia."

If I had any remaining doubt over Perri's gender, the looks they gave one another erased it completely. Their eyes might as well have been sending out tractor beams by the way they locked together. Colt's pale skin turned light pink. The dark stripes on Perri's forehead and cheeks grew darker still.

"Um, pleasure to meet you," Colt said, offering her hand.

"Yes," he replied. "It is." He grasped her hand, held it in his for a moment—clearly unsure what our customs were—then let go and said to me, "My delight with your ship grows with each passing moment, Captain."

Colt blushed even more. I felt myself grow slightly annoyed by the attention he was paying her. She was my yeoman, after all, and he was on a mission that could have serious consequences for his home planet. He had best keep his mind on business if he wanted to accomplish anything.

I didn't say so, of course. I merely said, "I was just showing Mr. Perri to his quarters."

Colt nodded. "Yes sir. I made sure guest suite number one was prepared. If you need anything else," she said to Perri, "just ask."

"I will," he replied, and I knew he would.

"Thank you, Yeoman," I said again, and I led the Aronnian away to his quarters.

He forgot all about Yeoman Colt the moment the door slid aside. "Oh," he said, stopping in the doorway and looking out at the starfield beyond the windows. The guest suite has three large windows in each of its two rooms. They lean outward, following the curve of the ship's hull, so a person can actually lie down against them and get the sensation of flying through space. The ship's artificial gravity gets a bit odd that close to the edge of the field, pulling to all sides rather than down, but that merely adds to the impression of free flight. Perri didn't try that right away; it was all he could do to step inside and let the door slide closed behind us.

He stood rooted to the spot for maybe half a minute. I didn't rush him. When a person encounters the vastness of the universe for the first time, he generally needs a while to soak it all in. Perri finally started moving again on his own, taking slow steps closer and closer to the windows until he stood right in front of one, holding on to the edge of the deep-set frame for support.

"Oh," he said again. I came up beside him and looked out. Aronnia carved out a white, blue, and brown arc below us. I noticed that the continents stood out in sharp detail under sparse cloud cover—Spock hadn't been making up that bit about "mostly desert." The atmosphere blurred the boundary between planet and space ever so slightly, softening the impression a little, but the planet looked harsh and uninviting to me.

Not so to Perri. He took a deep breath and said, "Many have died for a chance to see this. I have often wondered if we were right in pursuing such a risky dream, but now I know. This alone makes it worthwhile."

"The director of spaceflight, a skeptic?" I asked. "You surprise me again and again."

He turned away from the window to look at me. "Even the most vocal advocate can harbor doubts. When you control as risky a venture as I do, your doubts practically define your life. I worry about every mission as though my own children were at risk."

I remembered stories from the dawn of human spaceflight, when hundreds of controllers would fidget during a manned mission, entire rooms full of people smoking addictive tobacco to calm their nerves while they waited for disaster to strike the astronauts and cosmonauts in orbit. We had come a long way since then, but I imagined that some fleet captains back home still bit their nails to the quick for every starship they sent into the void.

For that matter, I worried enough about my own crew to understand how Perri felt. The *Enterprise* was far stronger than any of the Aronnians' ships, but we were still a fragile bubble of humanity compared to some of the forces waiting for us in deep space.

One of which might be waiting for us later today. Devernia was only a few hours away.

The sooner we got there, the sooner we would find out what we faced. I said, "It's time we were going. Would you like to accompany me to the bridge, or would you rather watch the trip from here?"

"Oh, the bridge by all means," Perri said, turning

nonetheless reluctantly away from the window. I suspected he would pull the bed over so the stars were right over his head when he slept here that night.

He seemed completely at ease in the turbolift this time, and when we arrived at the bridge he broke into a big smile. "It's round," he said. "And domed overhead. It looks just like the control pod on a titan." Then he took in all the science and navigation instruments and said, "Considerably more advanced, of course."

I introduced him to the bridge crew. He looked at Spock for a long moment, no doubt wondering about the Vulcan's pointed ears and green hue, but when he looked over to Dabisch his mouth fell open. The Galamite's transparent cranium, glowing fuschia eyes, and scaly purple skin must have seemed like a hallucination.

"Pleased to meet you," said Dabisch, who was used to it by now even though he'd only been on board for a few months.

His voice has a distinctive timbre to it, a hum like a low-frequency carrier wave that his vocal chords modulated for sound. "We spoke earlier," Perri replied when he heard it.

"Yes," replied Dabisch. "I did not use video when I set up the call. I have found that it leads to confusion when the rest of the crew turns out to be human."

"I can see how that could be a problem," said Perri. He turned back to me. "You do have an . . . um . . . interesting ship."

"Thank you," I said. Our regular navigator, Lieutenant Tyler, was back at the controls. "Mr. Tyler, set course for Devernia, warp factor seven. Let's go see what happened to the titan migration."

"Aye, sir," he said, calculating the coordinates and sending the information to Number One at the helm controls beside him.

I nodded toward the main viewscreen, on which the image from straight ahead was displayed. Aronnia curved away to left and right, and stars glinted steadily above. When Number One engaged the warp engines, however, all that changed in an instant. Aronnia whirled crazily around, first to the left, then overhead as the *Enterprise* came around to the right coordinates. Then it vanished like a punctured balloon and the stars leaped toward us in long white streaks.

Perri gripped the handrail that encircled the command and helm stations, but internal gravity had kept us from feeling a thing. He let go with visible reluctance, and said, "I don't believe it's this smooth riding a titan."

"I suspect not," I admitted.

Devernia was less than two light-years away, but we still had a few hours to kill before we got there even at warp seven. I let Spock and Dabisch show our guest around the bridge while I went over the supply report that Yeoman Colt had given me; then, when I was satisfied that we wouldn't starve before we reached our next starbase, we went back downship for lunch. Dr. Boyce joined us in the cafeteria, first scanning our guest with his medical tricorder to make sure none of our foods would poison him.

"Stay away from onions and garlic, but otherwise it looks like we're fairly compatible," Boyce told him when he was done.

I smiled when he said that, since I had just been thinking how his white hair was nearly the same color as Perri's. There was a certain similarity about their faces, too, though one was marked with stripes and the other with worry lines. Their size was their biggest difference. Boyce was taller and heavier, big even for a human. He may have been older than the average starship crewman, but he was all muscle. Perri was thin and wiry, but at first glance he and Boyce could have been father and son.

Boyce questioned him like a father grills a son who comes home late from his first date, that much was sure. "What kind of metabolism do these titans of yours have?" he asked before he'd taken his first forkful of vegetables. "How do you control them?" "How intelligent are they?" And so on.

Perri answered some of his questions, but diverted others. Titans were fairly intelligent, he said, but only in certain ways. They were very territorial, for instance, and would band together to protect their feeding grounds—which presented quite a problem for anyone who wanted to approach one of the Aronnian system's gas-giant planets. The titans scooped raw materials directly out of their atmospheres, dropping out of orbit to make a blazing, meteoric run through the upper regions with their immense mouths unfolded to ten times their body width.

"That must be quite a sight," Boyce said. "What are they going for in the atmospheres? Hydrogen? Or do they filter out life-forms for food?"

"Both," said Perri. "They use the hydrogen for fuel and reaction mass, and the tiny airborne creatures for nourishment."

"Pretty slick system. Must save you a bundle on fuel and construction costs. How'd you develop something like that, anyway?"

Perri was picking at his green beans, but I suspected it wasn't the food he was concerned with. "Um, yes, it certainly does provide cost-effective spaceflight," he said. "You must understand, however, that I cannot discuss the details of their production. That would compromise Aronnian trade secrets."

"Hmmph." Boyce was a scientist; he wasn't the kind to let trade secrets get in the way of understanding. But Perri was obstinate; he would tell us only that the creatures were a relatively new development, and that the population was self-sustaining once established. "We also use . . . um . . . by-products of the technology for manufacturing. It's an important part of our economy. We have considered exporting titans to other star systems," he said, "but naturally we want to make sure we retain control of the technology if we do. From what we've seen of the Federation we're a relatively young race, and that's the only real trade item we have to offer."

Boyce shrugged. "You never know what's useful and what isn't, except of course for booze. That outsells practically everything else. You got any good alcoholic beverages to export?"

"We're introducing a distilled liqueur through an independent distributor named Harcourt Fenton Mudd. He promised us a large return on our investment, but so far sales have been disappointing."

I didn't know this Mudd fellow from Adam, but I said, "Be careful of independent contractors. Most of them are reputable, but there are some shady characters out there. You're better off dealing directly with planetary governments."

"We are beginning to understand that," admitted Perri. "That is why we are proceeding more slowly with the titans."

"How come they migrate?" Boyce asked. "That seems to be a big weakness, especially considering your current situation."

Perri ate the last of his dinner roll and washed it down with coffee, though I could tell from his expression that he didn't particularly care for Centauri roast. "We do seem to have made a miscalculation, haven't we?" he asked. "I can only hope it isn't as serious as it seems." He turned to me. "Captain, it was late evening my time when you picked me up, and I find that this meal has made me somewhat drowsy. Is there time for me to take a short nap before we arrive in the Devernia system?"

"Yes, certainly," I told him. "I'll wake you before we get there."

"Thank you." He rose from the table, and Dr. Boyce and I got up as well, but he motioned us back down. "You need not interrupt your own meals. I think I can find my way. If not, there seem to be plenty of people to ask directions."

That was true enough. "Very well," I said. "Pleasant dreams."

When he left the cafeteria, Dr. Boyce said, "He's hiding something."

"He admits he's hiding something," I reminded him.

"I think he's hiding something else."

"Maybe. I'll be taking us out of warp with shields up, that's for sure."

"Good idea," Boyce said. "And I'm going to count our spoons while he's on board. I wish you hadn't given him free run of the ship."

I laughed. "Critical systems are always under guard when guests are on board, you know that. Besides, where can he go? Unless he's got a pocket full of titan seeds— and the whole cargo deck to grow one in—I think we've got him pretty well under wraps."

"I hope so," said Boyce. "But something about him doesn't feel right."

I'd learned to take his opinions seriously. He was one of the *Enterprise*'s first crew members, after all. He'd served under Captain April before me, and he'd examined more aliens more closely than I ever would.

"Okay," I said. "I'll keep my eye on him too. But I'm expecting more trouble from whatever's ahead of us than from him."

My hunch proved correct. When we dropped out of warp, Perri was rested and standing beside me on the bridge. The computer had reported him in his quarters the entire time. Whatever he might be hiding, he had caused no trouble so far, and he was as horrified as I was by the scene we encountered near Devernia.

There was an all-out battle going on. We had approached from a distance, far beyond synchronous orbit around the system's one habitable planet, but that wasn't far enough. The viewscreen was full of titans, their dark bodies eclipsing the stars and their rocket exhaust drawing bright lines through the darkness. Smaller spacecraft darted in and out among them, and the flash of deep-space explosions were visible even under low magnification. The collision alarm sounded almost immediately. "Incoming missile," Spock reported.

"Evasive action," I ordered, but Number One said, "It's too close. It's going to hit us."

"Red alert!" I said. "Brace for impact." I gripped the arms of my chair as the claxon began to wail. Perri, beside me, grasped the handrail. As I had promised Dr. Boyce, we had dropped out of warp with the shields up. They would absorb an explosion, but the inertial damping fields couldn't compensate instantaneously for the shock.

The viewscreen lit up with the flash, then went dark as the outside sensors were momentarily overloaded. The ship lurched, lights blinked, and sparks flew from the navigation controls. Lieutenant Tyler cursed and jumped up from his chair, but a second later he was back at his post, ascertaining the damage. Number One, beside him at the helm controls, had hardly flinched.

The ship steadied out, and the starfield slowly returned to view. In it we could see the ion trails of many small spacecraft under power, and hundreds of titans sweeping gracefully around them. Devernia was a bright crescent against the stellar backdrop, peppered with the black silhouettes of the swirling combatants.

"Damage report?" I asked.

"Navigation is down," Tyler reported.

"Helm's not responding," Number One said. "Switching to backup control systems."

"Shields at ninety percent and falling," said Spock. "Radiation damage to starboard warp nacelle. Warp engines off-line." The lights blinked again, and his screen filled with more information. "Impulse engines also off-line. Main power off-line."

We wouldn't last long under auxiliary power. I jabbed the intercom switch on the arm of my command chair, years of experience guiding my fingers almost instinctively to the right button, and said, "Engineering, get that power back on!"

A moment later I got my response. Unfortunately it wasn't the resurgence of power I wanted, but just a worried-sounding technician who said, "We're working on it."

The air stank of burned electronics. I turned to look at Spock, unsure I had heard him properly. "Radiation damage? What kind of radiation?"

"The missile carried a fission warhead. Relatively low yield—I estimate less than twenty kilotons—but the nuclear reaction produced a neutron and gamma ray flash that was nearly as deadly as the explosion itself."

I could hardly believe my ears. Bombs. The Devernians were throwing nuclear bombs at each other.

33

Chapter Five

THE SEAMAN SLAMMED his brandy snifter to the table, breaking the pedestal right off the stem. He hardly noticed in his agitation.

"That's exactly what I was afraid of!" he said. "The same reaction that could drive a ship around the world on an ounce of fuel could also wipe out a city in the blink of an eye." He noticed his broken glass, drained the brandy in a single swallow, then set the glass upside down next to its pedestal and said, "But your *Enterprise* was evidently made of sterner stuff. Why wasn't it vaporized in the blast?"

Captain Pike shrugged. "We would have been if we weren't shielded. Even so, we took damage. The shields are mostly good against phasers and photon torpedoes. We weren't ready for the radiation or the electromagnetic pulse. *That* was the real problem. Warp engines are essentially big coils of wire, you know—"

"No, I didn't," the seaman said.

Pike didn't let the interruption derail his train of thought. "They are. And the pulse induced an enormous current in them. It surged straight down the main power bus into the matter-antimatter reaction chamber, where it diverted the antimatter stream for a moment, which tripped all the alarms and shut down the engines. And that in turn put us on battery power in the middle of a battle. Plus another pulse traveled to the bridge on the navigation control lines and fried our helm."

Out of the corner of his eye he saw the Klingon woman at the bar and he suddenly realized she was listening intently to his every word. Of course she would be; details of how to cripple a Federation starship would be worth a fortune on her homeworld. "Of course we've upgraded our shield technology to prevent that from happening again," he said loudly.

She grinned at him with her pointed teeth. "Of course," she said. She held his gaze for a moment longer, then turned to the bartender and whispered something to him.

The seaman had contained his agitation. "I apologize, Captain," he said softly. "It was a great shock to learn that my fears as well as my triumph had already come to pass, but I see that they are apparently old news as well." He shook his head sadly. "I must have been on the prison island longer than I imagined."

Pike didn't know how to respond to that, so he decided to change the subject. "I don't know your name," he said. "Mine's Pike. Christopher Pike."

The seaman nodded. "I gathered that from your tale." He hesitated, frowned, then said, "Considering my current profession, I fear you will have to call me no one."

"That's not much to call a man you're drinking with," Pike said.

"It is if you spell it N-O-W-A-N," said the seaman. "Nowan is a family name of long-standing nobility."

"It just doesn't happen to be yours," Pike said, not bothering to hide his disappointment.

"Ah, but it is," said the seaman. "It describes me, and

I answer to it. The rest of my family is dead, so I leave nobody orphaned by my choice. I am Nowan."

Pike couldn't decide whether to point out the psychological implications of what "Nowan" had just said, or simply let it go. The Klingon woman decided the issue for him when she walked over from the bar with two more snifters of Saurian brandy and set them down on the table. "I noticed you were out," she said, gathering up Pike's empty glass and the pieces of the seaman's broken one.

"Thank you," both men said automatically. She didn't reply; merely turned away and walked back to the bar.

Pike took one of the glasses and sniffed it. No detectable poisons. Of course that left a couple of thousand undetectable ones she might have dropped in it, but he didn't think the odds of that were very high. She wouldn't risk an interplanetary incident just to kill a fleet captain. She was probably hoping to get him drunk and learn more about the *Enterprise*'s weaknesses.

Fat chance of that. Pike hadn't been born yesterday. He raised his glass slightly in her direction, nodded to her, and took a sip. The rush of evaporating spirits on his tongue felt the same as usual.

He wasn't going to get much more out of this Nowan, he could tell. And in truth, that was as good a name as any. So he leaned back in his chair and picked up his story. "As I was saying, we're better equipped to handle fission bombs now, but at the time we were dead in space, with more missiles coming right down our throats. . . ."

Chapter Six

WE HAD a few seconds before the next impact. We couldn't maneuver, but we did have weapons of our own. "Target phasers on those missiles," I ordered. "Fire."

Number One and Tyler both reached to their weapons controls. Red beams of energy shot outward, spearing the two approaching missiles and exploding them at a safe distance.

As the billowing clouds of superheated gas expanded into nothing, Number One consulted her instruments and said, "Sir, neither of those missiles were aimed at us. Nor the first one either, apparently."

"Who are they shooting at, then?" I asked.

"It looks like the titans. We were just unlucky enough to get in the way. Look." She pointed to the upper right corner of the screen, where the bright spark of another missile reached out for one of the magnificent beasts.

I could hardly hear her over the wail of the red-alert klaxon. "Cancel red alert," I said, "and expand that view." The image grew to fill the screen. The titan was

37

firing its fusion engine, turning to get away from the approaching missile. But it was running the wrong way!

"Go *across* the flight path, not with it!" I whispered, feeling the agony of anyone who has ever watched a cartoon hero try to outrun a rolling boulder. But the titan was smarter than I had given it credit for; it wasn't just running. It was using its fusion exhaust as a weapon, spraying the million-degree plasma into the path of the oncoming missile.

It would have worked if the missile hadn't been so small. The titan's superheated plume of exhaust swept across it once, but the missile dodged and kept coming, and before the titan could correct its aim, it struck.

For a moment it appeared as if the warhead was a dud, but then I realized it had merely been fused to go off *after* impact, so it would concentrate its force inside its target. That was an effective strategy; the entire rear half of the titan's body erupted in a white-hot fireball, throwing a spherical cloud of ejecta outward into space. The front half tumbled end over end, spewing blue-green blood and entrails and charred flesh in a vast pinwheel.

Perri, standing beside me, moaned at the sight. Number One frowned and looked away. I felt the contents of my stomach shift, but I forced myself to watch. I might learn something about Devernian battle tactics.

The ship that had fired the missile let the corpse drift without further assault. It was a small, primitive craft like the ones the Aronnians used for in-system flight, but it was light and agile. It darted around among the titans like a bee among flowers, never keeping to a straight path for more than a few seconds. The titans, being so much more massive, couldn't follow it—and for some reason they weren't using their warp drives to get away either.

Agility was about the only thing to recommend the Devernian ship. Its missiles were mounted in racks outside the hull, vulnerable to attack. They used simple reaction drives; I could see black streaks along the fuselage from their rocket exhaust. The ship had no shields, no warp engines, and from the way it maneuvered on tongues of bright yellow flame I suspected it used chemical propellant. I would have laughed at their rudimentary technology if the *Enterprise* weren't drifting crippled in space because of it.

"The titans," Perri said, his voice full of anguish. "We have to protect the titans."

"We'll do what we can," I said, "but we can't stop that many fighters. Mr. Dabisch, open a channel to one of those ships."

"Yes sir." I heard bleeps and whistles as the ship's computer tried to establish a connection, but after a moment Dabisch replied, "No one answers our hail."

"Are they talking with one another? Break into their communications channels."

"There is no regular message traffic. Occasional burst transmissions only. It appears each craft is operating autonomously." Dabisch turned back to his board, saying, "There is also considerable microwave emission coming from the titans themselves. I detect no meaningful patterns there, either. It appears to be a radar locating system."

"Is that how they navigate?" I asked Perri.

He nodded. "Yes. They also use the questing beam to locate food. And, one would hope, Devernian attackers."

"Doesn't look like it's doing them much good." I tried the intercom again. "Engineering, what's your status?"

The same junior tech who'd replied the first time said, "Uh . . . we've got a lot of fried circuitry down here, Captain, but we'll have main power back in a moment. Impulse power should be restored along with it. Warp power will take a bit longer."

"Keep on it," I said. "We may need those engines soon."

"Understood."

"There goes another one!" Perri exclaimed, pointing at the viewscreen where a tiny ship had fired a missile at another titan. "Captain, you must stop this carnage."

I didn't really want our first act in the Devernian system to be hostile, but neither did I want to stand by and watch more of this slaughter. And we *had* tried to communicate.

"Target that missile," I said. "And this time fire a warning shot across the bow of the ship that launched it, too. Don't hurt them, but I want to get their attention."

"Yes sir," said Number One.

The ship's phasers lanced out twice. The missile vanished in a puff of vapor; the second shot came close enough to fry the paint on the ship's forward hull.

"That was probably a bit tight," I said.

"Sorry," said Number One. "I forgot these ships aren't shielded."

The Devernian craft swiveled around with tiny bursts from its chemical thrusters until it was pointed at the *Enterprise;* then its main engine sprayed flame and it accelerated toward us. "Well, we certainly got their attention, anyway," I said. "Get ready for incoming missiles. Don't let them even get *close* to us."

"Yes, sir."

We waited nervously while the Devernian ship drew closer. I glanced over at Perri, who gripped the handrail next to my command chair. He was breathing hard and studying the viewscreen intently, but I thought I could see a faint hint of a smile on his face. Who'd have thought he would turn out to be the type who enjoyed battle? Or maybe he didn't understand how precarious our position was. Two other ships broke away from the titans they were chasing and came toward us as well. "This doesn't look good," I said.

"I detect low-power laser emissions from all three craft," Dabisch said. "Not a communication signal. Possibly guidance for their missiles."

"Jam it," I told him.

The first ship fired a missile. Number One didn't wait to see if it could lock on to us; she fired the phasers at it as soon as she had a clear shot.

Both of the other ships fired as well. They were farther away, though, so I said, "Hold up a second. Let's see what happens."

Number One waited with her finger poised over the fire button. The missiles raced toward us—but the first one veered ever so slightly to the left and the second one angled overhead. Our jamming signal was apparently doing something, at least.

"Let them go," I said. "Save power." The phasers drew energy directly from the main power banks; we didn't have much reserve without the matter-antimatter generators on line.

We watched the two incoming missiles search in vain for a target, but then the closest ship fired another one. It was near enough that I didn't want to take a chance. "Shoot that one down," I ordered.

She did so. The two other missiles swerved toward the explosion, then lost their focus as it dissipated. One must have struck a piece of shrapnel; it flared into a yellow ball of flame as its fuel tanks ruptured, but its nuclear warhead didn't explode.

The other one, however, suddenly locked on target and accelerated again—not at us or at the remains of the other rocket, but straight at the closest of the three Devernian ships.

"Stop that missile," I ordered.

Number One moved to comply, but just then the lights flickered again and her targeting computer lost its fix. The phaser shot went too high, and by the time Number One could fire again more accurately, the missile had nearly reached its target.

The explosion sent the tiny ship fluttering like a leaf. A white fog of escaping air billowed out around it. The hull had been breached.

I hit the intercom switch again, this time a couple of buttons down from engineering. "Transporter room, lock on to the disabled ship off our port bow. Transport any survivors out of there immediately."

Jerry Oltion

"Scanning for life-forms," came the reply. "I've found one. Transporting. . . . He doesn't look good. Sickbay, Dr. Boyce to transporter room one on the double."

The transporters and sickbay were both on the same deck for just that reason. The few seconds it took to get a patient from the receiving platform into the turbolift and out again could mean the difference between life or death.

Dr. Boyce would save the injured Devernian if anyone could. And just in case he wasn't as badly hurt as it sounded, I sent a security team to meet them and make sure we didn't let a hostile alien loose on board the ship.

In the meantime, we were still under attack from outside.

"That flicker had better have been main power going on line," I said.

"Affirmative," said Spock. "Shields are now at full strength. Impulse engines are operational again."

"Then take us out of here," I ordered.

Number One complied immediately. The safest place in a battle is usually behind your enemy; the viewscreen image swirled around with dizzying speed, then we shot right past one of the approaching ships before it could fire another missile at us. Number One didn't bring us around for a counterattack, however, but continued on into deep space.

"Where to now?" she asked.

"Back into the fray, of course," said Perri. "We must protect the titans!"

"There are thousands of them," Number One said. "And hundreds of Devernian ships. We can't stop them all."

Perri slapped the handrail. "We must! What they are doing here is insane. If we let them continue, they will exterminate the titans, and our livelihood with it."

He had a better opinion of our chances than I did, but I wasn't exactly happy with what I saw, either. I looked at the viewscreen for a moment, trying to get a handle on the situation. Activity seemed centered around the Devernian home planet. The titans had drawn into a dozen or so tight groups for protection from their attackers, a strategy that might have worked fine against an enemy similar to themselves, but against nuclear weapons it was the worst strategy possible. The Devernians only needed to shoot into the herd, and they were practically guaranteed to hit something every time.

Space was littered with the corpses of dead titans. At first I hadn't noticed, since their skin was so dark, but the more I looked the more I saw. Thousands—perhaps millions—of slaughtered beasts drifted through space for as far as I could see. I looked to the planet and saw long streaks of light in the atmosphere where some of them blazed in a meteoric funeral pyre.

Perri was right; we couldn't just stand by and let this continue. "Take us into the nearest group of titans," I said, and while Tyler and Number One worked on the course I asked Perri, "What do you call a bunch of them together? A pod? A herd?"

"A fleet, of course," he said, forcing a smile despite the carnage outside. "They are spacecraft, after all."

"Of course." I watched as we drew closer. "Get between them and the Devernians. Number One, you fly; Tyler, you shoot down the incoming missiles. Nuclear bombs aren't cheap; maybe after they lose a few dozen they'll decide to talk."

The Devernians knew we were coming. They veered toward us, but Number One easily outflanked them at full impulse power. Tyler didn't even have to fire at their missiles; their chemical rockets couldn't approach our top speed.

The titans saw us coming, too. I suppose I was expecting gratitude, but I realized my mistake the moment we came to a halt amid them. These weren't just strange-looking starships with humanoid crews. There were no control domes on these beasts, no Aronnians inside pulling the reins or whatever they did to direct them. These were wild animals. *Panicked* wild animals big enough to smash us to pieces, which was just what they tried to do.

Half a dozen of them came at us from all sides. The screen filled with the enormous mouth of the one in front, offering us a view down a gullet big enough to fly a dozen shuttlecraft through in formation. The inside was lined with scaly plates of material hard enough to withstand the intense heat of passage through a gas giant's atmosphere. Those plates were hinged to turn forward as well; it came at us with them projecting ahead like pointed battering rams. Under full thrust it could only produce half a gravity or so of acceleration, but once moving its mass gave it the momentum of a small asteroid.

Shields were no good against something like this. "Evasive action!" I ordered. Number One reached out to comply, but before we had moved an inch the *Enterprise* shuddered under a blow from behind, then another from the starboard side.

We began to turn aside just as the one in front slammed into us. We lurched backward and heard its jaws squeal against the hull; then Tyler fired the phaser straight into its mouth. He used low power at first, no doubt hoping to drive it away without hurting it, but it hardly felt the blast through all that armor. It lunged at us again, biting down on the edge of the saucer-shaped hull, so he increased power and fired again.

It felt that, but it still didn't back off. The ship rang with its fury as it thrashed and bit; then two more titans struck us from above and below.

"To hell with this," I said, hanging on for dear life. "Ahead half impulse power. We'll knock them loose."

That was easier said than done. The one in front hung on like a bulldog, jerking back and forth in an effort to tear us apart, while more and more of them piled into us from the sides and the rear.

"Full impulse!" I ordered.

The *Enterprise* leaped forward under heavy acceleration. The battering from the sides and behind stopped as the titans there fell away, though one of them must have clung to the starboard warp nacelle for a moment. Unbalanced by its mass, we spun halfway around under full thrust before it dropped off. That motion finally wrenched loose the one in front as well; a deep groan echoed through the hull as it slid free, taking a generous swath of antennas and sensor arrays with it.

Even then we weren't out of the woods. The titans pursued us at top speed, darting ahead on warp drive and rushing us, only to be driven back by Tyler's phaser fire. And the rest of the "fleet," as Perri had called it, joined in the chase.

Chapter Seven

"OH YES," said the seaman, Nowan. "I've seen many a ship battered to pieces by a pod o' whales. They get to playing with you and it's all over."

"These weren't playing," Pike told him. "They were trying to kill us."

"Ah, but that's often play to a man, now isn't it? Who's to say it's not the same to other creatures as well?"

"Point taken," Pike said. "Whatever their motive, these titans had it in for us. We'd already sustained enough damage to cripple the ship and still they came on; I imagined them cracking us open like a crab shell and sucking out the entire crew."

"A nasty image, that." Nowan leaned forward, his elbows on the table. "So what did you do, turn and fight again?"

Pike shook his head. "It wouldn't have done any good. We were hopelessly outnumbered. We had all the advantage of superior technology, but it was useless against the sheer bulk and determination of all those angry titans."

He took a sip of brandy and said, "Oh, we probably could have launched a few photon torpedoes at them and scattered bloody pieces halfway across the Devernia system, but we were there to help save them, not kill them wholesale. I wanted a better option."

"Did you have one?"

"Barely."

Pike looked up. Every face in the bar was turned his way. Even the felinoid woman seemed interested. He felt heat rush into his cheeks at the realization that he was now the center of attention.

Nowan didn't care. "So what was it?" he demanded. "Out with it! Did your Mr. Tyler save the day with his fancy harpooning? Did Dabisch suddenly learn to speak Titan? What?"

Pike laughed. "Nothing so prosaic, I'm afraid. I merely remembered what I had seen the Devernian ships do—darting around like bees—and I realized they had already discovered the titans' weakness. They were bulky, and thus slow to maneuver. The *Enterprise* wasn't exactly a stunt fighter, but we could outfly a titan. So I order a full stop, a ninety-degree rotation out of the plane of the ecliptic, and a return to full impulse power. That shook off the pursuit—at least for a few seconds. . . ."

47

Chapter Eight

WHEN WE WERE once again under way and the titans were still trying to catch up, I hit the intercom switch and said, "Engineering, now would be a very good time to get those warp engines back on line."

This time the chief engineer replied. He was a New Yorker named Michael Burnstein, but I just called him "Burnie." "We're working on it," he said, "but that starboard field generator is in bad shape. We can maybe give you warp two, but the two engines won't be putting out the same thrust. The unbalanced field would tear the ship apart if we tried any more than that."

"Warp two is better than nothing," I said. "Number One, you heard the man; get us out of here."

"Aye, sir," she said. I heard the doubt in her voice, but she didn't question my order. She just entered the command into the helm console, then said, "Brace yourselves, this is liable to be rough."

The *Enterprise* had already taken a beating unlike anything she'd been designed for. Now we torqued the frame with unequal thrust on top of all her other damage. A deep bass rumble shook us to the core, and we heard the squeal of metal sliding on metal somewhere within the walls, but Burnie knew our limits. The ship held together—and the titans dropped farther behind. Either their biological engines couldn't keep up or they just lost interest in the chase when we made it more difficult, and I didn't care which it was. We plowed on alone for another full minute before I finally said, "That's far enough. Bring us out of warp."

We came to a halt about fifteen light-minutes away from Devernia. Everyone on the bridge held their breath as Spock scanned the space around us, and when he said, "I find four thousand six hundred and twelve titans in the spherical volume of space one light-minute across." I heard a collective groan, but then he added, "But none seem to be concerned with our presence here," and everyone sighed with relief.

Into the silence I said, "That seems to me like an awful lot of titans."

Perri, apparently deciding that he wouldn't be shaken to the floor again soon, released his death grip on the handrail and said, "During their migration they sometimes seem to fill the entire planetary system, but that is largely an illusion. There are seldom more than a few million of them altogether."

"A few *million?*" I asked, incredulous. The entire Federation didn't have a million starships. The ones we had were more useful than these, to be sure, but still, there was something to be said for sheer numbers. The Aronnians and Devernians were apparently sitting on a gold mine.

Spock turned back to his science station for a moment, then reported, "Sensors indicate seven million, eight hundred and twelve thousand, six hundred and eleven spaceborne life-forms of size comparable to the titans in the Devernian planetary system. There are three million, two hundred and six thousand, four hundred and seventy-six smaller life-forms of one-quarter scale or less. Would these perhaps be their young?"

Perri said, "Three million of them? Impossible. That many have never hatched in one year before."

"Hatched?" I asked, surprised. "I naturally assumed they gave birth to live young. But they lay eggs?"

His brows furrowed, and I realized he hadn't intended to reveal that fact to us. I couldn't see how it mattered, but it was plain that it did to him. It was too late to hide it now, though, so he said somewhat reluctantly, "Yes, they do."

"Where?" I asked.

He looked from me to Spock to Number One, then back at me. "On, um, small, rocky worlds. Ones with liquid water."

"In other words, habitable planets," Spock said.

"Yes."

Spock narrowed his eyebrows. "How do the titans land? Their bodies do not seem designed for planetary surfaces."

"They aren't," Perri said. "They drop their eggs from orbit."

"How large are the eggs?" I asked.

Perri didn't like answering questions, but he had no good excuse not to. "About two or three times as long as you or I am tall, and maybe half that wide. They're oblong, with fins on the back and a heat shield in front for atmospheric entry."

"Fascinating," said Spock. "I surmise that this is how you domesticate them, then? By bonding with them when they are young?"

"That's right."

"How do you—"

Just then the intercom whistled for attention, and Dr. Boyce said, "Captain, I've got a very agitated patient here who demands to see you. You want me to put him out until you've got time, or what?"

"Just a moment," I said. I hit the engineering button and said, "How are those repairs coming?"

Burnie replied, "We're just getting started on the warp engine. It'll be three or four hours at least before it's up and running."

Some engineers pad their estimates so they look like heroes when they beat the deadline. Burnie wasn't that type. If he said it would take three or four hours, that's how long it would take.

"All right," I said. "We'll try not to need it before that. Sickbay, looks like we're not going anywhere for a while. I'll be right down." I stood up and said to Perri, "Come on, let's go see what he has to say."

Boyce was right about the "agitated" bit. When we got to sickbay we found the patient strapped to an examining table with wrist, ankle, and chest restraints, and he was still struggling. "You have no authority to hold me!" he shouted. "This is an act of war! I demand to speak to your commanding officer."

"Whoa, whoa," I said, stepping up to his side. "Calm down a minute. Maybe you didn't see what happened out there, but we rescued you from one of your own people's missiles. *You* were shooting at *us*."

"Who are you?" he demanded.

I took a good look at him before I replied. He had the same general build as an Aronnian, the same facial stripes and wide eyes. They were definitely from the same genetic stock. I couldn't tell from a sample of two if their populations still interbred, but it was obvious they at least had common ancestors not long ago.

"I'm Christopher Pike, captain of the *Enterprise*," I said. "Who are you?"

"Name's Lanned, independent pilot on loan to the thirteenth Devernian attack group. You entered our space without invitation. What is your purpose here?"

I nodded toward Perri and said, "We came to find out what had happened to the titans. It looks like we've found that out, but we still don't know why."

"Why what?"

"Why are you slaughtering them?"

"Because they're slaughtering *us!*" He glared at Perri. "You—you *Aronnian!* You didn't tell them that, did you?"

Perri swallowed hard. "Of course I didn't, because it's not true. You Devernians have blown the situation completely out of proportion."

"Tell that to the orphans whose parents were eaten by titans," snarled Lanned. "Tell that to the parents whose *children* were eaten. Tell that to the homeless whose cities were burned."

Perri stepped closer. "The threat is not as great as you make it out to be. If you exercised even the simplest precautions, you wouldn't—"

"You murderous idiot!" Lanned lunged for Perri, nearly jerking the exam table off its mount. His head had the most mobility; his teeth met with a snap only centimeters from Perri's hand.

Perri flinched backward. Lanned said, "You and your precious Federation. 'Got to have star travel to be a member,' you say. 'Got to breed titans to sell on the interstellar market.' Well, every one you harvest comes with a price *we* have to pay, and we're not going to put up with your greed any longer." He spit a piece of tooth at the Aronnian.

Perri clenched and unclenched his fists as if he might try throttling the Devernian. He actually reached forward until I held out my hands—careful to keep them out of Lanned's range—and said, "Gentlemen, gentlemen, let's lower our voices and discuss this rationally. There's obviously a great deal of misunderstanding here."

"Discuss it rationally?" asked Lanned. "While I'm tied to a table?" There was a black gap between two of his front teeth. The broken one must have hurt terribly, but he betrayed none of the pain.

I looked at Dr. Boyce, then back to him. "We'll let you up when you convince us it's safe to do so. But Mr. Perri is our guest, and if you threaten him you will have to stay under restraint."

He scowled. "Unlike the Aronnians, we Devernians don't want to kill anyone. But we will wipe out every titan in our star system, and neither of you had better try to stop us."

Perri sighed. "He's an extremist. They're all extremists. They refuse to listen to reason."

Maybe so, but I wasn't exactly happy with Perri, either. He'd known what we would find here. This sounded like an ongoing argument, and he'd apparently expected us to sweep in with our superior technology and rout the opposition merely because the Aronnians were members of the Federation.

"I don't like being used," I told him. I drew my hand laser, then nodded to Dr. Boyce. "Let him up."

He looked at me askance, but didn't say anything as he unbuckled Lanned's feet, then his chest, then his hands. Lanned let him do so without hindrance, then slid his legs off the exam table and stood before us, rubbing his wrists.

"Thank you, Captain," he said. "And thank you, Doctor, for repairing my wounds."

Boyce bent down and picked up the fragment of tooth off the floor. "Here," he said, "let me fix this, too. Nobody walks out of my sickbay with a toothache."

Lanned drew a breath to protest, but we all saw him wince as air hit the nerve. "I wouldn't want to compromise your reputation," he said, sitting back down on the edge of the table.

A few minutes later, his smile restored, I led Lanned and Perri and two security officers to a conference room. Spock met us there, and we got down to business.

"First off," I said, standing at the head of the table

with the star-filled windows behind me while the others sat, "I want to know what happened to the Aronnians who came here before us. Assuming you actually sent the ships you told us you did," I said to Perri.

"We did." The pained expression he had been wearing for the last few minutes intensified. "Captain, you really have the wrong impression of us."

"I think you have the wrong impression of us, too," I told him. "The Federation doesn't intervene in disputes between neighbors. We will assist in negotiating a treaty, but we won't fight your wars for you. Is that clear?"

"Very. That's all we ask," Perri said.

"Yet you deliberately let us come here under the impression that we were investigating a natural phenomenon, knowing what we would actually find."

"We had no idea what we would find!" Perri said. "That was the whole point of coming here! The Devernians didn't answer our signals. None of the titan riders we sent to investigate returned. I told you that."

"But you knew you had a dispute with the Devernians, didn't you?"

Perri nodded slowly. "Y-yes."

"And if your investigators didn't come back, you knew they had probably been killed in battle."

"Not so," he said. "You, with your glorious *Enterprise*, don't understand how dangerous it is to ride a titan from star to star. We sent eight riders. We expected four to make it here. Of those, we expected two to return with news."

Spock cleared his throat. "You lose *half* your interstellar missions?"

"We do," Perri said defiantly, daring him to comment. But Spock merely nodded and entered something into his datapad.

I felt the hair on the back of my neck stand up. Half their astronauts were lost in space! Yet people went out anyway, knowing the odds. I didn't know whether to admire them or pity them.

I said to Lanned, "So four of them presumably made it through. What happened to them when they got here?"

"What do you think happened?" he asked.

"I think you killed them. Did you?"

He shifted uncomfortably. "Not me personally, no, but we all have orders to shoot anyone who interferes with the eradication effort. If the Aronnians tried to stop us, they would have been fired upon."

"'Would have been,'" I said mockingly. "Were they or weren't they?"

"They were," he admitted.

"Which could only be considered an act of war," I pointed out.

"It was an act of desperation," he protested. "We have no other choice. It's either the titans or us, and anyone who tries to prevent us from doing what we must will be stopped. That includes you, Captain."

Perri snorted. "You have all kinds of choice. People have coexisted peacefully with titans for centuries; there's no reason why we can't continue to do so indefinitely."

Lanned didn't even reply to him. He kept his eyes on me as he said, "Did he tell you how they breed?"

"They lay eggs on your home planet," I replied.

"Has he told you what happens next?"

"No."

"Let me describe it for you. The eggs fall with the force of a small bomb." He slapped his hand on the table. "They don't usually kill anyone when they hit. Planets are big, and our population is small, which means we generally don't even see where they come down. Most often the first sign we have that one has landed is when the young hatch out.

"You've seen the adults. You've seen the tentacles on the ends of their guidance fins. Well the young ones are all tentacles. That means they're mobile, and as strong as they are they can move fast as lightning. And they're carnivorous. They have to build up a great deal of body mass before they return to space, so they eat practically anything in sight—including *us*."

Spock had opened his mouth, no doubt to correct Lanned for saying "carnivorous" instead of "omnivorous," but he stopped with his mouth open when the Devernian's final words registered.

"It used to be something we'd hear about maybe once a year," said Lanned. "It was always in some other city and everyone would say 'What a shame' and that would be the end of it. But as our population expanded and so did that of the titans, it became more common. Plus, as the titans who fed upon us matured and went into space, it seemed that they deliberately began dropping their eggs near cities. We had to kill them the moment they landed, or the hatchlings would pillage entire towns. They're nearly impossible to stop after they hatch. And if by chance anything survives their depredations, it goes up in flames the moment they launch themselves into space with their fusion engines."

Perri said, "They're not dangerous if you feed them. You could domesticate them if you wanted to. That's what we do with the ones that hatch on Aronnia."

"Oh, yes," said Lanned. "All three of them. We get thousands, and they each eat tons of food every day for weeks while they grow. Where is that supposed to come from?"

Perri shrugged. "We feed them fish. You have far more ocean than we do; that shouldn't present a problem."

"The oceans are barren! The titans ate everything in them before they started dropping their eggs on land."

"Nonsense," said Perri. "If you have trouble with your oceans, it's because of industrial pollution. If you had been more careful the titans would have stayed offshore and you wouldn't have a problem."

"What do you know about oceans?" Lanned asked. "Aronnia is a desert. That's the only thing that has saved you; you don't have enough water to support a breeding population."

"We could breed them if we wanted to. Until you messed things up so badly there was no need."

Perri and Lanned looked as if they might leap up from the table and come to blows, and I wasn't sure if I would bother to stop them if they did. I was rapidly losing sympathy for either side of their argument.

The two security guards by the door lowered their hands to their lasers, but Spock interrupted before the situation could escalate any further. Tapping his data-pad's screen for emphasis, he said, "When the Aronnians applied for membership in the Federation, you implied that the titans were the result of bioengineering. However, it is becoming increasingly clear that you had no hand in the creation of these creatures, nor even in their husbandry. I suspect that you discovered them already as they are, and merely took advantage of a natural resource. Is that not correct?"

Perri didn't answer. Lanned said mockingly, "Why don't you tell him?" He said to Spock, "The titans came to Devernia about five hundred years ago. To *us*, not to them. There *weren't* any Aronnians until a few Devernians foolish enough to domesticate the titans strapped airtight tanks to their backs and rode them from our star to theirs. We colonized Aronnia. And now they claim the titans as their own handiwork." He laughed. "And as for 'taking advantage of a natural resource,' do you want to know what they use them for? I mean besides riding around on them like the fools who started it all?"

"I would be happy to learn anything you wish to tell me," Spock said.

"They scoop up their dung."

"Their dung?" I asked to be sure I'd heard him properly.

"That's right. Adult titans feed in the atmospheres of gas-giant planets, and they filter dust and small particles out of the rings of any planet that has them. Devernia only has one gas giant, but Aronnia has three, so the titans migrate there to fatten up before they come back here to breed. But they don't need everything they eat. Their excrement is rich in rare elements, which the Aronnians gather for raw materials."

The stripes on Perri's forehead and cheeks darkened. I wondered if he was blushing, to have us learn this apparently humbling fact about his race.

"You use it too," he said to Lanned.

"Of course we do. We'd be foolish not to. But we don't base our whole economy on it."

"Nor do we." Perri took a deep breath, then said, "Captain Pike. Regardless of our differences of opinion, you can plainly see that the Devernians have embarked upon a campaign of indiscriminate slaughter that will adversely affect both our planets. As members of the Federation, we have asked for your help in stopping this carnage. You've seen what they're doing here; you can't approve of it."

I looked out the windows. Even from here, I could see the distant flash of nuclear explosions. Devernia was a bright crescent in the far distance. "You're right," I said, "I don't approve of it. But my approval isn't required. All that's required before I act on anyone's behalf is that I understand what's going on, but the simple truth here is that I don't trust either one of you two as far as I can throw you." They both began to protest, but I cut them off. "Save your breath. You've both talked enough. I want to examine the situation firsthand."

Perri looked puzzled. He said, "You have. You are here. What more is there to see?"

I nodded toward the bright planet in the distance. "Devernia itself. When you're looking for a solution, go to the source of the problem."

Lanned said, "You haven't been invited."

I replied, "Then invite us. You need our help just as badly as the Aronnians do. You can't really think hunting them down will work, can you? Spock says there's millions of them out there. Do you have any idea what exploding a million nuclear bombs will do to your environment? Radioactive debris will rain down on you for generations."

"What else do you propose?" he asked. "We won't stand by and let the titans destroy our cities any longer."

"I don't have a proposal yet," I told him. "That's why I want to go have a look for myself. Maybe my crew and I can figure out something more agreeable for everyone involved—including the titans."

Lanned snorted at my presumption, but he said, "Very well, Captain. I will show you Devernia, on one condition."

"What's that?"

He looked at Perri and grinned. "That this arrogant dung-sifter come with us and see for himself what it's like."

Chapter Nine

IN THE Captain's Table, Nowan chuckled softly. "I'll wager he nearly wet his pants at that, eh?"

Captain Pike smiled, but shook his head. "If he did, he hid it pretty well. He spluttered around a bit, of course, said it was a complete waste of time, but in the end he didn't have much choice. Lanned had shamed him into it."

"He no doubt enjoyed that. He strikes me as a rather crude fellow. From your description of him, I fancy he enjoyed laying waste to so many great beasts. No doubt it gave him a sense of power."

"I don't know if he enjoyed it or not," Pike said, "but he thought he had good reason for doing it."

"Oh, aye," said Nowan. "Every man who's ever thrown a harpoon has found some way to justify taking the life of a leviathan, but so many have done it that you will forgive me if I suspect their motives. It sounds to me as if the entire Devernian society had gone a bit mad, if they truly thought they could solve their problem through such massive slaughter."

Pike rocked his brandy snifter around in a circle on the wooden tabletop. "Like Lanned said, they were desperate. They didn't go out hunting titans just because they wanted to. But yes, I suspect the solution they picked answered an emotional need as well as a practical one."

"That is an easy trap to fall into," the seaman said. "After our escape from the prison island, my own crew wanted to avenge ourselves on every ship that entered the bay, be it civilian or not. I found it difficult to deny them, in part because I felt their desire myself. But a true man will rise above his bloodlust and not let passion rule his actions."

"Spoken like a Vulcan," Pike said.

"How so?"

Pike felt a moment's confusion. How could anybody miss that reference? "They're all logic," he explained. "They don't give in to emotion at all."

"An admirable trait," said Nowan.

From her stool at the bar, the Klingon woman said, "A cowardly trait, you mean."

Both Pike and Nowan looked over to see her leaning forward with her lips pulled back in a snarl.

"To overcome one's passion is in no way cowardly," said the seaman. "It often requires great courage."

"Passion is part of life," the Klingon replied. "Deny it, and you deny the very core of your being."

"Then you think the Devernians were right to slaughter the titans, merely because they felt the need to strike back at them?"

Her lips pulled back even farther. "The Devernians sound like cowards, too. There is no honor in fighting dumb animals with nuclear weapons. A Klingon would pit himself against them on more equal terms as a test of his honor."

Nowan's eyes narrowed. "Men who need to kill things to prove themselves have no honor," he declared.

The Klingon woman snarled at him, a sound like a

lion about to pounce. "What do you know of honor, prisoner? A Klingon would never allow himself to be captured alive."

They stared at one another for a moment, fire smoldering behind their eyes. Everyone else in the bar had frozen in place, Pike noticed, except for the felinoid woman, who laughed musically and scratched at her left arm beneath its iridescent covering. The Klingon looked over at her with open disdain, but her expression turned to surprise when she saw the tiny hand phaser the felinoid had drawn from its hiding place and now held with the business end pointed straight at her head.

"Zap," said the felinoid. "You're my prisoner."

"Hey!" shouted the bartender. "No drawing weapons in here, you know that," but the Klingon didn't wait to see if the cat-woman would put it away. With a scream that chilled the blood of everyone in the bar, she leaped from her stool, picked up a chair from the empty table in front of her, and swung it around in an arc that knocked the phaser from the other woman's grip.

The weapon flew through the air toward the piano, but disarming her opponent wasn't enough. She brought the chair back around for another blow, this one aimed at the cat-woman's head, but the moment she had leaped from her stool Captain Pike had also reacted with instinctive speed. He had his phaser out of his boot before the cat-woman's even hit the floor, and he leaped to his feet and shouted "Drop it!" while the Klingon was still raising the chair over her head.

The Klingon didn't even hesitate. The chair came down in a swift arc toward the surprised felinoid's head, but it never connected. Pike fired as soon as he realized she wasn't going to stop, and the chair vanished in a puff of dissociated atoms.

It was a split-second decision. He could have stunned her instead, but if she was part of a peace delegation that could have terrible consequences. Even disarming her might cost more than humanity was willing to pay, but he couldn't let her hurt someone when he could prevent it.

She whirled around to face him, her face full of rage, but he held his phaser on her and said calmly, "Emotion or logic? Your move."

Just then the fire popped, and one of the men at the table with the cat-woman flinched so hard his chair scooted back with a screech.

Pike felt his finger twitch on the phaser's fire button, too, but he held steady. The Klingon woman held her eyes on him a moment longer, and Pike was just beginning to think he might have to stun her after all when she threw back her head and laughed. Her voice rattled the bottles on their shelves behind the bar and her long black hair swung from side to side as she shook her head.

"Well done, Captain," she said, stepping away from the felinoid's table. "I would welcome the chance to spar with you hand to hand."

"Perhaps another time," Pike said.

"I look forward to it." She walked over to the piano and Pike was afraid she was going to go for the cat-woman's phaser, but instead of picking it up she merely crushed it beneath her heavy black boots. *Then* she picked it up, and carried the pieces back to the cat-woman. "Here's your phaser, dear," she said sweetly. She walked back over to the bar, took a long drink from her tankard of Warnog, then sat down again—but not in her original place. She deliberately scooted down to the end of the bar closest to Pike, which still left her well beyond arm's reach, but not far enough to suit him.

"Dammit, Hompaq," said the bartender, "if you do that again I'll kick you out of here so fast they'll hear the sonic boom halfway around Qo'noS."

Hompaq, Pike thought. Typical Klingon name to go with her typical Klingon bravado.

"I was provoked," she said.

"You were insulting and threatening my customers, and I won't have it. Behave yourself or find another bar."

She shrugged and looked away. Conversation slowly started up again. Pike sat back down and tucked his phaser back in the loop at the top of his right boot.

Nowan watched him in open-eyed astonishment. "I have no idea what I just witnessed," he said, "but I will tell you this: I am no longer inebriated."

Pike smiled. "Nothing like a little adrenaline to burn out the alcohol." He looked around the bar and shook his head. "This place is just full of surprises, isn't it?"

"That it is," said his companion. "That it is. But I fear this particular surprise has diverted you from your story. You had me hooked, sir; I am ready to be reeled in. What did you discover on Devernia?"

Pike had to think a minute to recall where he'd been. Devernia, Devernia. Ah, yes.

Chapter Ten

WE COULDN'T go down immediately, of course. The warp engines weren't repaired yet, and I wasn't about to try running the gauntlet of titans around the planet on impulse power alone. So I took the time to fill in the landing party on what we had learned. To accompany me I chose Spock, one of the two security officers who had already overheard much of our discussion, and Yeoman Colt.

Perri was delighted to see her again, and Lanned seemed equally smitten, but they both expressed surprise that I would choose a petite young woman for the mission. I confess that when I had first seen her I had shared their skepticism, but she had long since proven herself to me, and I told them so. She blushed prettily at my words of praise, which only made her seem even more fragile and beautiful, but when I began issuing our equipment she took on a somewhat different appearance. A phaser rifle held at parade rest puts a certain edge on anyone's character.

I wondered if rifles would be enough. After seeing how

little effect the ship's phasers had on an adult titan, I knew a hand laser wouldn't be worth much against a juvenile, but I wasn't sure if a phaser rifle would be much better. Unfortunately it was the best I could do without hauling around a full-fledged phaser cannon, and I didn't think the Devernians would appreciate that. The rifles were going to be problematic enough.

I asked Lanned if he needed to contact his commanding officer, but he only laughed and said, "You presume a great deal more order than actually exists, Captain. I haven't had a commanding officer for weeks."

"You haven't?" I asked. "Who coordinates the battles? Who arranges for supplies? You must have some kind of leader."

He shrugged. "I'm sure someone back home fancies himself a leader. There might even be some who follow him. But anyone left who's worth following is out on the front lines in a ship of his own, battling the menace from space."

"Your chain of command has collapsed?" I asked, stunned at the prospect of a leaderless planet in a time of crisis—and at how cavalier he was about it.

"We all know what needs to be done," he said.

"So you think," said Perri. He was looking at our phaser rifles enviously, but I had declined to issue one to him or Lanned. I didn't want to have to protect myself from them as well as from titan hatchlings.

I did outfit everyone with survival equipment: medical kits, a day's rations, warm clothing. With all the activity in space around the planet, I didn't know if the *Enterprise* would be able to stay on station continuously. If there was no central authority to grant us permission to approach, there might be times when Number One would have to take her out of orbit to avoid hostilities.

I wondered what kind of reception we would receive on the ground, but Lanned said we would be welcome so long as we didn't try to interfere with their efforts to eradicate the titans. I didn't know whether or not to believe him, but I had little choice but to beam down and see.

At last, after the promised three and a half hours, Burnie pronounced the warp engines ready for flight. I led my landing party to the transporter room, then called the bridge on the intercom and said, "Take us in, Number One."

Lanned had given us coordinates for his home city, a seaport called Malodya on the south end of a large island. I waited nervously while Number One brought us into position directly overhead, darting in at warp three to slip past the titans and the Devernian warships without detection. The moment we re-entered normal space over the planet, however, she said, "Whoops! Here they come. Titans incoming at warp one point six, and Devernians following at full impulse power. We've got about thirty seconds before things get exciting."

"We're on our way," I told her. "Take the *Enterprise* out of range as soon as we're gone and wait for our pickup signal."

"Aye, Captain. Be careful down there."

"You be careful up here." I stepped up onto the transporter platform, where the others were already waiting. "Energize," I said to the technician at the controls, and a moment later the *Enterprise* faded away—

—to be replaced by a muddy street with gray stone buildings on either side of it. A line of scraggly yellow trees grew between the most traveled part of the street and the face of the buildings, but there was no sidewalk, no demarcation between vehicular and foot traffic. The street had apparently been covered with stones at one time—either that or it had never been cleared of them—but now so much mud had worked up around them that they presented more of an impediment than an aid to travel.

There were fifteen or twenty Devernians on the street, either walking or riding in ungainly wheeled vehicles that looked like they had all been assembled out of spare parts. No two cars looked alike. Some were improbably tall and narrow and looked like they would tip over at any moment, while others were wider and lower to the ground. They were all angles, apparently made out of stamped sheet metal and riveted or bolted together. The sound of them clanking and rattling down the uneven street assaulted us like an earthquake in a restaurant kitchen, and the air was thick with the aroma of partially burned hydrocarbons.

At least half of the vehicles had no paint that I could see beneath their thick coating of brown mud. The sea air—I could smell the salt from where we stood—was busy rusting them out. Besides the rust, their only common features were wide, large-diameter wheels that presumably helped them churn through the muck. I looked out at the oozing brown surface, then up at the gray sky that threatened to drop more rain on it at any moment, but I held my tongue. I had learned as a cadet that one doesn't criticize alien societies on first impressions. Maybe they had a good reason not to pave their roads.

We had materialized in a parking lot. Only one Devernian had witnessed our arrival—an old woman who had been tying down a pile of wooden crates on the back of a flatbed truck. She looked at us curiously, still tugging on the rope; then she narrowed her eyes and peered intently at Lanned. "Ortezi, is that you?" she asked.

Lanned shook his head. "No. I'm Lanned, Ortezi's brother. Ortezi was killed three years ago by a titan."

"Ah," she said, nodding sadly. "I thought so, but the way you all popped up from nowhere, I . . . ." She trailed off and finished tying her knot, asking as she worked at it, "How did you do that?"

Lanned held his hand out toward me and my four crew members. "These people are from the Federation.

That's how they get from place to place. They came here to stop us from killing the titans."

"Did they now?" Her expression grew cold.

"We're here to help you solve your problem," I said quickly. That wasn't strictly true, of course. The Prime Directive prohibited interfering in a society's development, either for good or for bad. If Aronnia hadn't been a member of the Federation we couldn't do anything at all, but they were and they had asked for help, and Devernia was arguably part of their society, so I felt comfortable at least investigating the situation. Whether or not we acted on it, however, depended on what we learned.

The old woman didn't warm up any, but she said, "Hah. If you could make 'em all vanish the way you appeared just now, you'd be welcome enough. Can you do that?"

"No," I replied. "I'm afraid that's beyond our ability."

"Pity," she said. She looked back to Lanned. "Your brother was a good boy. I used to hire him to help me skin trinis at harvest time." She rapped a wrinkled knuckle on one of the crates, and whatever was inside hissed loudly through the vent hole in the side.

Lanned smiled at her. "He showed me the scars. How is the farm doing now?"

She spat on the ground, which was spongy but hadn't given over to mud there in the parking lot. "Can't complain. People still have to eat, even when the sky's falling around 'em. I could do with a bit less rain, though." She looked again at the four of us from the *Enterprise* and said, "I don't suppose you can do anything about that, can you?"

"No, sorry," I said.

"Not much good to us then, are you?" she asked pointedly.

I saw Yeoman Colt trying to stifle a grin and I gave her a warning look, but that only made it harder for her to contain.

I looked away lest I start laughing too, and our surroundings quickly robbed any mirth from the situation. I said to the old woman, "We'll do what we can."

"See that you do," she said. She checked her knot, then climbed into the cab of her vehicle. The engine started with a belch of black smoke and a whine that rose in pitch until it howled painfully just near the threshold of hearing; then, with a clashing of metal against metal and a momentary spinning of wheels, the woman put it in gear and drove away.

Spock wiped a bit of mud from his pants leg, but considering our surroundings it seemed a futile gesture.

Perri didn't even try to hide his disgust. "What a trini pen!" he said, wrinkling his nose. "How can you people live this way?"

Lanned gave him a withering look. "What's the matter, desert dweller? Can't take a little moisture?"

"It's not the water, it's the—the *miasma* that's so disagreeable. Have you people no pride?"

"We don't have time for pride," Lanned said. "Unlike you—"

"And we don't have time to stand here insulting each other, either," I said before they could take off on another riff. "Come on, let's have the tour."

Lanned seemed happy to drop it. Perri's comment had apparently stung. I wondered if life here had always been like this, or if we were seeing evidence of the decline Lanned had spoken of. He didn't elaborate; he just said, "Very well," and walked toward the street, leaving the rest of us to follow or not as we wished.

It's hard to be unobtrusive when you're carrying phaser rifles. Some of the Devernians carried weapons, but they were usually handguns, and the few rifles we saw were definitely projectile weapons rather than directed energy beamers. At least our dark jackets covered our blue and yellow and red shirts, but people still gawked at us as we marched along the street, stepping carefully to avoid sinking to our ankles in mud. The locals wore mostly subdued browns and grays themselves, probably because they were going to *get* brown and gray within a block no matter what color they started out. Every horizontal surface was covered with mud, and every vertical one with dark soot. When I caught glimpses of the skyline between buildings I could see plumes of smoke rising into the clouds, smudging the already-dark sky. Even the rain was probably dirty, I imagined.

I tried not to be judgmental. Earth had gone through a period like this. Two of them, actually. We'd climbed out of it once, then bombed ourselves back into it again before Zefram Cochrane invented the warp drive and lifted us out of the squalor once and for all.

I wondered if the titans might do the same for the Devernians, but if Lanned was to be believed then the titans were responsible for the situation in the first place.

Or maybe they were responsible for more than that.

I stopped dead in my tracks. Yeoman Colt, who had been speaking quietly with Perri, bumped into me from behind and jumped back.

"Oh! Sorry, sir."

"My fault," I told her. "Lanned, how old is this city?"

"Malodya?" he asked. "Seventy or a hundred years, maybe. Why do you ask?"

"How old is the oldest city on Devernia?"

He shrugged. "I don't know. Old. Maybe four hundred years?"

Four hundred years was *old*?

"And how long ago was Aronnia colonized?"

Perri answered that. "Two hundred and seventeen Aronnian years ago. That would be about one hundred and eighty-something Devernian years."

Colt said what I was thinking. "You're so young! How could anybody go from the birth of cities to spaceflight in two hundred years?"

Lanned laughed softly. "The spaceships were free. We only had to develop the sealed containers to ride in. And the titans provided the raw materials for that, too. Their bones are mostly metal, and their eggshells make excellent refractory crucibles for smelting it."

That's what I had thought. I could easily imagine tribes of hunter-gatherers or early agrarian farmers watching the creatures come and go on their fusion flames, wondering how they did it and making their own experiments with fire. Two hundred years was fast, but it would be long enough for them to learn to work metals and build the machinery of civilization—even their own spaceships—if they had an example to strive for.

Any problem I had with the Prime Directive paled in comparison to the interference that had already happened here. Now I wondered which would be worse, helping them eliminate the titan influence or leaving them alone.

Spock had been taking tricorder readings since we had arrived. Now he spoke up and said, "Ion dating of the building materials supports Lanned's figures. This section of the city is forty-seven years old."

"You want to see the oldest part?" Lanned asked.

"It might help us understand your culture," Spock replied. I didn't really know what we were looking for, but I supposed looking at the city's history might give us a direction to expand our investigation so I said, "Yes, let's have a look."

Lanned led us down the block to the intersection with another muddy street, turned right, and headed toward a cluster of ten- to fifteen-story buildings that I assumed was the center of town.

I looked at the smaller structures we passed on the way, and I noticed a peculiarity in their design. There were no windows at all on the ground floor, and the doors were heavy sheets of steel, banded for strength. "Are those doors designed to keep hatchling titans out?" I asked.

Lanned shook his head. "Nothing will keep them out if they decide there's food inside. The doors are only designed to delay them long enough for someone on the opposite building to get a shot at them." He pointed to the roof of the building across the street from us, where I saw a notch in the waist-high wall and in the notch the round end of what looked like a medieval cannon pointing at us. It must have had a bore the size of my fist.

I turned to my security officer, Lieutenant Garrett, who nodded grimly. He saw it too. And now that we were looking, we could see them atop every building all the way down the street.

I didn't see anyone up there with the cannons, so I assumed that they were left unmanned until someone sounded the alert. "How often do you need to fire one of those?" I asked.

"We test them every week," Lanned replied. "So far we haven't actually had to shoot a titan this far into town, but there's always a first time. We're ready."

That they were. I shivered at the thought of needing a cannon on every rooftop, but it probably made the city's inhabitants feel safer.

We continued walking toward the downtown area, but we turned aside before we got there. After crossing several muddy cross-streets, we came to a wide, tree-filled park, and the moment he saw it Lanned suddenly smiled and said, "Oh, the *big* gun! Of course you must see that." He led the way under the canopy of yellow leaves toward a circular pond in the middle of the park.

When we reached the edge of it, Lanned said nothing; he merely turned to look at us, a peculiar smile on his face. I looked at the black surface of the pond, maybe five meters across and ringed in rusting metal about knee high; then I turned once around and examined the park. Wide-leafed trees, bushes here and there, a low ground cover that looked more like tiny fern fronds than grass— but no gun.

Was the pond the remains of its turret, perhaps? Maybe there had been some kind of artillery emplacement here and this was all that was left. It was circular enough to be a turret, and the rim of metal around it could be a track . . .

Or a barrel.

I looked into the black water again, trying to spot the bottom. If there was one, I couldn't see it.

"How deep is that, Mr. Spock?" I asked.

He was already examining it with his tricorder. "I read two hundred and seventy-four point three meters," he said.

I felt my insides tighten up as if I'd just been transported to the top of a cliff. I backed away from the edge and looked to the side to keep my balance. What kind of people would leave a hole that deep in the middle of town without a fence around it? Even if it was full of water. I said to Lanned, "You can't mean to tell me this is a gun barrel."

"Oh, but it is," he said, grinning wide now. He glanced momentarily at Yeoman Colt, then looked back at me. "I'm glad to see that something we did can impress you Federation people."

"You've certainly managed . . . two hundred and some *meters?* What in the world did you *shoot* with it? And what did you shoot *out of* it?"

"Titans," Lanned said. "Titans to both questions. Their eggs make excellent projectiles going up as well as coming down. We just sent them back upward with considerably more velocity than what they arrived with."

"But straight up? You'd have to be incredibly lucky to hit anything with it."

Lanned said, "Not so lucky as you might think. The eggs shatter under the stress of the explosion, so it's really a cloud of fragments rather than a single egg. That means less impact when it hits something, of course, but when your target is moving at orbital velocity all you really have to do is put the projectile in front of it."

Spock's tricorder made whistling sounds as he continued to take readings. "That would be an effective weapon. An egg fragment weighing only a kilogram would strike with 28,543,209.88 joules of energy."

"How much is that in kilotons?" Colt asked.

"A lot," I told her before Spock could make an equally precise conversion. "Did it work?"

Lanned nodded. "Oh yes. We shot down twenty-six titans with it before the barrel cracked."

"Fascinating," said Spock.

"Of course, that was before we developed our own spaceships. After that we just carried rocks into retrograde orbit and pitched them out. That meant they hit with *twice* the power. Much more effective."

"But you gave that up, too, in favor of nuclear bombs," I said. "Why?"

Lanned lost his grin. "We kept hitting too many of our own rocks. Projectiles from the gun fell back into the sea if they didn't hit anything, but orbital debris stays up there for months. Besides, by the time the titans get into orbit, they're already close enough to release their eggs. We had to take the fight farther out."

"You realize, of course," said Spock, "that by attempting to drive them from Devernia you have disrupted their migration pattern and caused them to remain here year-round instead."

"We know that now. We didn't expect it to work that way when we started killing them, but we're trying to take advantage of it and eliminate them while we've got the chance."

I edged closer to the enormous gun barrel and looked down into the water again. My reflection stared back out, just as awed as I. These people weren't afraid to think big, that much was certain.

Just then I saw a flash of light in the sky reflected in the water, and a moment later we heard a whistling sound overhead, followed by a concussion we could feel in the soles of our boots. I blinked and saw another flash—no doubt the afterimage in my retinas. Concentric rings rippled outward into the middle of the flooded gun barrel.

"What was that?" I asked, knowing the answer already.

Lanned confirmed it. "Eggfall!" he said, and the tone of his voice carried both fear and satisfaction.

Chapter Eleven

CAPTAIN PIKE paused to take a drink, and found that his brandy snifter was empty again. So was his drinking companion's. They eyed one another for a moment, then Pike looked over at the bar where the Klingon woman, Hompaq, sat. The other bar patrons had gone back to their own conversations and their own concerns, but she had hardly moved for the last quarter hour. She didn't even look as if she was paying attention to Pike anymore, but he doubted that she had forgotten their confrontation. She was probably just waiting for the chance to stick a knife in his ribs.

Nowan knew exactly what he was thinking. "Armwrestle you for it," he said.

Pike laughed softly. "No, it's my turn. Be right back." He picked up both glasses and stood up.

"I'm right behind you if there's trouble."

"If there's trouble, I'm probably going to be on my back," Pike said, not really sure he was joking. He squared his shoulders and walked over to the bar anyway, setting the glasses down on the polished wood with a soft click. Hompaq bared her teeth at him, and he felt his skin crawl as she reached down to scratch her bare midriff, but she brought her hand back up empty.

The bartender had been restocking the cooler midway down the bar. He turned his head at the sound, and Pike said, "Two more."

He nodded, but finished transferring dark green bottles of ale before he stood up.

"Relax, tiger," the Klingon said. "If I was mad at you, I'd have let you know it before this."

He looked sideways at her. "How? By swinging a chair at my head?"

"I never use the same tactic twice. It's bad form. No, if I were angry at you, I'd probably do something disgustingly personal and very painful." She grinned again, showing all of her pointed teeth. "Of course to a Klingon, that's practically indistinguishable from making love."

"How charming," he said. Was she coming *on* to him? Impossible. Wasn't it?

The bartender took down the curved brown bottle of Saurian brandy from the shelf, got two fresh glasses from beneath the bar, and poured.

"Maybe we should just take the bottle," said Pike.

Hompaq chuckled softly. It was all she needed to say; Pike felt warmth in his cheeks.

The bartender shook the bottle gently, said, "Actually, there's not much left in this one," and poured the rest into the glasses, leaving them each a centimeter shy of the top. "Want a fresh one?" he asked.

Good grief, thought Pike. Had he actually drank half a bottle of Saurian brandy already? On an empty stomach? No wonder he had phasered the chair out of Hompaq's hands. And no telling what he would do after a whole bottle. "No thanks," he said. "That's probably more than we need."

"Try some Warnog," said Hompaq, raising her tankard. "It'll grow hair on your chest."

Pike couldn't resist. He looked back at her, let his gaze slide deliberately down from her face to the rounded targets her half-exposed breasts made, and said, "Hasn't worked on you yet."

She looked down in surprise, then burst out laughing. "Ha! Very good, human. I think I like you." She slapped him on the back hard enough to make his teeth rattle.

Pike thought of half a dozen replies to that as well, but he prudently let them all slide. Picking up the brandy snifters, he raised one slightly toward her, said, "Cheers," and went back to his table.

"Well done," Nowan said when he sat down.

Pike shrugged. He'd gotten past her without violence, but he wasn't particularly proud of the accomplishment. There'd been a time when he would have welcomed the chance to wipe the bar with her. That wasn't necessarily better, but he felt somehow let down by the thought that he was mellowing out, and he suspected that Hompaq felt the same disappointment. Nothing would please her more than a good brawl.

She was still watching him. He winked at her. Let her wonder what it meant.

"So now, where was I?" he asked Nowan. "Had Colt fallen into the gun barrel yet?"

"No!" Nowan exclaimed. "Did she?"

"Nope." Pike grinned at him. "Just checking to see if you were listening. You sure you want to hear all this?"

Nowan drew himself upright in his chair. "Sir, if you leave me stranded at this point I will join the scantily clad woman in rending you limb from limb. Proceed at once. The egg had fallen. What did you do?"

"I'll tell you what we *should* have done," Pike said. "We should have run away while we had the chance. . . ."

Chapter Twelve

BUT OF COURSE we ran toward it. It was hard to tell where it had come down, what with all the buildings in the way, but Spock kept scanning for life-forms with his tricorder and he kept us pointed in the right direction. We couldn't follow the locals; Devernians were running every which way. I eventually realized there was a pattern to their movement—parents and their children going one way and people with guns going the other—but that wasn't apparent at first. All I saw was a city that looked like a kicked anthill, an anthill full of angular ground vehicles with bad brakes.

We were nearly run over half a dozen times as we sprinted toward the fallen titan egg. Once we came upon an intersection that was clogged with crumpled cars, and I realized with horror that they had no structural integrity fields, no artificial gravity, not even crash harnesses to restrain their passengers. Only the poor condition of the streets prevented a worse disaster; nobody could drive fast enough through the rutted mud for a collision to be fatal.

At last we rounded a corner and found the impact site. The egg had struck a building at a low angle and smashed right through a second-story wall, crashed through the floor inside, and come to rest in a ground-floor room on the other side of the building. The cannons from the buildings around it were useless in this situation, but a couple dozen Devernians had climbed to the roof of the one that had been hit and were busy removing the gun from its mount so they could carry it inside to fire point-blank at the egg.

"Make way!" Lanned shouted as we neared the crowd of onlookers on the ground. "Coming through!"

There were hundreds of people milling around with their hand weapons drawn, but so far nobody had fired one at anything. Those nearest to us turned to see who had shouted, and when they saw us following Lanned, armed with our phaser rifles, they backed away. They had probably never seen a phaser before, but the rifles were deliberately designed to look deadly, and that apparently was just what they wanted to see. "Inside!" some of them shouted. "Blow it up! Kill it! Kill it!"

"How long—" I asked, gasping for breath after running so far. "How long before it hatches?"

"Who knows?" Lanned answered. "It used to take about nine days, but now that we're keeping the mothers at bay they're developing further before they drop. Sometimes it's just hours. Others hatch on the way down."

We pushed our way into the building just as a loud *boom* shook it. We heard shouts from within, and I thought the egg must have hatched, but when we reached the room where it had fallen we saw that it was still intact, an oblong spheroid big enough to hold a full-grown elephant. It was scorched black by its fall through the atmosphere, it surface crinkly and stinking of hot metal and complex organic compounds. Its nose was buried in the floor and its tail stuck up through the ceiling, the fins on the back making it look for all the world like a cartoon bomb.

The noise we'd heard had come from a more realistic bomb that someone had placed beneath the egg and touched off, but that had had no effect other than temporarily deafening everyone in the building and scattering shredded paper like confetti all around the room. It had apparently been an office a few moments ago. I noticed a few other people with clumsy-looking grenades as well as slug-throwing handguns dangling from their belts, but it was clear that those kind of weapons were no match for what we faced here.

"Out!" Lanned shouted, waving everyone away. "Get out of here! We'll take care of it."

Of course nobody left, but nobody tossed another grenade, and the ones closest to the egg backed off to make room for us. Spock stepped forward and ran his tricorder along the surface of the egg. "What's he doing?" someone asked.

"Ascertaining the danger," Spock replied. He stepped around the egg, sidling along the wall where it was a tight fit, his tricorder whirring the entire time. The novelty of it held the Devernians at bay until he had made a complete circuit.

"Well, Spock?" I asked when he didn't speak right away.

"A moment, Captain." We were standing under one of the fins; he frowned at his tricorder's display and moved around to the side of the egg again. It was warm, I noticed, but not as hot as I would have expected from its fiery passage through the atmosphere. Its shell must have functioned as an ablative heat shield, the outer layers vaporizing and carrying away the energy before it could cook the layers below.

"I read intense metabolic activity," Spock said finally, "but I do not detect any motion. I believe the embryo is still developing."

"Good," someone said. "That'll give us time to blast it apart."

Lanned was looking at Spock and the tricorder. "You can see through the shell with that thing?" he asked.

"Only on Q-band," Spock said. "It is opaque to all other frequencies, but Q-band is designed for high-penetration and long-distance scans, so it does allow me to take at least some readings."

"How about the other way around? Can you put energy *into* it?"

Spock considered his request. "That would theoretically be possible, but not with this unit. I assume you wish to irradiate and sterilize the embryo?"

"That's right."

"Given its biomass and its resistance to heat, I suspect it would take more energy than even a phaser battery contains to assure its destruction through irradiation alone. Molecular disruption remains a much more cost-effective option."

Perri had been catching his breath at the back of the room, but now he spoke up. "What are you talking about killing it for? If it's not due to hatch right away, then this is the perfect opportunity to domesticate it. Get some food handy so it will have something to eat when it crawls out of the egg, and it'll bond with the first person it sees."

"Are you volunteering to be that person?" asked Lanned.

Perri swallowed, and I was sure he would find some way to weasel out of it, but he surprised me. "Yes, of course," he said. "If no one else wants a starship of their own, I certainly won't turn it down."

Lanned was just as surprised as me. "I—well—" he stammered, looking from Perri to the others and back, "I—we don't have the food even if we wanted to let you," he said.

If Perri was relieved by that news, he didn't show it. "You're letting a priceless resource go to waste," he said.

The other Devernians looked at him as if he'd just sprouted horns, and one of them raised his handgun threateningly, but Lanned waved him back and said, "Maybe in a different time they were a resource. Now they're only a menace. Captain Pike, can your phaser rifles kill this egg before it hatches?"

"I don't know," I said. "Spock?"

He consulted his tricorder, frowning at the results. "The shell is composed of an unknown organic molecule with a hyperconnected bond structure. It is a superconductor of heat and electricity, and is opaque to most frequencies of electromagnetic radiation. Our phasers will not penetrate deeply, but they may be able to burn through under sustained fire." He looked up at me. "However, since there is no immediate danger, doing so prematurely will only destroy a valuable opportunity to study the development of a titan embryo."

"What good will that do?" one of the Devernians asked. "We already know how to kill 'em. Cannons don't do it on the first shot either, but if you hit 'em enough times in the same spot, you eventually punch through."

Spock raised a single eyebrow. "I am sure you do," he said. "However, additional knowledge can only improve your ability to deal with the titans, either to exterminate them more effectively or perhaps to discover a more benign way of handling the situation. In either case, knowledge is more useful than indiscriminate action." He reached out to touch the blackened surface of the egg just ahead of one of its fins. "For instance, were you aware that this egg has a defect right here which reduces its strength by twenty-six percent?"

"It does?"

"It does. It also has a tracery of microfissures emanating from this point here"—he stretched to tap a spot high around the curved surface—"which I presume is the pressure point that allows the egg to be opened from within." He took another tricorder reading, and nodded. "The position of the embryo lends support to that hypothesis. All its tentacles are clustered beneath this region, presumably to assist in pushing it outward."

"Hmm," said the Devernian. "What else do you see in there?"

Spock never got the chance to answer, because the team of men who had dismounted the cannon from the roof arrived with it just then. "Stand back!" they shouted. "Gun coming through!"

That cleared the path. Six Devernians, carrying the cannon between them like a coffin, struggled through the doorway with it and set it on its tripod a few steps from the surface of the egg. Now that I had a closer look I could see that it was a little more sophisticated than my first impression of it; it had a hinged breech for loading, and the gunners carried cartridges the size of their forearms tipped with armor-piercing slugs.

Even so, it was the wrong tool for the job. "You can't actually be thinking of shooting that thing in here," I said. "The ricochets would be more deadly than the titan."

"You've got a better idea?" one of them asked, mopping sweat from his forehead.

"Yes, as a matter of fact I do," I told him, raising my phaser rifle, but careful to point it toward the ceiling. "We'll take care of the egg when the time is right, but in the meantime Spock is studying it for weaknesses."

"He's already found a soft spot," the man who had been arguing with him before said.

"Then let's shoot it in the soft spot and be done with it!" the cannoneer said. "Where is it?"

"Right here," the other man said, slapping the weak area ahead of the fin.

"Yeah!" someone else shouted, and other people took up the cry as well. "Kill it! Kill it now, before it hatches!"

"Wait!" I shouted, but my voice was lost in the din.

The cannoneers aimed their gun at the side of the egg, and one of them pulled back a cocking lever. "Take cover!" he yelled.

"Wait!" I shouted again, but it was plain that they weren't about to.

So I did the only thing I could do. I shot the cannon. It wasn't made of a hyperconnected organic molecule; it was simple iron, and its atoms dissociated instantly under the blast of a phaser rifle.

There was a shocked silence, into which I said, "We've got the situation under control."

We didn't, of course. The Devernians weren't big on authority, and they weren't happy at all about losing a cannon to some upstart alien. I heard angry muttering and knew that in a moment it would become an angry roar. And most of these people were armed.

Yeoman Colt and Lieutenant Garrett held their phaser rifles ready, but it was all for show. We couldn't shoot these people, not until they shot one of us, and by then we'd probably all be dead.

I could only think of one thing that might appease them. "Sorry, Spock," I said, raising my phaser rifle and firing at the egg's weak spot. They were going to kill it in a few minutes anyway, I told myself, right after they finished with us.

An area about the size of my outstretched hand began to glow. Red at first, then orange, intensifying through yellow and green and blue to white. Sparks, then whole tongues of flame shot out from the target site, but it didn't burn through.

"Add your phasers to mine!" I ordered, and two more energy beams converged on the spot as Colt and Garrett fired. Spock continued recording, since a fourth rifle shouldn't have been necessary. There was enough energy pouring into that one spot to punch through a small asteroid, but the egg still resisted. I felt my phaser grow warm in my hands, but I kept firing.

Sparks and flames continued to gush from the incandescent spot; then at last, just as I was beginning to wonder if our power would hold out, we cut through to softer tissue. In one last gout of flame our beams lanced into the creature within, which convulsed in a frantic attempt to break free. The spot that Spock had identified as the fracture point bulged outward; then a piece the size of a dinner plate blew free with explosive force, barely missing his head. It clanged off the ceiling and fell at Lanned's feet, and a mass of writhing tentacles reached a couple of meters out through the hole. One of them caught the arm of a Devernian who stood too close and wrapped around it with incredible speed, then yanked the man off his feet and smashed him into the side of the egg.

I shifted my aim to the tentacles and held my finger down on the trigger. Even they were amazingly resistant to our energy beams, but they weren't as tough as the shell. Within a second or two they began to crisp, and the creature dropped the Devernian and yanked them back inside. All four of us continued to fire while the egg rocked back and forth and the baby titan screeched in agony, but at last it subsided and after a few more seconds for good measure we let off. Smoke rose from both holes in the egg, and the air reeked of cooked flesh. The titan was dead, but even with that much continuous fire we hadn't managed to vaporize it. I checked my phaser charge: I was down to twenty percent.

The Devernians' anger at us had given over to awe at the pyrotechnic spectacle. "Where can I get me one of those things?" one man asked.

"I think your cannon would probably have done a better job," I said, disgusted with our poor showing.

That was apparently the right thing to say. The man who had asked the question laughed, then someone else joined him, and pretty soon the whole room full of people were laughing and slapping one another on the backs. The man who had been grabbed by the arm got up and dusted himself off, wincing when he moved but laughing nonetheless. Colt and I and Garrett even exchanged wide grins. No matter who had done the actual job, the titan menace had been stopped, and that was cause for celebration.

Except for Spock, of course, who was still taking readings of the corpse with his tricorder. And frowning. He turned away from the egg and stepped through the office debris to the wall farthest from it, his tricorder still whirring softly as he waved it from side to side.

"Problems, Spock?" I asked.

"I am still detecting metabolic activity consistent with a titan embryo," he replied. "Not, however, from this egg."

"You mean there's another one nearby?"

"That is affirmative."

I felt a chill run up my spine. I had seen a second flash in the sky, but I had thought it was just an afterimage. Apparently it had been another egg. If I had sounded a warning, the Devernians could have taken care of that one as well.

Maybe they had anyway. We couldn't tell what was going on even a block away from where we were. But I knew we had better have a look.

"Let's go!" I said. "Spock, how far is it?"

"That is difficult to ascertain, Captain. Perhaps three or four hundred meters. As we draw closer I will be able to pinpoint it more accurately."

"Lead on," I said, sounding a great deal more confident than I felt. Now that I'd seen what we were up against, I had a lot more respect for the danger. Those tentacles coming out of the egg would haunt me for weeks. Plus we were about out of phaser energy, and we couldn't just run back to the *Enterprise* to recharge.

It took a moment to get out of the building. The Devernians farther away from us had no idea what was going on; they thought the action was still inside. We managed to push our way out, and once they saw a group of their own people following a tall, pointy-eared alien with a humming instrument in his hand, they joined in and we became a good-sized mob advancing up the street. We were a fairly slow mob, since Spock set the pace and he couldn't watch his tricorder and his footing at the same time; plus it was hard to run in the muck.

Lanned was right beside me as we slogged along after Spock. I asked him, "Isn't it a bit coincidental that two eggs dropped on the same city at the same time?"

"There's no coincidence about it, Captain," he replied. "They followed your ship in. Since we began shooting at titans in space and driving them away, whenever one nears the planet they drop as many eggs as they can."

I groaned. "Oh, wonderful. You're saying we actually *brought* them here."

He nodded. "Don't be too hard on yourself. I suspected it might happen. You wanted to see what the titan threat was like on the ground; I thought this would be as good a way as any to show it to you."

"You could have warned us," I said.

He gave me a calculating look. "And why should I? You have to agree that the surprise is part of the experience."

I supposed it was that, but I could definitely have done without it. Of course that was Lanned's whole point. All of Devernia could do without it, and that's why they were doing what they were doing.

Yeoman Colt had overheard our exchange. Now she said to Lanned, "It sounds to me like you just need to run a blockade rather than hunting titans with bombs. If you can keep them from coming near enough to lay their eggs, then you don't have to actually kill them. You could even let a few titans through the blockade over uninhabited places if you wanted."

"Whatever for?" asked Lanned.

"To keep the population going," she answered. Lanned snorted derisively, but she pressed on. "You and the Aronnians both need them for raw materials. If you kill them all, both your economies will suffer. What's wrong with a blockade, if it will keep them from dropping eggs on your cities?"

Lanned held his arms out wide. "You of all people should be able to understand the sheer magnitude of an entire planet. It's costing us everything we have to keep them at bay even now that we have reduced the population by half. If we don't kill them all this year, we won't have the resources to keep up the effort next year. How could we maintain a perpetual blockade?"

He had a good point, at least from the Devernian point of view. But Colt said, "How about a network of phaser satellites? I know phasers aren't much good against eggs, but they did seem to sting what was inside it. Automated satellites could fire on any titans that came close, except over whatever breeding ground you set aside for them. Pretty soon they'd get the idea."

Lanned considered it. "Aside from the fact that we don't have your less-than-wonderful phaser technology, how many satellites do you suppose that would require?"

"I don't know," Colt said, "but I'll bet it would be a lot fewer than the number of missiles it takes to blow them all up."

Spock hadn't appeared to be listening, but now he lowered his tricorder and said, "Aside from the obvious Prime Directive violation, the number of satellites is not trivial. A typical phaser cannon of the magnitude that could be installed in a satellite has an effective range of perhaps a thousand kilometers. To guard the surface of a spherical volume of space within synchronous orbit around a planet of this size, even with minimal overlap, would require seven thousand and fifty-six satellites."

"Oh," she said.

Spock turned back to his tricorder, the issue settled as far he was concerned. "I believe the second egg is somewhere in the next block," he said. "Twenty degrees to the right of the street's path and seventy meters distant."

I estimated the range. There was a three-story building about that far away; twenty degrees to the right of the street would put the egg just behind it. As we jogged toward it we heard shouts and a sharp *pop, pop, pop* that I assumed was the report from Devernian handguns.

"Sounds like someone else discovered it already," I said.

Just then a screech like a wounded tyrannosaur split the air.

Lanned turned white. Even the dark stripes on his face faded to practically nothing. He reached instinctively to his side for a weapon that wasn't there—he hadn't been wearing one when we beamed him aboard the *Enterprise,* and he hadn't picked up one since—then turned to me and said, "It has hatched already."

"I kind of gathered that," I told him, checking to make sure my phaser rifle was still set on maximum output.

Colt and Spock and Lieutenant Garrett did the same, and we advanced toward the source of the noise. Most of the Devernians who had followed us did so too, but I noticed a few backing away. Even some of the ones with weapons. Not a good sign.

Chapter Thirteen

"WHAT'S A TYRANNOSAUR?" the Klingon woman asked.

Pike looked over at her. So she was still listening, eh? Of course she was. And of course she wouldn't know what a tyrannosaur was.

"It's a big lizard," he told her. "About fifty meters tall, carnivorous, with a mouth big enough to park a shuttle-craft in."

"Where are they found?" she asked eagerly. "They sound like they would make interesting pets."

"They're found underground, these days. Fossilized. They lived on Earth a hundred million years ago, but they died out after an asteroid impact."

"Oh. Pity."

Pike laughed. "I'm not sure about that. Especially after what I saw on Devernia. Big monsters and people don't mix."

"What happened?" Nowan asked. "Who got killed?"

"Who didn't?" Pike asked, sobering somewhat. "I mean, think about it. The Devernians had a pretty decent planet, from what I saw of it. Their ancestors were minding their own business, making their own discoveries and working toward their own particular style of civilization, when all of a sudden these huge, ravenous beasts started dropping out of the sky. You can imagine what happened to the first guy who grew curious about an egg. And the first settlement near a landing site. Devernian history is full of death and destruction, all of it because of the titans."

Hompaq nodded approvingly. "Which no doubt strengthened them beyond measure. If you humans had lived when these tyrannosaurs did, you would have a more adventurous spirit."

"You think so?" asked Pike. "That's not what I found on Devernia. What I saw there was a society in collapse. They'd risen a long way, certainly, but they were on their way back down when we got there."

"Then they did not have a warrior's heart," Hompaq said, as though that were a moral failing worth damning an entire race for.

"You're right about that," Pike told her. "The only good thing I can say about the situation is that the Devernians had never discovered war. Oh, they knew about it. They understood the concept. They might even have gotten around to having one or two, if they could just take care of those pesky titans first. But their common enemy united them like nothing else could."

Nowan pursed his lips, considering that statement for a moment, before he said, "Perhaps that was not such a bad trade-off, if the outside threat truly eliminated warfare. Think of all the suffering humanity would have been spared if only we had fought against nature rather than one another."

Pike shrugged. "Eaten by dinosaurs or blown up by bombs; dead is dead."

"But the moral price to society is far less acute."

"True enough." Considering where this guy said he'd come from, Pike wasn't surprised he felt that way. "I agree with you," he said, "at least in principle. But when

I remember what it felt like staring into the mouth of a wounded titan, I'm not so sure I would have appreciated the distinction at the time."

"So it did attack you?" asked Nowan.

"Oh yes. And everyone else within reach, too. We had quite a time with it."

" 'Quite a time'? A monster from the gates of Hell attacks and you had 'quite a time'? Sir, I'm afraid I must accuse you of understatement, if not false modesty as well."

Pike cocked his head sideways, and an impish grin slowly crept across his face. "Okay, then, we had a hell of a time. Bodies everywhere. Blood and guts and bullets and phaser beams flying back and forth, and the titan snarling and coming on like a runaway hovercar and the wounded screaming to be put out of their misery and heroic action on all sides and—"

"Enough, enough! I preferred 'quite a time.' "

Pike laughed. "I thought so. But it really was that."

"So divulge your secrets forthwith. Who went down the beast's gullet? This is your tale, so we know who played the hero, but who helped you bring it to its knees?"

Hompaq said, "It didn't have knees."

"I was speaking metaphorically," Nowan replied. Of Pike, he asked, "What did it look like, then? Like an octopus, perhaps?"

"A little," Pike replied. "Or a spider. Of course it was moving so fast what it mostly looked like at any given moment was a muddy ball of snakes. With big, triangular teeth . . ."

Chapter Fourteen

WE COULDN'T go through the building; the people inside had slammed the heavy steel doors and weren't willing to open them for anyone. So we had to run down a narrow alley between that building and the next one. I expected the titan to rush toward us at any moment and catch us in the cramped space, but we made it to the alley in back without incident.

What we found there, however, was just as chilling as what I'd feared. The egg had come down in a courtyard garden, splashing up a wall of muddy soil which the hatchling now hid behind while it gulped down the body of a luckless Devernian. The mud had blocked off a corner of the courtyard, so the titan had two walls for protection behind it, and the mud in front. Fragments of eggshell sticking up from the mud also helped shield it from attack. All I could see of it was its mouth, round and lined with concentric rings of triangular teeth which all pointed inward to prevent their prey from escaping. The Devernian was beyond trying; only his legs stuck out now, and they betrayed no sign of life.

The others were firing a nearly continuous barrage from their projectile guns, but the beast kept too low for them to hit anything vital. The muddy bank spattered with ricocheting bullets, and I heard a few of them whiz past over our heads as well. I looked upward to see why the cannoneers on the rooftops hadn't fired yet, and I realized that the ones on the building right beside the creature couldn't shoot straight down on it. The building across the alley was only a single story tall, which gave the cannon there little better vantage than what we had from the ground. They were no doubt holding their fire for a clear shot.

The baby titan finished swallowing; then snarled again and stuck its head up over the edge. The cannon roared and the titan jerked backward, but I couldn't even see a wound where the projectile had struck. I saw where it bounced to, though; from the titan's nose it smashed into the stone steps by the building's back door, which acted like a perfect right-angle reflector and lofted it right back at the gun that had fired it. Fortunately gravity and air resistance had taken their toll, and it merely struck the building below their feet and fell to the ground, hissing as it cooled on the mud.

"Spock," I said, leaning close so he could hear me over the barrage of gunfire. "Can you find the weak spots here, too?"

"Affirmative, Captain," he replied, looking up from his tricorder. "Its body appears to be a compressed version of the adult form—an aerodynamic oblong with a large ramscoop mouth at the front and four small fins at the back which end in three tentacles per fin. Its skin is made of overlapping scales of the same material from which the eggshell is made, but it has four eyes set at equidistant points around the base of its mouth. The eyelids are also shielded, of course, but much less so than the rest of the body. If we could burn through the lids, the sockets beneath offer access directly to the brain."

"Great! How big are those eyes?"

"Approximately ten centimeters across."

"Oh." Maybe it wasn't so great after all. Ten centimeters across was hardly bigger than the palm of my hand. I was a fair shot with a phaser, but to hit a spot that size on a moving target, and hold the beam there until it burned through to the vital organs beneath, wasn't going to be easy.

We had to try it, though. I turned to Colt and Garrett and shouted, "Next time it shows itself, aim for the eyes!"

I considered moving closer, but that would put me in the path of the Devernians, and they didn't seem to be very cautious in their aim. What I really needed was high ground, but there were no trees in the courtyard and the building was smooth-sided and windowless. So we just shouldered our rifles and waited for the titan to rise above its shelter.

We didn't have to wait long. One Devernian was apparently not enough to assuage its hunger, or maybe it was smart enough to realize it couldn't stay hidden forever, but whatever the reason, it leaped out from behind the mud bank and raced toward us, its mouth open wide and its tentacles churning like multiple jointed legs to propel it along.

All I could see was mouth. I fired a quick burst at that, hoping to turn the creature aside, but its overlapping teeth were made of the same stuff as the eggshell and it hardly felt a thing. The Devernians fired dozens of shots directly into its gullet as well, with no more effect.

Colt and Garrett split apart to try and flank it. Even Spock clipped his tricorder back on his belt and raised his phaser rifle, but he held his fire until he could see an eye.

The rooftop cannon roared again, but the shot fell behind the creature. It was moving fast, covering the fifteen or twenty paces between its hiding spot and its attackers in a couple of seconds. They didn't stick around for it, however; the crowd split apart in two separate waves racing in either direction down the alley.

The titan turned to the right, toward us instead of broadside to us, which meant we still didn't have a good shot at it. And now it was coming straight at Lieutenant Garrett.

He fired his phaser down its throat. I aimed for the tentacles, the only other part of it I could see. Colt, off to our left, fired at its flank.

The triple combination definitely got its attention. And that probably saved Garrett's life, because the titan couldn't see what it was charging with its enormous ramscoop mouth opened wide. It slammed the mouth closed and turned its head sideways to get a better view of what had stung it, and all four of us immediately fired on the exposed eye.

The titan whipped around again, opening its mouth and roaring in pain. Our shots hadn't penetrated deeply, but we had definitely blinded that eye. And now that it had turned toward Spock and me, Garrett had a clear shot at the eye on the other side. His red energy beam lanced out, and the titan screeched and whirled around toward him, which let us have another shot at the eye we had already hit.

It had stopped advancing, but now it held its eyelids closed over its two damaged eyes, and the way it shook its head from side to side we couldn't hold our fire long enough to burn through to the brain.

The rooftop cannon fired once more, and this time the shot had an effect. The gunners were also aiming for the creature's eyes, and even though they missed the top one the massive slug struck with enough force to drive the titan's head momentarily to the ground. The armor-piercing core had ripped a ragged hole in its scaly hide, from which thick bluish green blood began to well up.

We took the opportunity to fire once more on the eye we could see, burning away the eyelid before the titan whirled around and fled for cover again.

"One more shot and we'll have it!" I shouted to the others.

That was easier said than done. The titan had hunkered down between the mudbank and the stone building and didn't present so much as a tendril for us to shoot at.

Perri and Lanned had both stayed with us during its charge. I felt flattered at their confidence in our ability, but considering how hard these things were to kill I also thought that confidence was a bit misplaced. My phaser was down to seven percent now. I had about two more good shots before I might as well start using it as a club.

Lanned didn't know that, of course. He said, "Come on, let's get closer. It's half blind now; we should be able to get within easy range."

"Getting within range is only part of the battle," I reminded him. "Surviving to do any good once we're there is just as important."

The look he gave me said "Chicken!" just as clearly as words. I believe he would have walked right up to the wounded titan and fired at it point-blank if I had given him my phaser, but I didn't.

Yeoman Colt had come back toward us again, and was looking toward its hiding place with a thoughtful expression on her face. "Captain?" she said.

"Yes?"

"What about those fragments of eggshell?"

They were still sticking up out of the ground on our side of the mud bank that the entire egg had splashed up when it struck. And some of them were big enough for a person to hide behind.

"The titan could flatten those in an instant," I said.

"Not that curved piece."

There was a hemispherical section of shell resting on its side near the top of the mud slope. A person could crouch down beside it, and if the titan rushed him the shell would fall over and cover him like a bomb shelter. Maybe. If the titan didn't rip it away and eat him instead.

"There's got to be a better way than that," I said,

looking around at the courtyard to see what it might be, but the building was no more scalable than it had been before, and no trees had grown in the few minutes since we had arrived.

A few Devernians trickled back down the alley toward us, but the courtyard had grown quiet as we all—even the titan—waited for something to happen. Every moment we waited, though, gave it time to regain its strength, maybe even to heal the wounds we had given it. I had no idea how fast it could do that, but I didn't want to learn the hard way.

I picked up a fist-sized rock near my feet and flung it over the embankment. It hit the titan with a loud crack, but the creature didn't raise a tendril. Could we have killed it? We couldn't be that lucky. No, it was just too smart to leave cover again without good reason.

"Trade me rifles, Mr. Spock," I said, holding out my phaser to him. He didn't protest; he simply exchanged his nearly charged phaser for my nearly depleted one, then said, "The upper and lower eyes are still functional. Be careful."

"Right. The rest of you get close together so you can all aim for the same eye we hit before. Fire the moment it comes into view." I took a couple of steps toward the eggshell.

"Wait, Captain." I turned around. It was Colt. "You can't . . . I mean . . . it was my idea."

"And it's a good one," I said. "If it works, you'll receive a commendation."

"That's not what I meant, sir," she said stiffly.

"I know it isn't." I smiled. "When you're captain, then it'll be your turn to have all the fun."

I turned back and walked toward the egg, stepping lightly so the titan couldn't hear my approach. For once the soft ground helped out; I couldn't have made noise if I'd wanted to.

The eggshell stank. I didn't care; I didn't plan to stay there long. I approached it cautiously, made sure I knew where to jump if I had to, then peered around it to see if I could spot the titan.

It was looking right at me. The eyes on either side of its head were black and bubbling, but it held its head up so it could use the lower one. For a split second we stared at one another, then the titan roared a challenge and leaped up. I fired at its good eye, held the beam as long as I dared, then jumped for cover. As I flew through the air I saw three more phaser beams converge on a spot right over my head, and I had just enough time to curse my stupidity for taking the most fully charged phaser with me before the eggshell slammed down around me and the world went dark.

Devernia tasted terrible. I spit out a mouthful of salty mud, then pulled my arms and legs in close to my body. I didn't have room to get to my knees; I had to lie on my left side and hold the phaser rifle next to my chest. The eggshell muffled sound, but it couldn't block it completely, and I could hear the titan screeching right overhead. I expected it to crush the eggshell and flatten me into the mud at any second, but the noise went on and on and I felt only a few thumps against the shell. I heard a distant boom and knew that the cannon had fired again, then more screeching and the ground shook like jelly.

The eggshell slammed downward, pressing me deeper into the mud. I tried to move my feet, tried to raise my head, but I was pinned. I could move my hands just enough to feel that I had less than an arm's reach of space in any direction, which meant I had enough air for maybe five minutes at most.

The way it stank, running out might be a blessing.

I still held the phaser rifle. Its emitter was right near my head, and I didn't have room to turn it around. I didn't want to fire it in the enclosed space anyway; I had seen how long it took to burn through the eggshell material, and I didn't want to breathe the fumes it would generate while it did.

No more noise came from outside. They must have killed the titan, then. Much good would that do me; I suspected its body was lying directly on top of me.

I tried scratching at the ground to see if I could dig my way out, but the eggshell had been driven deep into the muddy soil and I could only dig a little ways before the hole began to fill again.

Suddenly I heard three soft thumps on the shell. Someone was out there! I thumped back with my fist, but it was like hitting a boulder. I could barely hear it even on my side. I grasped the phaser rifle and swung its butt against the shell near my knees and that did the trick. I pounded out three sharp raps in reply.

There were a couple more thumps from outside, then silence. I listened for a voice, but if anyone was calling to me, the shell blocked the sound.

"Hello!" I shouted, just in case they could hear *me*. "I'm okay, but I'm running out of air!"

Nothing. I thought I saw light, but then I realized it was phantom tracers in my own eyes. I didn't have much time left.

I tried to think of something I'd missed, but it was getting hard to keep my mind on the problem. I was getting sleepy, and I could hear a great rushing sound in my ears as I started to black out.

Well, I thought, *at least they're not going to find my body next to a full phaser rifle.*

I held the emitter up to the surface of the shell as far from my head as I could, and pulled the trigger. Bright light nearly blinded me as layer after layer of the tough polymer vaporized under its blast, but there was more shell than I had strength for. The phaser wavered, cutting a wide groove, before I braced my arms and held it on the original spot again. The tracers in my eyes grew worse, and my lungs felt as if they were on fire, but I held my finger on the trigger until the phaser beam sputtered and flared out.

The light didn't die. I saw a tiny circle of white,

decided it had to be an afterimage in my eyes from staring at such an intense glare, but then just as I was about to lose consciousness the thought struck me: Afterimages of bright spots were dark, not light.

I awoke to a wet, sucking sound that I thought at first must be the noise a body makes as it slides down a monster's throat, but after a moment I realized I was still under the eggshell. Light was pouring in through a ragged hole in its side—light and sweet, wonderful air.

The sucking sound came again. Somebody was lifting the shell off me! Air rushed in through the hole to fill the partial vacuum created as it rose, and I stuck my face into the stream and breathed greedily. Who cared what it smelled like; it held oxygen!

Then I had a bad thought: What if it was the *titan* prying up the eggshell? I had just used up the last of my phaser charge.

I didn't have more than a few seconds to worry about it before the shell slid free of the mud and flew up over my head. I uncurled and sat up, ready to shove the rifle down the creature's throat ahead of me, at least, but instead of its ravenous mouth I saw dozens of people encircling me.

"Captain!" shouted Colt and Garrett. A cheer went up from the Devernians. I rose shakily to my feet and said, "Thank you!" but nobody could hear me.

There was so much shouting and backslapping that I was afraid the Devernians would finish the job that the titan had started, but they stopped just short of breaking bones. Colt offered her arm to steady me as I staggered under the assault, and I managed to stay on my feet.

On top of the embankment lay the body of the titan. Smoke rose from the side of its head where its right eye used to be. Its tentacles lay limp now, dangling from undeveloped stabilizing fins that would never guide it through an atmosphere. I supposed I should have felt bad about its death, but at the moment I couldn't. I looked over at Perri, but the Aronnian looked more stunned than dismayed.

He also looked completely disheveled. So did everyone else, now that I thought about it. I looked down at my own clothing, which was covered in mud all along the left side. I had mud in my hair as well. I must have looked even worse than the others, but at the moment I didn't care. The titan was dead and I was alive.

When things died down a bit I noticed Spock—who barely had a hair out of place—scanning the body with his tricorder again. His expression was that of a scientist making a major discovery.

"What is it, Spock?" I asked him.

"Fascinating," he replied. "In addition to its digestive organs and nervous system, this immature titan already has a partially developed warp engine, a fully operational fusion engine, and a microtubule hydrogen storage tank of surprising capacity. The tank is empty now, but next to it is an osmotic filtration system capable of filtering enough deuterium from seawater to completely fuel it within two weeks' time."

Its fusion engine was already developed? "We're lucky it wasn't fueled when it hatched," I said, "or it could have fried us all in a heartbeat."

"That is true," he replied, "but luck may have played less of a role than simple evolutionary pressure."

"Evolution?" I asked. "How so?"

Spock continued scanning with his tricorder as he answered. "Deuterium is a precious resource in space, but it is relatively abundant on planets. Since the hatchling would not normally need flight capability until it was ready to leave for space again, there would be no reason for the mother to deplete her own supply of deuterium by providing any to the developing egg."

"I guess that makes a certain amount of sense," I replied. "Although I find it hard to believe that anything could evolve a fusion engine in the first place."

"Nevertheless," Spock said, "I find considerable evidence that the osmotic fueling system, at least, is a relatively new addition to their genetic code. I have a theory, based on my study of the unhatched egg and this more developed specimen. Are you familiar with the concept of neoteny?"

I realized I was standing there in the middle of a devastated courtyard, tired and wet and covered with mud, while my science officer was about to expound on the origin of the creature that had nearly killed me. "No, Spock," I said. "I'm not familiar with it, but I don't think this is the time to go into it. I want a hot shower first, and a good meal."

He nodded stiffly, obviously disappointed that he couldn't share his theory with everyone, and went back to gathering more information.

I took my communicator from my belt and flipped it open, but it didn't respond. Not surprising; it was full of mud.

I sighed. "Yeoman, could you please call the *Enterprise* and request beam-out?"

"Yes sir," she replied. She took out her communicator and opened it with both hands. "Colt to *Enterprise*. Come in, *Enterprise*."

"Enterprise here," Dabisch replied.

"Six to beam up."

"We're on our way, but it'll take a few minutes. These titans have been chasing us halfway around the system."

"Understood." She paused a moment, then said, "Captain, if they come in over the city again, the titans who follow them will just drop more eggs."

She was right. "Tell them to stay over the ocean and beam us out from there," I said.

She relayed the order, then closed her communicator.

Lanned said, "I'm not sure I want to go back to your ship. I've got a planet to help defend here."

I couldn't argue with him. Not after what I'd seen. Even Perri didn't seem inclined to protest.

Spock, however, said, "If my theory about their origin

is correct, we may have need of someone who understands their habits."

"So what's your theory?" Lanned asked.

"The short version," I said. "We've only got a few minutes."

"Understood. I think it is quite obvious that the titans are not indigenous to the Devernian nor the Aronnian planetary systems. Their metabolic processes share nothing with the local biology, and we have Lanned's own testimony that they appeared only five hundred years ago. They must therefore come from a neighboring system. From the stages of development that I have studied, I find evidence that they are evolving at a rapid rate. This indicates to me that they are adapting to a new ecological niche, which in turn indicates that they had a considerably different living arrangement wherever they came from."

"So?" asked Lanned. "It's what they're doing here that concerns us."

"Just so," said Spock. "What they are doing here, essentially, is breeding without check. Yet they cannot breed like this everywhere they go, or they would have overrun the galaxy already. Therefore, if you wish to stop them from doing so here, I suggest finding out what keeps them in check elsewhere. If we can do that, we can perhaps stabilize their population at a less dangerous— and ultimately more useful—level."

"I'm not sure I want to find something big enough to eat a titan," Perri said nervously.

"And I'm not sure I'd want it in my solar system if we found it," Lanned said. "It could easily cause more trouble than even the titans do."

"Predators do not have to be larger than their prey, nor even more fearsome," said Spock. "On my home planet, Vulcan, the sehlat is our most efficient predator, yet it is no larger than me and gentle enough to be kept as a pet. On Earth, where Captain Pike comes from, wolves are a similar predator. There are also parasites and disease to consider, either of which can limit the population of creatures far larger than themselves."

Lanned thought it over for a moment. I heard a murmur run through the crowd around us as Spock's idea passed along from person to person. I was thinking about it, too, but from a different angle than they were. I was trying to decide if we had a Prime Directive problem on our hands.

The Prime Directive stated that Starfleet personnel were prohibited from interfering with the normal development of a society. Generally that meant no interference whatsoever, but the key phrase in the rule was "normal development." Devernia hadn't enjoyed anything like "normal development" since the titans had arrived. How bad was an outside influence to correct another outside influence?

I could have radioed Starfleet Headquarters for advice. They would mull it over for a year or three, kick it up to higher authority for review, and eventually come to a decision about the time the last Devernian was eaten. And if that happened it would be my fault, because *I* was supposed to be the higher authority. It was my job to be Starfleet's representative on the scene. I knew the rules as well as anyone, I knew the exceptions that had been allowed before, and I knew the disasters that had happened when they were ignored. I also—at least theoretically—knew the situation at hand better than anyone else.

So it was my call. If I made the right decision, I could become a hero. If I made the wrong one, I could face a court-martial, though I might still be a hero to the people my decision saved.

When I thought about it that way, the choice didn't seem that difficult to make.

Lanned must have been thinking along the same lines. Besides which, I could see the same gleam in his eyes that I had seen in Perri's when he had first arrived on board the *Enterprise*. Lanned had been in space before, but he had never ridden a titan. The prospect of an interstellar flight definitely appealed to him. And if he returned home a hero, well, so much the better.

"Very well," he said. "I will accompany you on your search for the home of the titans."

Chapter Fifteen

In the Captain's Table, the seaman who sat across from Captain Pike had the same gleam in his eyes. He shook his head slowly, in the manner of a man who doesn't know whether or not to believe what he's just heard. "Sailing from star to star," he said. "What man wouldn't jump at the chance?"

"Oh, lots of them," Pike replied. "Even nowadays there are millions of people who won't leave the planet."

"Millions? That implies that millions have the choice, does it not?"

"Well, sure, but even when spaceflight was limited to just a few trained astronauts, there were millions of people who didn't want *them* to go either. Humanity has always had its share of stay-at-homes." He looked over to Hompaq and said, before she could make the obvious snide comment, "And so do the Klingons, or your homeworld would be a ghost planet."

She had indeed been about to say something, but she stopped with her mouth open, then laughed softly and said, "That's not necessarily true. We could all come and go."

"You could. But you don't, do you?"

"No."

Nowan looked at the two of them for a moment, biting his lower lip while he worked up his nerve to say something. Pike noticed his hesitation and asked, "What?"

He breathed deeply, exhaled, then said, "I mean no offense, but when you first began your tale I felt confident that you were merely a skilled fabulist. The very things you described lent credence to that theory, for I knew they could never actually happen. Yet you speak so convincingly of them, and pile detail upon detail, until I can no longer maintain my disbelief. You *do* voyage among the stars, do you not?"

"I did," Pike admitted. "Nowadays I've got a desk job just up the street."

"And this disturbs you. You have lost something valuable, a part of your life that you are afraid you may never recover."

"Guilty," Pike said, surprised at how obvious his melancholy must be.

"That merely caps the edifice of credibility you have been constructing all evening. Somehow, in some way I cannot yet fathom, you travel the stars. She also travels the stars. And this . . . being over here—" he nodded toward the reptilian humanoid near the door, who blinked one eye and dipped a long, orange tongue into his blood-red drink "—could only come from another star himself. For you, this apparently isn't even unusual."

Pike laughed softly. "Oh, it's unusual enough. I've never seen our friend by the door's species before, nor the curvaceous cat-woman's, either. Klingons I've seen aplenty, but finding one in a bar half a kilometer from Starfleet Headquarters is a bit out of my experience as well." He looked around the bar as he spoke, slowly building up his own nerve to ask the question that had now become foremost in his mind. He felt a bit silly actually voicing it, but he could no longer ignore the evidence. "I imagine my confusion is slight compared to yours. Tell me, what was the stardate when you entered this bar?"

"Stardate? If you refer to the Julian method of calculation, that has been out of vogue for more than a century. In the Gregorian reckoning, today is August twelfth, 1861."

The only surprise Pike felt came when he realized how little Nowan's words surprised him. He had already suspected something like this. He had no idea how it could be possible, but he knew this guy was the genuine article.

Nowan, too, was ready to believe. "And what was the date when you entered?" he asked. "No, wait, let me guess. Your *Enterprise* is the size of a small city. It is the pride of your star fleet, but it is not the only one of its kind. Millions of people have traveled in ships like it, or had the opportunity. For this to happen, I would guess fully two hundred years must have passed between my time and yours."

"Good guess," Pike told him. "But you didn't figure on two world wars before spaceflight even got started, and a whole generation of people who thought it was more expensive than it was worth, plus the Eugenics Wars and another world war after that. When I woke up this morning it was stardate 1626.8. In the Gregorian system that would be, let's see . . . times eight, carry the six . . . October third, 2266. Or is it the seventh? I can never remember the conversion factors."

It didn't matter to Nowan. "Good God! Over four hundred years. I am dust and bones to you."

"Maybe, maybe not," Pike said. "You're here now." He turned to Hompaq. "How about you?" he asked. "What's your era?"

She bared her teeth. "I could dance on your grave, Captain Pike, if I could reach it."

"Do tell," he said casually, but inside he felt as if he'd just grasped a live plasma conduit. She could be playing games with him, but he didn't think so. There were too many discrepancies in this bar for him to be in the right time either. And it was all fine and good to think of the poor seaman as a castaway on the shoals of time, but when he suddenly found himself the anachronism, things became a great deal more personal.

He couldn't let it go, though. "Where am I buried?" he asked.

"Do you really want to know?"

Did he? Probably not, but he'd always hated those hokey tri-vids where the characters backed away from information that later turned out to be vital. The location of his grave was probably the most vital information he was likely to get, so he said, "Sure. Where am I buried?"

"Remember Talos IV?" she asked.

"How could I forget?" For Nowan's benefit he said, "Yeoman Colt and Number One and I were captured by aliens there once. They had the power to completely cloud our minds, to make us see anything they wanted us to. We barely got away." To Hompaq he said, "Talos IV has been interdicted. It's a capital offense even to communicate with the Talosians. Why would anyone take my body there?"

"Maybe you're not dead when you go," she said.

Again he felt that shock of dissonance. How easily she spoke of his demise! Killed by Talosians after all. What a rotten way to go. And the worst part of it was, he would probably not even know he was there. They would make him think he was back on the *Enterprise*, or horseback riding in Mojave, while he was really strapped to a dissecting table in their filthy underground warrens.

"Why would I ever go back?" he asked. "Can they lure

me there over this kind of distance? If so, then nobody is safe."

The bartender had been listening quietly, but now he spoke up. "Calm yourself, Captain," he said. "Talos is no threat to anyone. But you could be, if you followed that line of thought."

Pike didn't even have to ask what he meant by that. An entire career of interstellar duty had driven home the Prime Directive and all that it implied. Partial knowledge could be more dangerous than ignorance. If Pike thought the Talosians were mounting an attack on the Federation, he could set into motion a preemptive strike that would drain Federation resources at a time when they were already facing threats on too many fronts. Not to mention starting a battle with someone who might not deserve it—though Pike had no love for the Talosians.

Nor Klingons, when it came to that, yet he found himself strangely attracted to Hompaq. He looked more closely at her. That heavily convoluted forehead wasn't normal for Klingons. At least not Klingons of his era. Nor, he suspected, was it the result of an accident. Hompaq must have been from far enough in the future that her race had actually evolved into this form. Or maybe this was a cosmetic thing, a personal choice she had encoded into her own genes for amusement.

Or for battle. He would hate to butt heads with her in a dark alley.

"So tell me, are we at war with one another?" he asked her.

"In whose time?"

"In—" He stopped, realizing how utterly meaningless his question was. They weren't at war yet in his time, and Hompaq could be from anywhen. He looked back to the bartender. "What date is it *here,* right *now?*"

The bartender shook his head. "I can't answer that."

"Why? Prime Directive?" Pike asked him.

"More like meaningless question."

"Okay, then, *where* are we?"

"Equally meaningless."

"Then how did I get here?"

"You walked through the door. And if you ever want to find this place again after you leave, that's about all the more you want to ask about it."

"Why?" Pike asked. The bartender rolled his eyes, and Pike realized he was being a pest. And maybe he was jeopardizing something truly special. He had heard of places like this before, in legends of fairy rings and disappearing magic shops. Always the newcomer was warned not to inquire too closely into the secret. He was the newcomer here, and he had just received the same warning, but he had never been satisfied with the legends and he wasn't satisfied now. "What does it matter if I know where this place is, or when it is?" he asked.

The bartender sighed. "When did you say you were from? 2266?"

"Yeah."

"Then you are familiar with the Heisenberg Uncertainty Principle."

"It's impossible to know both the position and the velocity of a particle at any given time. So?"

"So that's three variables. The velocity of the envelope of space-time that encompasses this bar is negligible. That means you can either know its position or the time, but not both. Take your pick, but hold on to your hat if you decide on the time."

"That's—we have Heisenberg compensators on our transporters to get around that very problem."

"We don't," said the bartender. He looked at Pike with a steady gaze, waiting for him to decide.

"So I'm just supposed to relax and accept it?" Pike asked at last.

"That's the general idea." The bartender smiled, then turned away and began to polish his glassware.

Pike looked at Hompaq, who also smiled in her pointy-toothed way, then he looked at the other bar patrons, who all wore amused expressions as well. Even the seaman at his own table was grinning.

"Why do I feel like the ghost at the banquet?" Pike asked him.

"It appears we're all ghosts at this particular banquet," Nowan replied. "And while I have never heard of this Heisenberg mystery you refer to, I suspect our esteemed host has the right of it. My inquiry, and yours following it, have proved to be a herring in the path of our Devernian fox. We turn aside at our peril, and disappoint all who follow the hunt."

Pike saw that everyone else in the bar had once again stopped what they were doing to follow what he and Nowan were saying. He felt a bit put on the spot. Didn't these people know that it wasn't polite to eavesdrop on someone else's conversation?

At least it wasn't polite in Pike's time. But customs varied from time to time and place to place, and as he had been gently informed just now, he wasn't in Kansas anymore. Nor San Francisco, most likely. Nor, for that matter, in 2266.

But if any custom was likely to be universal, he imagined it was the one that said it was impolite to stop telling a story in the middle.

There would be time enough later to unravel the mystery of the Captain's Table, if he decided to pursue it.

He took a cautious sip of his Saurian brandy—he had drunk quite enough of that for a while, but he did need to lubricate his throat a bit—then said, "Very well, the Devernians. Let's see . . . Spock had decided that the titans had opened the wrong door and wound up someplace they didn't belong, so we were about to head off in search of their rightful home. Fortunately we didn't worry about the Heisenberg Uncertainty Principle, or we might never have tried. . . ."

Chapter Sixteen

I STAYED IN THE shower for a good half hour, letting both water and ultrasonics scour away the memory of Devernia. I suspect the rest of my landing party did the same; none of them surfaced again for at least an hour after our return. Except for Spock, of course. He was already on the bridge when I got there, poring over star charts for the local region of space. I settled into my command chair and said to Number One, "Status?"

"All systems operational, sir," she reported. "Engineering is still repairing minor subsystems all through the ship, but the engines and helm controls are back up to specs. Shields are functioning at one hundred percent, and energy reserves are at full capacity. We're ready for space."

"Good. Mr. Spock, have you figured out where we should go yet?"

"I have identified seven stars as likely candidates for the origin of the titans," he said. "Unfortunately my selection criteria must remain rather crude until I receive further data, so these seven are merely the ones that are closer to Devernia than Aronnia and which also possess gas-giant planets."

"I would think that would include half the galaxy," I said. "How did you narrow it down to seven?"

"By factoring in the calculated speed and maximum range of the titans. Their energy source is deuterium fusion, not matter-antimatter annihilation, so they have a much more limited range than we do. By calculating the size of their fuel tanks and estimating the efficiency of their warp engines, I came up with a figure of fifteen light-years as their maximum range without refueling."

"Very clever," I said. "So which one of our targets is the closest of the seven?"

Spock put a star map up on the main screen, and used the computer's pointer to indicate one of the myriad stars on it. "This one here, which is actually a G2-F6 double, designated merely by a survey record number of L2334.45."

"A double star, that's good," I said. "Two chances of finding something in one place."

"It also has the advantage of being on the edge of an unexplored sector," said Spock. "I assume that we would have records of titans from other survey teams if anyone had encountered them; therefore it seems likely that what we seek is in unexplored space."

"Very likely indeed," I said. "Mr. Tyler, you have the coordinates. Number One, take us there, warp factor seven."

"Yes sir." As soon as Tyler keyed in the course she engaged the warp engines and the *Enterprise* leaped away from Devernia. I wasn't sorry to see it fall away behind us when we switched the viewscreen back to the exterior view.

I busied myself with the detailed ship's status report that Dabisch had prepared for me, noting that a work crew had gone out in a shuttlecraft to check the damage we had received to the outer hull when the titans had physically attacked us. The video of that was pretty sobering: dents in the duranium from direct impacts, long gashes from the titans' armor-plated ramscoop mouths, sensors torn entirely free . . . it would take months to repair it all. The video tour zoomed in on one window with a star-shaped crack in it and I wondered if anyone had been inside the room when it happened. Possibly; the damage report indicated that the window was in observation room J-12, which might have held off-duty crew members interested in watching our approach to Devernia. Somehow what they would have seen seemed even scarier than what I had faced on the planet, though I couldn't explain even to myself why the prospect of being sucked into space by explosive decompression and then eaten was any worse than simply being eaten.

The repair crew had not yet repaired the window; until they could get to it they had merely covered it with an external sealant and closed the room to use. It wouldn't have done anyone much good to go in there now anyway, I noticed, since the sealant was black.

When I finished the status report and still hadn't heard from either of our guests, I asked the computer to locate them for me.

"Both Perri and Lanned are in the cafeteria," it replied in its synthesized female voice, which I had always thought sounded just like Number One's. I sometimes kidded her about it, telling her that it must mean she had the theoretically perfect pitch and intonation for easy understanding, but this time the computer's words robbed all thought of teasing from my mind.

"Uh-oh," I said. The two of them together unsupervised sounded like a good way to start a food fight.

"Number One, you have the conn," I told her as I headed downship to stop it.

When I got there, however, I found them both at the same table, chatting happily with Yeoman Colt. All three of them glowed from recent showers, and Colt glowed even more from all the attention she was receiving. I felt a momentary pang of annoyance, but I quashed it immediately. It was part of her job to help entertain guests; if she happened to enjoy it, so much the better.

I almost turned away to leave them to their conversation, but Perri looked up and saw me at the door before I could go. "Ah, Captain," he said. "I see we are under way already." He nodded out the windows to where the white starlike streaks that formed the subspace representation of interstellar space were sweeping past.

"No sense wasting time," I replied. "There's a lot of places to search, and not much time if we want to save both Devernia and the titans."

He nodded. "After seeing conditions there I must say I'm not sure how both can be saved, but I agree we must try."

Lanned made a rude noise with his lips. "Such a selfless position, for someone who stands to benefit greatly if we succeed."

"As will you," said Perri. "You seem determined to declare yourself at cross-purposes with me, but the truth of the matter is that we are both now interested in the same thing."

"Indeed," said Lanned, and he turned his attention back to Colt.

She laughed. "You had better keep your minds on the titans."

"What's the hurry? It will be a day at least before we arrive at the first star system. A great deal can happen in a day."

"Can it really?," she asked innocently, but she kept smiling.

"Well," I said, "it looks like you've got the situation here under control. I'll leave you three to it." I turned away, then remembered where we were and turned back to Lanned. "I don't know if Dr. Boyce mentioned this to you yet, but you can't have onions or garlic. You either, Mr. Perri. Don't forget."

Lanned said, "Yes, I received the unfortunate news.

And now of course my tongue yearns for this exotic flavor that's forever denied me." He said to Colt, "You will have to describe it to me in full sensual detail."

"Onions?" she asked. "Sensual?" Then she got a mischievous look on her face and said, "Well, maybe so. Under the right circumstances."

"See?" cried Lanned. "I knew it. Ah, cruel fate!"

"Be glad that's the only thing you're denied," I told him, then I took my leave.

He seemed a bit taken aback at my tone of voice, but I didn't even try to explain. Maybe Colt could explain it to him, but I really didn't know.

As I walked back to the turbolift I thought about the strange quirks of fate that put some people in position to enjoy a thing that someone else could not. It could certainly be frustrating. I imagined it seemed quite unfair to anyone caught on the receiving end of a Prime Directive problem, for instance. Or the not-receiving end, as it were. It would be tough enough to discover someone who had solved a problem that still loomed large in your own society, but how much harder it must be to watch them leave without telling you how they'd done it.

I wondered if that was what we would find somewhere ahead of us. Spock said he'd found evidence that the titans were evolving, but I had a hard time imagining what they could have evolved *from*. The way I figured it, they had to be genetically engineered, and that implied a society somewhere ahead of us that could do it. Ahead both spatially and technologically.

The *Enterprise* had already met a few superior races, and without exception those encounters had been unpleasant. We'd been captured, toyed with, dismissed, and demoralized more than once, and I didn't want it to happen again. Yet it could happen at any moment out here in uncharted space. No Federation ship had ever been to this star we approached now; we could find just about anything there.

Lanned had been right: at warp seven it would be a day before we arrived. I knew I should try to get some sleep before then, but I was too keyed up. If I tried in this condition, I would just toss and turn and feel worse than if I didn't bother.

Fortunately I had learned a good trick for putting myself to sleep when I needed to. The gym was on the same deck as the cafeteria; I walked around the curved corridor until I reached it, then went inside to tire myself out lifting weights.

We approached the G2 component of the double star system first. Not because we suspected any more likelihood of finding anything there, but simply because it was a tenth of a light-year closer to Devernia than the F6 star at this point in their orbit.

We dropped out of warp with our shields down. It was always a gamble to do that, but the energy attenuation fields cut the effectiveness of our sensors, and I preferred being able to see what was out there rather than hunkering down and waiting for it to come knock on our shell. At Devernia I had chosen the opposite tactic and it had paid off, but a captain learns to play his hunches, and I had a hunch we wouldn't find a war in progress here.

Spock was ready at the science station. The moment we emerged into normal space, he said, "Scanning for energy signatures. . . . No spaceborne sources within sensor range. Scanning planetary surfaces. . . . No artificial sources there either. Scanning for life-forms. . . ."

It took a little longer to do that, but the result was the same. "No life-forms registered in the entire planetary system."

"What do we have here for planets?" I asked.

"Two class K, marginally habitable, one gas giant, class T, and asteroid fields of astonishing density in each of the interorbital spaces between planets." He frowned and adjusted a sensor. "The asteroids are unusually uniform in size. They are, in fact, the same size as adult titans."

"But no sign of life?" I asked.

"None, sir."

"Take us closer," I said to Number One.

We swept into the system under impulse power, and as we approached the first asteroid belt, I said, "On screen, high magnification."

The view expanded, stars rushing off the screen to be replaced by tiny, dim points of light. As the *Enterprise* drew closer, they grew from points to tiny oblongs, and from tiny oblongs to bigger oblongs.

Perri and Lanned stood on either side of my command chair, having finally allowed Yeoman Colt to escape their attentions. I didn't allow myself to wonder if either of them had succeeded in winning her affection. I said to them, "Look familiar to you?"

"They are titans," Perri said softly. "Millions of them. All dead."

"What happened to them?" asked Lanned.

"Spock?" I asked.

Information flowed onto his monitors faster than a human could follow, but he seemed to have no problem interpreting it. "I see signs of violence. Fins torn away, some bodies partially eaten. Others seem intact, but thinner than desiccation alone would account for."

"How long ago did all this happen?" I asked.

He consulted his instruments. "Exact dating is difficult, but from the amount of heavy ions deposited by the solar wind, I calculate no more than a thousand years. Perhaps as little as two hundred."

"So these could have been the ones that seeded the Devernia system."

"That seems likely."

"And then they all died out."

Perri grew agitated. "Could this happen to our titans as well? Spontaneous death of the whole species?"

Spock said, "Death is seldom spontaneous. I believe

we can safely assume that this many creatures died of some external cause."

"What is it, then?"

"I do not know—yet." Spock turned back to his monitors.

"Take us to within ten kilometers," I said to Number One. "Get ready to raise shields."

"Yes, sir."

If something external had killed them, I didn't want to find out what it was the hard way. But as we drew closer, it became more and more apparent that most of the titans were still intact. They looked thin, though. I could see their skeletons through their scaly hide: hexagonal and pentagonal matrices like geodesic domes, narrowing down to their bulging engines at the tail.

"They look emaciated," I said. "Did they starve to death?"

"That appears to be the case." Spock consulted more instruments, switching to different sensors and frowning when he realized the ones he wanted were gone. "Though I cannot rule out poisoning or pathogens."

"What about the ones that are damaged?"

"The wounds are consistent with the bite patterns we suffered when titans attacked our ship. It looks as if they tried to eat each other."

Starving creatures often did that. It sometimes even worked, if there was a possibility of rescue or if the survivors could last until the famine ended. But nobody had come to rescue these poor beasts, and apparently their food supply had dried up for good.

Then I remembered what they ate. "How could they run out of *hydrogen?*" I asked. "We're talking about the atmosphere of a *gas giant* for a food source here."

Spock said, "The titans need more than just hydrogen. Spectroscopic analysis of their bodies reveals carbon, sulfur, potassium, and seventeen other trace elements."

"All of which are found in gas-giant atmospheres, aren't they?"

"Normally that is so," Spock said. "However, this system's gas giant is atypical. It is class T, which means it is mostly helium and heavier gases surrounding a rocky core. That core, however, displays many of the internal characteristics of a class-U planet, which has a significantly higher ratio of hydrogen, methane, and ammonia in its atmosphere. I theorize that this once *was* a class-U planet, until its hydrogen and hydrocarbons were consumed by titans."

I couldn't believe it. They skimmed off an entire planet's atmosphere? Then I looked out at the drifting carcasses, millions of them—probably billions of them—filling the solar system. There were so many they actually formed rings around the star. They reminded me of Saturn's rings, with their gaps where shepherd moons orbited and kept the particles from drifting away. Except each of these "particles" was two-thirds the size of the *Enterprise.* Suddenly it didn't seem so unlikely that they could have consumed an entire gas giant's hydrogen supply.

"I wonder what they did to the terrestrial planets?" I asked.

Spock put an image of one on the screen. The planet was mostly brown, with small ice caps on the poles. There didn't seem to be much cloud cover, but then there didn't seem to be a lot of water to create clouds with. I didn't see any evidence of oceans. I couldn't see much other detail; on that scale it was hard to see anything smaller than a few square miles.

"Take us in for a closer look," I told Number One. The planet was a third of the way across the system, so she had to fly us up out of the plane of the ecliptic to get past the ring of titans. While we traversed the seemingly infinite plain of dead bodies, I said to Perri and Lanned, "Looks like there's a lifetime supply of free fusion drives and warp engines out there if someone could figure out how to harvest them and adapt them to a conventional spaceship."

"We have tried," said Perri. "Without the circulatory system to provide them with nutrients, they break down."

"Break down? As in 'malfunction' or 'decompose'?"

"Decompose," he replied. "There appears to be an enzyme in their cellular structure that triggers the process after they die." He considered his words a moment, then said, "However, studying them is how we learned to build our own fusion engines."

"But not warp engines," I said. "For those you still use live titans. Why?"

"Well, um . . ."

"Because we can't figure them out," said Lanned.

"That's not true!" Perri protested. "We just don't—"

"It is so," Lanned said. "You managed to fool that Federation first-contact group into thinking you built the titans, but the fact is you don't know the first thing about them."

"That's no surprise to me," I told him. "Nor is it any concern of mine, other than simple curiosity. You possess interstellar flight capability; that's one of the criteria for membership in the Federation. Unless you stole it, which doesn't seem to be the case, how you got it is not an issue."

Perri looked surprised, and I laughed. "You've been trying to hide your ignorance from us all along, but it really doesn't matter. The Federation is as inclusive as we can be without interfering in a society's development. We're not going to kick you out because you get your spaceships for free."

"I would hardly call it 'for free,'" Lanned said.

"Good point."

We were approaching the planet by then. Its gravity had cleared a wide space in the ring of titan bodies, so Tyler set up a standard polar mapping orbit four hundred kilometers above the surface and Number One brought us in. Spock locked the telescope onto a spot below and increased the magnification until we were looking straight down on a dry streambed that cut through a rocky desert. I didn't see anything growing, nor any evidence that anything had ever grown there—except for titans. Bodies of young ones as well as old littered the ground, the old ones crumpled up in the middle of craters that attested to their inability to land once they achieved adulthood. They must have been so desperate they tried it anyway, or else they knew they were committing suicide.

As we swept around the planet in our orbit, the telescope lost its lock and began to show us a moving image of the surface directly below. We saw more and more titans, some of them piled up in drifts, for thousands of kilometers.

A steep cliff swept past; then the character of the ground changed from the heavily eroded badlands we had been looking at to a smoother surface. Wind blew dust into swirling tornadoes a kilometer high. Then I saw a few flat-topped mesas with little mountains on the tops of them and I realized what this had to be.

"Those are islands!" I said. "Spock, freeze that image."

He did so, and I pointed to the fried-egg features on the landscape. "See the reefs around the edges, and the long, gentle slope that used to be beach? This dusty ground used to be seafloor, and that cliff we saw a minute ago had to be the continental slope at the edge of what used to be land."

Spock said, "I believe you are correct. Deep-penetration radar shows a much thinner rock crust in this area, which is consistent with a seafloor. We must assume that the oceans have dried up."

"Been swallowed up, more likely," I said. "By baby titans filtering deuterium from seawater."

Lanned said softly, "This is what Devernia will look like in time."

"Not if we can help it," I said. "This is just more proof that the rest of their ecosystem didn't come with them.

It's obvious they can't live without an outside influence to keep their numbers in balance. We'll find out what it is, don't worry."

"Don't worry?" he said. "Captain, this sight will haunt me to my dying day, whether we find a solution to the problem or not. Just knowing this *could* happen to us will always make me worry."

I shrugged. "Maybe that's smart. You're less likely to be surprised by the next thing fate drops in your lap. Mr. Spock, unless you need to take more readings, I suggest we continue our search."

"I believe my sensor log has recorded sufficient detail here," he said.

"Good. Tyler, set course for the other half of this binary system. I suspect we'll find the same thing there, but we're so close we might as well look and see."

"Yes sir." He supplied Number One with the coordinates and she brought us out of orbit, then engaged the warp engines, and we left the devastated planet and the rings of dead titans behind.

Chapter Seventeen

NOWAN SHOOK HIS head sadly. "That must have been a sight. I've seen an entire bay filled with whales slaughtered for their oil, but I've never seen anything of the magnitude you describe."

"Neither had I," Pike told him. "It was a pretty sobering sight. Rings clear around a *star*, all made up of dead bodies. It gave me the creeps."

"'The creeps.' An interesting phrase. Evocative. I may steal it."

"Feel free," said Pike. "It's not original with me."

Nowan laughed. "It no doubt comes from a century or two before your time. That would make me only two or three centuries ahead of mine when I use it." He shook his head. "I will no doubt take away more than just that from our discussion here today. But there is one thing I am afraid I must leave behind."

"And what is that?" Pike asked him.

"The brandy!" Nowan laughed at his own joke, then scooted his chair away from the table and stood up. "If you will excuse me for a moment, I must find the necessarium."

"Of course," Pike said.

Nowan turned once around, looking for the proper door. When he looked toward the corner beyond Hompaq, she tilted her bony forehead toward the back of the bar instead. "Behind there."

"Ah, thank you." He hurried away.

Pike got up and carried their empty glasses over to the bar. "Two more, please," he asked the bartender, who was mixing something green and fuming for one of the men at the cat-woman's table.

"Coming up."

He felt less nervous standing next to the Klingon woman now, though he really didn't know any more about her than he had before. Less, actually. She could be anyone, from anywhere. If this bar was like the places of legend, then she might have stepped into it from the Klingon homeworld, or from halfway across the galaxy.

He looked at the other patrons' reflections in the mirror. Even the humans could be from anywhere, or anywhen. He wondered how many of them recognized him. How many of them knew his fate.

Hompaq apparently did, though he had a hard time believing he would wind up on Talos IV again. The fact that she even knew about the place argued that she knew something about him, though. He wondered what else she knew.

"So tell me," he said, "has anyone made it safely through the Galactic Barrier yet?" Just last year Captain Kirk had discovered an energy field around the outer edge of the galaxy, an enormous barrier that prevented ships from crossing either in or out without serious damage to ship and crew. If it turned out to be a serious threat, the galaxy could become a pretty crowded place in a few millennia.

Hompaq shrugged. "It's been done a few times, but

always at high cost. Not many people think it's worth trying. There's a lot of nothing on the other side."

"There's the entire *universe* on the other side," Pike said.

"And it's over a thousand years to Andromeda even at warp nine."

"So we haven't found anything better than warp drive, then."

She swiveled around on her stool to face him more directly. "Define 'we.' There's evidence that somebody has done it. One of your Starfleet ships will even find itself in the Delta Quadrant by accident."

"What? Which ship? In the *Delta* Quadrant?" It would take them a century to get home from there at conventional warp speed. Pike had to prevent that from happening! After all, looking after the welfare of the fleet was his *job*.

She shook her head. "I don't remember the name." But there was just the trace of a grin on her lips.

"You do too," Pike said.

"And so what if I do? Cap's right." She nodded toward the bartender, who had finished the fuming green drink and was now pouring Pike's brandy. "We could turn this place into a great big traveling trans-chrono anomalizer, or we can stop fishing for information and enjoy our time here."

"Yes, but—"

"No 'but.' "

"Innocent people will be hurt."

"Innocent people are always hurt. You stop this one and something else will happen to somebody else. Maybe this ship in the Delta Quadrant will discover something you need to know."

"Like what?"

She shrugged. "Like how to kill Borg, maybe."

"Borg?"

"See? It's an infinite regression. Galactic Barrier, warp drive, Delta Quadrant, Borg, Q, Trelane, *tribbles*"—she

scowled in distaste at that word—"and so on indefinitely, but you probably don't recognize half the refer-
ences. Each one will lead you to another fistful of
concepts you don't understand, and so on for as long as
you'd like to go. Or"—she picked up his brandy snifter
and took a sip, then scowled almost as badly as she had
over the word *tribble*—"we can ignore all that and enjoy
one another's company without giving ourselves indiges-
tion. Want some Warnog?" She held her mug up under
his nose where he could smell its oily, almost petrochem-
ical odor.

"Uh, no thanks."

"Smart man. Want to arm-wrestle?" She thumped her
right elbow on the bar, forearm held high.

Pike laughed. He and Dr. Boyce had sometimes arm-
wrestled in the forward lounge after hours. Boyce was a
big man, but Pike lifted weights almost daily; he usually
won. That was a long time ago, though. He hadn't lifted
anything heavier than a reference book since he'd taken
the desk job. Still, he hadn't gone completely to seed yet.

"Sure," he said, carefully scooting the brandy snifters
down to the end of the bar where they wouldn't get
knocked over. There was a cup full of pens there. Clear
plastic ballpoints with octagonal barrels, by the looks of
them. Pike had never seen one of those outside of a
museum.

Hompaq didn't give him time to investigate. "You're
not as smart as I thought," she said with a sneer as she
leaned forward eagerly and wiggled her fingers to loosen
them up. Pike did the same, then sat down on the stool
next to her and took her hand in his. Her skin was
warmer than he'd expected, and softer. Apparently being
a Klingon warrior didn't mean you had to mistreat
yourself.

They adjusted their grip, then gave a tentative push to
make sure they were ready. "Okay," Pike said. "On the
count of three. One . . . two . . . *three.*"

Hompaq lunged so quickly his knuckles nearly rapped

the bar, but he recovered just in time and struggled to bring his hand back up. He felt himself slipping off his stool, wrapped his left leg around its post, and held on.

Hompaq growled and pushed harder, but Pike leaned into it and slowly brought their hands back up to vertical, then beyond. She leaned forward as well and stopped him from going any farther, but neither of them could gain any ground after that. They strained for fifteen or twenty seconds, both of them starting to shake with the effort.

Then Pike noticed what else was shaking. He'd been concentrating on the contest so hard he hadn't realized where he'd been staring until the jiggling motion became impossible to ignore. Hompaq must have realized it just about the same time, because she laughed and shook her body even harder. A moment later his hand smacked painfully against the bar and it was all he could do to keep from falling backward off his stool.

"Treachery," he said, letting go and rubbing his forearm with his left hand.

"A warrior should learn to keep his mind on the battle," she told him, grinning wide with her pointed teeth.

Just then Nowan came back around the corner from behind the bar. He saw Pike next to Hompaq, and came over to stand beside them, a bemused expression on his face. "I expected considerable advances in plumbing," he said, "but I must confess I still expected *plumbing.*"

Both Pike and Hompaq laughed, and Nowan added, "I must have spent five minutes trying to decide what went where. I hope I did it right."

"You're still here," Hompaq told him. "If you'd gotten it wrong, you'd probably have been sucked into an alternate dimension."

"That sets my mind at ease."

Pike shook his fingers to get the circulation going in them again, then picked up his brandy snifter. Nowan took his from the end of the bar and went back to their table.

"You could, uh, come sit with us, if you'd like," Pike said to Hompaq.

"I could, could I?"

"If you'd like."

"How do I know you won't shoot my chair out from under me?"

He shrugged. "I never use the same tactic twice. It's bad form."

"So it is." She rapped her mug on the bar. "Hey, Cap. Top this off for me, will you?"

The bartender did so, filling the mug from a tap rather than a bottle. Klingons must come here fairly often, Pike thought. Either that or Hompaq drank too much.

They went back over to the table by the stairs. Pike took a quick peek up the dim stairwell before he sat down, but he saw only a landing and the beginning of a hallway leading off to the left.

"Interested in what's up there?" Hompaq asked playfully. She had taken the chair with its back to the room, but she had turned it so she sat sideways to the table.

"I don't know what's up there to be interested in it," Pike said.

"You want to find out?"

He settled into his chair. "I thought I wasn't supposed to poke too deeply into the mysteries of this place."

"Hah! True enough. Besides, you weren't finished with your story. You'd found the great titan graveyard, and were about to investigate the companion star. What did you find there?"

"You sure you're supposed to know this?" Pike asked her. "It could lead to an infinite regression. Titans, Bork, K, Tremaine—what if we found tribbles? Whatever they are."

133

"You didn't."

"You know that for certain, don't you? Maybe I should let you tell the rest of the story."

She scowled. "Maybe you shouldn't. I don't know everything about you, Captain."

"That's encouraging."

"Good. So tell your tale."

He took a sip of brandy, then shrugged. "All right. Let's see, we were headed for the F6 star. It was just a few minutes away at warp seven . . ."

Chapter Eighteen

... So WE DIDN'T HAVE much time to wonder what we'd find. Of course we had trouble even before we got there. Titan bodies kept looming up in the sensors, and Number One kept having to dodge them at warp speed all the way across from star to star. They must have eaten every source of raw materials in both systems—every moon, every asteroid, every meteor—and then they had spread out to eat the comets. And those weren't in a nice flat plane, so we couldn't even rise up over them the way we had deeper in-system.

We slowed to warp six, then to warp five, and on down the scale as the titan density increased. Spock scanned ahead with long-range sensors and found the gaps where planets had swept their orbits clean, and we aimed for the first of those, dropping back into normal space just a few light-minutes from the outermost planet.

At first glance it looked like a terrestrial world, not much larger than Earth. It was too far from its sun—even a brighter F6 like this one—to ever support humanoid life, but it showed definite signs of titan influence. Their bodies littered the surface here, too, though we found no young ones this time. There were a great many unhatched eggs, all split open from impact. The cause was readily apparent: there was no atmosphere left at all to slow their fall.

I couldn't see any evidence that this planet had ever had continents or oceans. It looked more like Mars than Earth, only much darker and without the heavy cratering that Mars endured. I wondered why it hadn't been bombarded by asteroids early in its life, but Spock soon gave me the answer.

"Fascinating," he said, finally looking up from his monitors. "This planet used to be a gas giant."

"What?" I asked. "How could that be? It's bare rock now."

"This is the core of a class-S planet, much like your Saturn. It did at one time have a metallic hydrogen envelope surrounding it and a gaseous hydrogen and helium atmosphere, but that appears to have been entirely removed by the titans, as have the atmospheres of all the planets inward from here. When I calculate the mass removed and compare it to the estimated mass of the titans in both star systems, I find that the two figures agree within three percent."

"My god," said Number One. "They completely stripped the planets."

"Take us inward," I told her. "Let's see what else they've done."

Now that we were within the planetary disk, where gravitational perturbation would keep loose bodies in the plane of the ecliptic, we could rise above the rings of titan bodies and move steadily inward, scanning the planets as we went. The next two were just like the first, rocky cores of what had once been huge gasballs, but the fourth one had the familiar characteristics of a class-M planet. It still held its atmosphere, probably because nitrogen and oxygen weren't useful to the titans in quantity, but it had suffered the same fate as the class-K planet we had examined in the other star system. Titans had filtered every bit of water out of the oceans, and they had blasted the surface to rubble.

"Any life-forms at all?" I asked Spock as we dropped into mapping orbit.

"None," he said. "However, I do show a power signature of some sort."

"What kind of power?"

"Electrical. Nearly a megawatt. It just cleared the horizon."

"On screen."

At first I saw just a jumble of rock and dead titans, but then I realized there was a pattern to the rubble. Straight lines ran outward in six directions from the center, meeting with other lines to form a hexagonal array.

"A *city?*" I asked.

"It would appear so. The power signature is coming from a geothermal generator six hundred meters below the surface. I suspect it provided electricity to the buildings, when they were standing."

"Any sign of the inhabitants?"

"The titans are the only biological form in evidence larger than microbes."

"Figures," I said. "Any indication that the inhabitants might have gotten away before this happened?"

"Unlikely, Captain. The level of technology displayed in the power turbine is lower even than the Devernians' or Aronnians'. No offense intended," he added to our guests.

"None taken," said Lanned. "I know where we stand in the overall scheme of things."

"Are there any other cities?" asked Number One.

Spock consulted his sensor displays. "Now that I know what to look for, I find several. None have operating power sources, and none show any surviving above-ground structures at all."

"Anything interesting underground?" I asked.

"A few open spaces that might have been parking facilities for ground vehicles," Spock said. "Subway tunnels. Storage space."

I had been considering a landing party, but that didn't sound promising. I said, "Whoever lived there obviously didn't have the answer to the titan problem. I don't see what good it would do to investigate firsthand. Let's mark this on the charts for an archaeological mission and go on to the next candidate star. Mr. Spock, which one would you recommend next?"

He put the map on the screen. "There are three stars within seven light-years of here—half a titan's maximum range. We could go straight ahead, farther from Devernia, turn twenty degrees to galactic south, or turn seventy degrees to galactic north."

It didn't take long for me to decide. We'd found titans on our first stop; that meant they came from somewhere in this direction. I didn't see any reason to turn aside. "Straight ahead," I said. "Let's see if we get lucky twice in a row."

"You call this luck?" asked Perri.

"We came out here to find titans," I told him. "We did that."

He shivered. "Yes, we did, didn't we?"

It took us another day to cross the immense distance between stars. Our guests spent the time competing for Yeoman Colt's attention—and doing it so blatantly that I took her aside on the pretext of going over the damage reports with her and asked her straight out, "Are those two bothering you?"

We were the only people in the conference room, me seated at the table and her standing beside it. I assumed she could give me a straight answer without embarrassment, but she blushed when I asked the question and I realized I must have overstepped my bounds.

"If they aren't, it's none of my business," I said hurriedly, "but if they are I'll put a stop to it. You shouldn't have to put up with unwanted advances from anyone."

She played with a loose strand of her reddish blonde hair, winding it around her finger and letting it slip free. She didn't look at me, but instead addressed the window behind me. "It—it's all right. I can't say I'm not flattered. If I thought it was going to go on for long I'd probably feel different, but we'll only be doing this for what, another week or two? To be perfectly honest, that will be just about right." She glanced at me, then back out the window. "I actually find them attractive in a strange way. The lure of the exotic, I suppose. Neither one of them is really my type, but they're both interesting."

She tucked the loose hair into her ponytail and lowered her hand. "I appreciate your concern, sir."

"Just doing my job. I think."

"You are."

I sighed. "Thanks for saying so."

She looked at me quizzically.

I fumbled for an explanation. "I . . . what I mean to say is . . ."

"Sir?"

I laughed. "Maybe you should sit here and I'll stand over there and it'll be easier to say."

"How about if we both sit?" she asked. She pulled out a chair and spun it around so she could lean forward against its back.

"That's the same way Yeoman Leon used to treat a chair," I said, smiling at the memory.

"Oh. I'm sorry." She moved to get up.

"No, that's fine," I said quickly. "That's what I wanted to say, actually. It's fine. You are. I mean, you're doing a fine job." I plunged ahead with reckless abandon, knowing I'd better elaborate or look even more foolish than I already did. "I know I said some pretty harsh things when you first came on board. Leon was a

139

good friend as well as my yeoman, and losing him was hard. I didn't want someone to take his place, and when Starfleet assigned a young woman to the job I thought they were crazy, but I can see now that they knew what they were doing. And so do you, as it turns out. I just want to make sure you know I realize that. You're doing great, and I'm sorry I ever doubted you."

She tilted her head a little, embarrassed again. "Thank you."

"And don't worry about being compared to Leon all the time. I haven't done that since your first few days on board. You've got your own way of doing things, your own personality, and I appreciate that."

"That's . . . a relief."

"I thought it might be." I realized I was tapping my fingers nervously on the table and forced them to stop. "That's all I had to say, besides making sure you weren't being bothered by our guests."

She nodded, but she didn't move to go. I didn't want to chase her out, either, so I waited for her to say what was on her mind. When she did, it wasn't what I'd expected.

"Why did you join Starfleet?" she asked.

That was a tough question. I was still trying to decide if I wanted to answer it when she elaborated.

"I have this theory that there are two kind of people who join. There's the duty and honor and glory guys who want to be part of something great, and there's the strange new worlds people who want to see what's out there. I'm guessing you're the strange new worlds type, but if I'm going to work closely with you it occurs to me that I should know for sure why you're here. It might make a difference sometime when we have to understand each other in a hurry."

"It might," I admitted. I had been about ready to jump on her for getting too personal, but she had a point. Leon and I had known each other that well. In fact, he could probably have answered her question easier than I could, since I had to get past all the internal clutter that hid my true motives even from myself. She had made a pretty good guess, though. "I think you're right," I answered. "I came out here for the adventure. I inherited the duty and honor bit when I became an officer."

"Thought so."

"That's not to say duty and honor isn't worthwhile," I pointed out. "If we all came out here for the adventure we'd probably get the whole shipload of us killed the first planet we came to."

"Maybe."

She started toying with another strand of hair. I watched for a few seconds, hypnotized; then I broke away and said, "How about you? Adventure, right?"

"Right."

"Which is why Perri and Lanned don't bother you."

She grinned sheepishly. "Guilty."

"Have an adventure, then," I told her. "But be careful you don't get hurt."

"I will." She straightened up on her chair, then stood and flipped it back around under the table. "Thank you, sir," she said again. "Will, um, will that be all?"

"Yes," I told her. "Carry on."

She giggled. It was the first time I had ever heard her do that. "So to speak," she said.

I shook my head. "So to speak."

She turned to go, and I watched her walk to the door, wondering if I had overstepped my bounds as far as it felt like I had. I had no idea. A captain and his yeoman should be able to talk about anything, at any time. As she had said, it might make a difference sometime when we had to understand each other in a hurry. So why did I feel like I'd just navigated my way without sensors through an asteroid belt?

Our next star proved disappointing. It was an A-type, big and bright and hot, and the rocky planets close-in were just that: rocks. All the water had been boiled off epochs ago, leaving nothing for titans or anything else to use. The outer planets held more volatiles, but they were all giants, which left no breeding ground.

"I suppose they could have come through here on their way to that last system," I said when Spock delivered the bad news. "Adults could refuel in those atmospheres, couldn't they?"

"They probably could," he replied.

"So we still don't know whether to go on, or to try galactic north or south."

"No, sir. Except the stars to the north are more densely packed, which means we could search more of them in a shorter time if we go that direction."

"Sounds good to me," I said. "North it is."

Our luck changed at the very next star. It was a K-type, dimmer than Sol, and with a wider range of planets. When we dropped out of warp, Spock almost immediately said, "I read titan fusion drives throughout the system."

"Proximity?" I asked.

"None within one hundred thousand kilometers."

Good. I didn't want a repeat of what had happened to us when we'd arrived at Devernia. "What does their population density look like?"

"Not as high as what we found around L2334.45, but significantly higher than that around Devernia."

"Other life-forms?"

"None register at this distance; however, simple spectrographic analysis indicates life other than titans on at least two of the inner planets."

Life. I thought of what Colt and I had talked about earlier, how we were both in Starfleet to see what we would find in the depths of space. Thousands of people had discovered life on alien planets, starting with the first expedition to Mars even before Zephram Cochrane invented the warp drive, but it still gave me a little thrill to do it again. I looked over at Colt, standing behind Number One. She was smiling too. "What kind of life?" I asked.

"Impossible to determine from here," Spock replied calmly, his Vulcan heritage momentarily winning out over his human half and preventing him from betraying any emotion he might have felt. "All I read is a molecular signature similar to chlorophyll."

Most likely plants, then, but I understood Spock's reluctance to say for sure. We could find a planet covered with green animals just as easily as anything else.

"Take us closer," I said to Number One. "But be ready to get us out of here in a hurry if there's trouble. Mr. Spock, is there any indication of power generation?"

"None yet, but the titans' energy signatures may be masking anything more subtle."

"Any communication signals, Dabisch?"

"Only the microwave bursts coming from the titans themselves, the same as those we found around Devernia."

That would be their primitive radar beams. "Still no information content?" I asked, just to be sure.

"None," he confirmed.

We accelerated toward the inner planets on impulse power, watching carefully for any sign of aggression from the titans or anyone else, but we came within a half-million kilometers before they even noticed us.

When they did, the reaction was immediate. There had been thousands of them orbiting the planet; a hundred or more whose orbital motion was aimed near our position suddenly lit their fusion engines and accelerated toward us.

"Interesting," Spock said, examining the monitors. "I detect a significant disturbance in the stellar magnetic field. I believe they are using that as well as their rockets for motive power."

"They're coming fast," said Number One.

"Shields up," I said. That hadn't made any difference the last time, but it wouldn't cost us anything but sensor range to power them up, and we already knew the titans were coming. I didn't like waiting for them without some kind of defense, however ineffective it might be. And in the back of my mind was the thought: If they could manipulate the stellar magnetic field, what else could they do that we hadn't seen yet?

"Mr. Perri," I said, "do you know anything about this magnetic propulsion?"

He said, "The only magnetic effects we have observed are the containment fields for the fusion reaction chamber and the subspace effects of the warp coils."

"Lanned?"

"He's right as far as I know."

"Spock, did you notice anything like this in your sensor scans around Devernia?"

"Negative, Captain."

"One hundred thousand kilometers and closing," said Tyler at the navigation console. "Seventy-five. Fifty."

As tightly as a fighter squadron flying formation, the titans spun end-for-end and decelerated toward us on their fusion engines. The plasma stream from their exhaust struck our shields, the flash momentarily blinding us until our sensors shifted to a wavelength they could see in. I was glad I'd raised our shields; the hull could take fusion exhaust without harm from this distance, but the radiation wouldn't do the crew any good.

"Magnetic activity increasing," Spock said, watching his monitors carefully. "Plasma stream is being affected. It is drawing tighter. Curious. That would reduce the efficiency of—"

Suddenly the viewscreen lit up with a red flash so bright that some of the individual pixels blew out before the automatic gain control could compensate. I blinked and saw afterimages, and when I looked back to the screen there were dark spots where the elements had failed.

"Hull temperature rising," Spock said. "Shields unable to compensate."

"Get us out of here," I said. "Warp eight." I had no idea what had just hit us, but I didn't want to find out the hard way.

Number One complied instantly. The warp fields wrapped around the ship and hurled us a couple of light-minutes across the planetary system within seconds.

"Any sign of pursuit?" I asked.

"None, sir," Spock said.

"Full stop," I ordered. When the stars settled down and we ascertained that no more titans were in the vicinity, I said, "All right, what hit us back there?" I looked around the bridge: Spock busy correlating all the information available to him on his science station, Number One checking fire control and helm response, Tyler scanning nearby space. Colt and Perri and Lanned were gripping the handrail and looking at the forward viewscreen, which showed a serene starscape that betrayed none of the violence we had just endured.

Dabisch looked up from his communications board and said, "I picked up an incredibly strong signal at the low end of the visible-light spectrum. All carrier wave, though; there was no information in it."

"It was not a communications beam," Spock said. "It was a simple laser."

"A *laser?*" I asked. "Was there someone riding those titans?"

"Negative."

"Then where did it come from? That was one almighty powerful laser to punch through our shields like it did."

"It came from the titans themselves," Spock replied. "Or more precisely, from their fusion drive exhaust stream. Observe." He switched the main viewer to the aft sensor array and increased the magnification until I saw a gleaming white starship on one side of the screen and a fleet of a hundred or so titans approaching it from the other. It was the *Enterprise* and the titans that had attacked it; the light from the event only now catching up with us.

The titans flipped over and sprayed rocket exhaust at us. "Most of the plasma comes from atomic hydrogen," said Spock, "mixed with a small amount of helium from the fusion reaction. It is harmless, except when compressed magnetically to a uniform density, as you see here." Sure enough, the jet of gas grew narrower, becoming a bright red pencil-line drawn between titans and starship.

"At this point, with energy still pouring into it from the fusion engines, the gas conduit lased at a wavelength of 670 nanometers."

I stared open-mouthed at the screen as the red line suddenly increased in brilliance a thousandfold, bathing the *Enterprise* in scintillating fire. Our shields flared like a nuclear blast, radiating most of the energy outward, but unable to reflect every erg of it. I knew from the design specs that the leakage was less than one percent, but with a laser that size, even one percent had nearly cooked us.

The ship on the screen winked out of existence. That was when we'd engaged the warp engines. The titans released their magnetic hold on the exhaust stream and braked to a halt where we had been, milling around like hunting dogs looking for a downed bird in tall grass.

"My god," Number One said, "that's more firepower than *we* have."

"It is an impressive capability," Spock said.

Lanned made a soft humming sound deep in his throat. "I've never seen them do that before."

"You're lucky," I said. "A laser that size could fry one of your ships in a second."

"How could it be that these titans have lasers and the ones around Devernia don't?" asked Colt.

"I don't know," I said. "Spock, any ideas?"

"None at this point, Captain. I would need further data on which to base a theory."

"I was afraid you'd say that. Where do you want to look first?"

"The nearest planet would be most logical," he replied. "We will want to investigate them all if possible."

"If we survive that long," said Tyler, but he keyed in the coordinates.

Chapter Nineteen

"You actually went *back?*" asked Hompaq. "I'm impressed."

Pike gave a little shrug. "It wasn't as dangerous as it seemed. We could always outrun them."

"Until they burned out something vital."

"True. We tried hard not to get hit a second time."

"I'll bet you did. Too bad you didn't have a cloaking device."

"A what?"

"Invisibility, Captain. It blocks visual, electromagnetic, even subspace emissions. Very useful in sneaking up on something."

"I bet it would be!" Pike said. "How long are we going to have to wait before that becomes available?"

She looked nonchalantly up at the ceiling. "A while."

Nowan cleared his throat, then said, "For him, or for me? 'A while' for him is forever for me. Assuming I go back where I came from when I leave this drinking establishment."

"You do," said Hompaq.

"Invariably?" he asked. "What if I leave with one of you?"

She shook her head. "You still go back to your home time and place. You think Cap's gateway can't handle two people at once?"

"Cap, that's the bartender?" asked Pike. He looked over to see the man watching them with a thoughtful expression on his face.

"It's his place," said Hompaq. "It's the Captain's Table, so we all just call him 'Cap.'"

Pike looked back to her. "How often do you come here, anyway?"

"Often enough."

"Why?"

"Not to answer your questions," she said pointedly.

He took a deep breath, let it out slowly. "All right, I'll stop prying. But this place has got me damned curious."

"Good," she said. "You're supposed to be curious, but the mystery is yours, not mine or anyone else's. You wound up here because of something inside *you*, not me. If you have to figure out anything about this place, figure out why you're here first."

Pike chuckled. "Like I told this fellow here, I came in because it was raining and I was cold."

"Sure you did. And you went back into that mess of titans because you told Perri and Lanned you'd help them solve their problem. But that's not the real reason."

"What was the real reason?"

"You just told us not ten minutes ago."

He tried to remember what he'd said. "Did I? If so, I must have forgotten it."

She snorted loudly. "Your yeoman knows."

Comprehension dawned on his face. "Ah. Adventure. Yes, perhaps you're right. It's a good thing Spock and Number One were there for duty and honor, or I probably would have gotten us all killed, just like I told Colt."

"Why?" asked Nowan. "What did they do?"

149

"Called it quits when the going got too tough," said Pike.

"What?" demanded Hompaq. "This is heroism?"

"No," said Pike. "It was realism. And logic."

"Logic," she spat. "Vulcans value it far too much."

Pike took a sip of brandy. "Well, it proved valuable to us, or I wouldn't be here to tell you about it."

She sighed heavily. "Very well, tell me how this Vulcan's *logic* saved the day. But you had better figure in heroically again or I will make you regret wasting my time with this prattle."

"No pressure, eh?" asked Pike. He stretched, rubbed his neck, then said, "All right, here's heroism for you: I went in with our shields down, knowing we'd have a few seconds to bring them up again before we were attacked, and knowing that Spock could get better sensor readings in those few seconds. How's that?"

"That's bravery. Heroism is bravery when you expect to fail."

"Oh," said Pike. "Then that came a bit later. In fact, the first time through was a piece of cake."

Chapter Twenty

WE WENT BACK into the system at warp six. It was too hard to stop exactly where you wanted to at warp seven or eight, and the way we intended to do things, precision counted more than speed. The Devernian titans' top speed had seemed to be about warp two, so unless these differed from them in that regard as well we probably could have gone in even slower than that, but we didn't know if they could detect us in motion so I decided to catch them completely by surprise if I could.

Spock had already gotten sensor readings of the outermost planet before the titans had chased us away, so we went to the next one in from there. Tyler calculated a course that let us drop out of warp only a thousand kilometers above its surface—a banded, churning, Jupiter-like surface—where we got about ten seconds of scanning time before the local titans noticed us and closed in. When the first hint of fusion exhaust licked out toward us, I told Number One, "Next planet," and she took us away before they could start their laser.

We did the same thing there. There was no time to do more than monitor our scanners; we would be hours going over the recorded data once we were clear of the titans. At the third planet, however, where Spock had found evidence of life, he kept his eyes on the life-form readouts as they scrolled past.

"Time to go," I said when the titans rushed toward us, but he said, "One moment, Captain."

I gave him his moment, then said, "Go," and Number One took us to the next planet, but Spock said, "We must go back. There was evidence of land-dwelling animals."

"Other than titans, you mean?" I watched the screens warily while our sensors automatically scanned planet number four.

"That is unclear, which is why we must return for closer examination." He spoke without looking at me, still watching his monitors. "And now I find similar life-forms here."

"You've got about fifteen seconds to do something about it," I told him, watching the titans gather. "Ten. Five. *Go.*"

We went.

The inner planets contained no surprises. When we had scanned them all, I had Number One take us out of the ecliptic, over the south pole of the star, while we decided what to do.

"How much more time do you need?" I asked Spock.

"At least thirty seconds," he replied. "A minute would be preferable. Our rapid scan indicated life-forms on both inhabited worlds, neither of which fit the immature titan profile. I must locate and do a full scan on at least three of each type in order to determine their genetic makeup."

"Why three?" asked Colt.

"Because any single specimen could be a mutant. Only by comparing multiple samples can the true genotype be mapped with any degree of confidence."

"We're not going to *get* a minute," I told him. "And by the way they're behaving, I doubt we'll get even thirty seconds. Look." I pointed to the main viewscreen, on which Dabisch had put a magnified image of the inner solar system. The space surrounding each of the planets was abuzz with milling dust motes, from which tiny lines of red light speared out.

"It looks like they're fighting among themselves now," Lanned said.

"Or just rattling their swords," said Number One. "Are they actually hitting anything?"

Dabisch expanded the view of one of the planets Spock wanted to return to. Now we could see individual titans and their odd magnetically induced laser beams, but as Number One had suspected, they weren't shooting at each other.

"We certainly got them worked up," I said. "But I think we can still manage to catch them by surprise. Mr. Tyler, set a leapfrog course for those two planets, and try to pick a region where the titans are least active to jump into. We may have to run through each system a few times, but we'll get our data even if it's a piece at a time."

"Course laid in, sir," he said.

"Spock, are you ready?"

"Ready."

"All right, then, engage."

We streaked toward the first planet under warp power, then stopped only a hundred kilometers above its surface. Spock started his scan while we watched out for titans.

They saw us instantly. Unfortunately one happened to be pointing almost directly away from us, and it wasted no time in firing its fusion jet at us. Magnetic fields constricted the jet a few seconds later. There was only the one titan this time, so we might have been able to withstand its lone weapon, but I didn't want to guess wrong. "Go," I said, just as the plasma lased and the beam shot out at us. The viewscreen flashed again and hull temperature sensors sounded the warning, but Number One already had her finger on the button and we streaked away to the other planet before we took any serious damage.

We had only a few more seconds there before the titans spotted us. This time three of them fired from three different angles, and we took another hit before we jumped free.

"Spock? Did you get anything?"

"One life-form detected and scanned at each planet," he replied. "Three samples of each type of life-form are required for unambiguous speciation. We will need two more passes to ensure good data."

"Great," I said. "Mr. Tyler, again, please. Pick a new spot near each planet. Maybe they'll all be looking for us where we were last time."

"Yes, sir." He calculated the coordinates, fed them to Number One's control board, and she took us back in.

Space was filled with titans. We had to dodge half a dozen of them before we even broke out of warp, and by slowing down to do so we evidently gave ourselves away. They were waiting for us when we arrived, their fusion flames crisscrossing the space in front of us. The moment we stopped they all went into laser mode, blasting us from at least three sides.

"Abort!" I shouted over the howl of alarms. Number One slapped her control panel and we jumped into warp again, skipping the other planet and rushing back out into interplanetary space. Some of the titans followed us until we increased speed to warp five and left them behind.

"I'm beginning to take this personally," I said when the alarms shut off. "Tyler, try a polar approach. Maybe they won't be looking up."

"Aye, sir," he said. He sounded dubious, but he set the coordinates.

"Ready, Spock?"

"Ready. However, I believe that shields will not impair our sensor efficiency enough to make their use counterproductive."

I wasn't going to argue with that. "Shields up, then. Take us in, Number One."

We streaked inward again, arching up out of the ecliptic and down over the planet's north pole, but the titans were on the alert all around the globe. They gave us no more time than on our last pass before their lasers struck again and I ordered us away.

"I'm tempted to paint a shuttlecraft silver and go in with that," I said. "Let them shoot at a mirror for a change."

"Even silver paint would not reflect one hundred percent of all impinging light," Spock pointed out. "It would burn through within seconds, and the shuttlecraft's hull would take little longer."

"How are they *finding* us so fast?" I asked. "Can that microwave radar of theirs possibly be that efficient?" Starfleet hadn't used radar since the invention of subspace field distortion sensors, but I supposed it could still be useful in normal space.

Spock checked his long-range scanners. "Microwave field intensity has increased among the titans who are most alarmed," he said.

"Can we jam it?"

"Possibly," Spock said. He played with the science station's controls for a few seconds, frowned, and said, "They use two frequencies, one at the natural resonant frequency of deuterium oxide molecules, the other at a much shorter wavelength. The first one will be relatively easy to block with an anti-phase return wave, but the second one will be much more difficult."

"Why is that?" I asked.

"Its frequency is high enough that it is nearly in the infrared light spectrum. As we have seen with the laser beams, we cannot mask ourselves completely from light, nor can we send a return beam of sufficient complexity to cancel our reflection. At best we can attenuate it by a factor of two."

"Let's try it anyway," I said. "Maybe it'll give us the few extra seconds we need to get a good scan of those planets."

"Very well," he said. He worked at the controls for a few minutes, during which time Number One said, "Is this really worth it?"

"The data I have already received seems to suggest that something with the same metabolic processes as titans is living on the surface of these planets," said Spock while he worked. "Since we came here to learn about titan ecology, it would be useful to know more about them."

"It would be useful to know why they attack us on sight, that's for sure," Colt said. "Do we look like some ancestral enemy, or do they just hate spaceships?"

"A good question," said Spock. "Unfortunately that will be difficult to answer with just one ship to experiment with."

"Yours attacked us too," I said to Lanned, "but I had assumed until you started shooting at them they left your ships alone. Was I wrong?"

"No, you're right," he said. "They tolerated our ships at first. Of course when we started killing them they swarmed the planet and attacked anything that rose above the atmosphere, but we didn't mind. That way we didn't have to waste fuel tracking them down."

"I wonder if your size made you appear less of a threat, until you proved yourselves otherwise."

"Maybe. We'd never seen how they react to bigger ships until you showed up, and by then they were mad at everybody."

"Perri?" I asked. "How did the titans around your planet react to the first Federation survey ship?"

He rubbed his forehead as he tried to remember. "I

believe all but the tame ones had migrated to Devernia at that time."

Lanned laughed. "Incidentally making it easier for you to claim the few remaining ones as our own creation."

Perri nodded. "It was a misconception which we did not attempt to correct. I have admitted that, and Captain Pike has said it made no difference anyway."

"Not to him."

Before Lanned and Perri could get into another argument over it, Spock said, "I am ready with the jamming signal."

"All right, let's do it. Mr. Tyler, let's try the other planet first. They've had more chance to calm down over there."

"Aye, sir," he said, and he entered the course.

"Number One, engage."

She did, and we raced back in-system one more time. When we popped out into normal space above the planet, I held my breath while we waited to see if we would be spotted. There were hundreds of titans within easy striking distance, but they didn't seem concerned. I counted ten seconds, fifteen, twenty—then one of them suddenly turned toward us.

Dabisch said, "They have shifted frequency!"

"Spock, can you compensate?"

"Not in time."

"Number One, get ready to take us out of here."

The news of our arrival spread like a ripple on a pond. Titans turned first toward us, sending their radar beams out ahead as they accelerated on magnetic fields and fusion power, then they flipped over and fired their plasma streams at us.

"Time to go," I said.

We left, but not before their lasers clipped us. Our shields flared, and another few pixels of the main viewscreen blew out. Then the hull-breach alarm wailed for attention.

I slapped the control to silence it. "Damage report?" I asked when we dropped back into normal space at the edge of the star system.

Dabisch listened to the in-ship communications link for a moment, then said, "Pressure loss in observation room J-twelve. No injuries."

J-12. That was the same room that the Devernian titans had damaged. The repair crew had sprayed black sealant on the window, which, since it now absorbed any light that struck it, had undoubtedly grown hot under each laser blast we had received. It would have cooled down while we prepared for another approach, only to be heated again by the next laser, expanding and contracting each time until the already-cracked window shattered under the stress.

"It's all right," I said. "Isolated incident. I assume the pressure doors are holding?"

"They are. A repair team has been dispatched."

"Tell them to paint the patch silver this time," I said. "It may not work for long, but it's better than starting out black." I turned to Spock. "How much more data do you need?"

"How much more can we *afford?*" asked Number One.

Spock looked at his displays, on which I could see several genetic maps scrolling past side by side. "Actually," he said, "I believe I have gained sufficient information. The land creatures we discovered are degenerate forms of titans, rather than a distinctly different species."

"What do you mean by 'degenerate forms'?" I asked.

"They have evolved into their present shape so recently that they share their entire genetic code with the spaceborne form. Only the expression of certain features has changed, such as the atrophy of the fusion and warp engines in favor of greater tentacle strength and a body more balanced for running."

So they had given up spaceflight and adapted to life on land. At least some of them had. The others, apparently, had evolved laser weapons. "What about those lasers?" I asked. "Why didn't the ones around Devernia have that capability?"

Spock recalled the data from there and compared it with what he had just recorded. "I did not detect any magnetic field manipulation in those specimens, other than in the fusion engine. My study of the embryonic and neonatal forms on Devernia indicated that the magnetic containment field coils developed first, followed by the fusion engine. The adult titans we observed here have much less efficient fusion engines, but they make up for that by using their ability to manipulate magnetic fields as a propulsion system."

"And to create that laser effect in their exhaust plumes."

"Correct. Evolutionarily, it would be a fair trade."

I shook my head. "I have a heck of a time believing that anything, even if it had somehow evolved a fusion engine in the first place, could evolve a *laser.*"

"Actually, I was thinking in the other direction," said Spock. "Losing the laser effect is a fair trade if it results in a more efficient engine, so long as the solar system in which they live contains no natural enemies."

"Like Devernians?" asked Perri. "From the titans' point of view they must certainly look like enemies."

Spock nodded. "They are indeed, but that is a new threat. The titans have not had time for evolutionary pressure to alter their genome to meet it, but I suspect it will eventually shift back to providing them with lasers now that the threat has become evident."

Lanned's eyes grew even wider than usual. "How long before it happens?" he asked.

"That is impossible to predict. Evolution typically takes generations, but the titans seem to evolve quickly, on the order of years rather than millennia, and the genetic code they need is already there to be expressed. It could happen with the very next hatchling."

Lanned's knees buckled, but he caught himself on the

railing and pulled himself back to his feet. He turned to me, his striped face as pale as my own, and whispered, "We have to go back!"

"And do what?" I asked.

"Warn them!"

"What would you do differently? Stop killing the titans? They would overpopulate and destroy Devernia as surely as they did the double star we investigated two days ago."

"Then you must go back and help us exterminate them quickly, before they mutate into these—these fire-breathing monsters."

I looked at the viewscreen again, once more showing the star system with its myriad dust motes winking with ruby threads of light. "We don't have that kind of firepower. Your nuclear bombs are probably more effective than our phasers, when it comes to killing titans. Photon torpedoes would probably do the job, but we don't have enough of them to even put a dent in their population."

"But we must do something!" Lanned said. "The threat is even worse than we realized."

"We're doing it," I said. "We're learning more about them every day. Somewhere out here is the answer to your problem. Out here, not back at Devernia."

"You hope," he said.

"I'm sure of it," I replied confidently. Not that I believed it, of course, but it's a captain's duty to keep his crew inspired. Before Lanned could say anything more, I turned to Spock and said, "What's our next target star?"

Chapter Twenty-one

PIKE PAUSED in his story to take another sip of brandy. Then, scooting back his chair, he said, "If you don't mind my pausing for a few minutes, I think it's my turn to visit the head."

"We should make you stay here until you're done," Hompaq said, grinning evilly.

"Oh," said Pike. "All right, then. Let's see, at the next planet we found a transdimensional entity with godlike powers who agreed to go back to Devernia with us and turn all the titans into giant space butterflies instead. Fragile as cobwebs, of course, but beautiful. Now Devernia is a popular tourist attraction for people who want to see the famous veiled sunsets."

Hompaq growled deep in her throat. "If that's the end of your story, I will throw you headfirst into the fireplace."

"And I will help," said Nowan.

"Hmm," said Pike. "Perhaps I can come up with something a bit more exciting. Let me go think on it for a moment." He stood up before either of them could protest any further and stepped through the door marked HUMANOID MALE at the back of the bar.

Nowan had been right; there was no plumbing, not even in the sink. Instead of a washbasin, there was just a flat metal plate on the countertop. Pike waved his right hand over it and heard the unmistakable hum of a transporter. His hand tingled momentarily, but nothing prevented it from continuing through its arc. On a hunch he dug into his pocket for a pen, drew an "X" on the palm of his left hand, and waved it above the plate. The transporter hummed again, and when he looked at his hand the "X" was gone.

"Amazing," he said aloud. Yes indeed, they did some interesting things with transporters these days. Whenever "these days" were.

He heard a bang from out in the bar, then Klingon laughter. Had she thrown another chair at someone? He opened the door a crack and peered out, saw her still sitting at the table, and opened the door the rest of the way.

Nowan was rubbing his arm and saying, "You have an unconventional way of wrestling, madam."

She nodded toward Pike. "Like I told the storyteller here, a warrior should keep his mind—and his eyes—on the battle."

Pike settled into his chair again and said, "Yes, let's. We were just about to head for yet another star system. . . ."

Chapter Twenty-two

WE INVESTIGATED five more in the next five days. Finding titans was never the problem. Avoiding them long enough to collect any meaningful data was the difficult part. In every star system where we encountered them, they were without exception hostile.

They all had laser capability, which led Spock to believe that that was the standard from which the Devernian titans had evolved. Other characteristics, however, seemed completely variable. Some populations had bigger ramscoop mouths than others, and that seemed to vary with the density of the atmospheres they scooped nutrients from. Some, like the Devernian titans, had teeth within the ramscoops, which appeared to arise when there were planetary rings or asteroids to feed on. The tentacles had atrophied on one species which lived in a system with no rocky planets to breed on. There the adults laid their eggs on comets instead, and the young fed on the ice until they were ready to launch themselves into space.

163

"This is a classic example of evolution in action," said Spock on the afternoon of our fifth day. "Like the finches on Earth's own Galápagos Islands that convinced Charles Darwin of the theory, I find each star system filled with a population perfectly adapted to local conditions." He had just discovered a correlation between the strength of the titans' radar signals and the availability of deuterium in the water of their hatching grounds. "Here, for instance, they use the low-frequency radar signal to locate deuterium sources for their young, and then drop their eggs in areas of highest concentration. Yet in planetary systems where there is no concentrated deuterium source, they lose that ability and instead adopt a cometary birth strategy."

Number One and I were looking over his shoulders at the data. Perri and Lanned had tired of the study and had gone off to explore the ship some more, and Colt had gone along to keep them out of trouble. Number One said, "The problem with your evolution idea is that none of these populations are stable. They're all headed toward overcrowding and eventual starvation."

"That does seem to be the case," said Spock. "I can only assume that we are seeing the same problem repeated here as we saw on Devernia: none of the ancillary life-forms that evolved with these creatures has managed to cross the interstellar gulf with them. Even with the rapid rate of evolution we have witnessed here, one species in isolation cannot evolve fast enough to provide the necessary diversity to keep the ecosystem in balance."

"You're making one big assumption," she said.

"And what is that?"

"The assumption that they *did* evolve. What if they were made?"

Spock thought it over. "My argument still holds. Even

an artificially produced organism cannot exist in isolation. If the titans were genetically engineered, other organisms were also created to feed them, and to feed *on* them."

"They seem to find plenty to eat on their own," I pointed out. "It's just the latter part that's missing."

"No," said Spock. "Dr. Boyce has helped me identify developmental abnormalities among all the races I have studied. They are missing key nutrients, which has led to weakened internal organs and shorter life spans than they might otherwise have."

I wasn't sure if a longer-lived, stronger titan was a good idea, but I imagined that Spock and Boyce probably knew what they were talking about. "That still doesn't give us any idea where the rest of this ecosystem of theirs *is*, does it?" I asked.

"Perhaps it does," Spock said. "One thing that seems universal among them is the low-frequency radar with which they seek out deuterium sources. That is a very specific signal, and while it would be quite weak at interstellar distances, it would still be detectable."

"So we can scan this entire sector of space and we'll know which stars have titans," said Number One. "We could have done that all along."

"We could have, but since we found titans at all but one star so far, we have not wasted our effort. What I propose now, however, should cut our search down even further."

"Good," I said. "What's your plan?"

"I am assuming that what works for titans would work for other creatures as well. In space it would be very useful to search out nutrients with radar before expending significant amounts of energy to go harvest them. However, other creatures would presumably need other nutrients than titans do, and therefore their radar frequencies would be different from the titans'. If we search for a planetary system from which multiple frequencies emanate, there would be a high likelihood of finding multiple species there."

"I don't know," I said. "The titans a few planets back already used two different frequencies themselves, and they shifted to a third when we riled them up."

"That has so far been an isolated case. All the other titans we have studied have used only one frequency."

"Well, I guess it wouldn't hurt to try it," I said. "Scanning is a lot quicker than actually going to look at every star in the sector." I turned to Dabisch at his communications board, ready to give him the order, and saw that he was already working on it.

He put his results on the viewscreen as they came in. The blown-out pixels had been replaced, so the picture didn't have gaps in it anymore. I saw a scattered starfield, on which one star after another turned red as Dabisch found the "standard" frequency of radar emanating from it. I had expected to see a spherical distribution, but it looked more like a cancer with long arms reaching out from various barely connected nodes. I saw that Devernia was at the tip of one such arm, down which we had traveled maybe a third of the distance.

"I'll bet what we're looking for is in one of those joining points," I said, just as the one farthest from us lit up in red, then green, then yellow. "Multiple frequencies there," Dabisch announced.

"That's twenty light-years away," I said, looking at the scale on the bottom of the screen. "Over a week of travel time. Keep scanning."

Dabisch did so, but it soon became apparent that Spock had been right: the homeworld—if that's what we were seeing—was unique in all the sector.

It was so deep in unexplored territory that it didn't even have a catalog number. I sighed. "Mr. Tyler, set course for that star. Looks like we're going for a bit longer trip than we'd hoped."

* * *

We spent the week making repairs to the ship. We couldn't go outside while under way, but we could reach all the critical sensors through the Jefferies tubes and access hatches, so by the time we arrived at our destination we were back in fairly good condition. Not full battle specs, but after what we had endured I felt glad to have as much working as we did.

Of course that lasted about an hour. It would have been even less, but I brought us back into normal space well out of our target system so we could scan for lifeforms before we proceeded inward. The monitors lit up like Christmas trees, color-coded dots showing different types of creatures scattered all through the system. I could see free-flying dots at random between planets—those I assumed were titans—but there were heavy concentrations of life-forms in the gas-giant atmospheres, in their ring systems, and in the three separate asteroid belts between planetary orbits. The terrestrial planets didn't seem to have many life-forms on them, but the gas giants and the asteroids more than made up for that lack.

"How many species?" I asked when the map finally stabilized.

Spock said, "At least six. Perhaps as many as ten. It is difficult to ascertain true species differences with long-range sensors."

He sounded happy—at least as happy as Spock ever sounded. But I was disappointed. "That few?" I asked. "I had thought we would find hundreds, if this is where they originated."

"This is far more than we discovered anywhere else," he pointed out. "And the population densities seem consistent with a stable ecosystem."

"How so?"

"The smaller creatures exist in the greatest numbers, with population density decreasing in inverse proportion to the mass. This would seem to indicate that the smaller species provide nourishment for the larger ones, all the way up the food chain to the titans."

"It's a pretty small food chain with only six links in it." I leaned back in my command chair and looked at the screen. With all that color-coding it looked complicated as hell, but I had never heard of an ecosystem with so few species. "Dabisch, is there any sign of civilization here?" I asked.

"No communication signals. If there is power generation, it is masked by the titans' own power signatures."

"I guess we'd better go in for a closer look," I said. "Are the titans using just the one frequency of radar here?"

"Affirmative," said Dabisch.

"Then maybe we'll have a better chance of slipping in undetected. Get ready to start our jamming signal. Number One, kill our exterior beacons. We're going in dark this time." I pressed the shipwide intercom button. "All hands, this is the captain. We are going to stealth mode two. Extinguish all lights visible from the exterior of the ship, and opaque all windows."

I didn't really think that would matter much—the hull was painted white, after all—but every little bit might help. Especially if we could stay out of the light.

"Do you have a preferred starting point, Mr. Spock?"

"This gas giant." He used the pointer to indicate the third one in toward the star. "It has the greatest biodiversity of any one planet, with separate species in its ring system and on each of its moons as well as in the atmosphere. It seems to be a microcosm of the entire system."

"All right. Mr. Tyler, Number One, are you ready?"

"Ready."

"Ready."

"Approach at warp five. Bring us to a stop in the shadow of one of the smallest moons. Be prepared to raise shields, but leave them down until we're attacked. And don't wait for my command if you see a threat."

"Yes, sir," they said in unison.

I looked to either side of my command chair. Lanned, Perri, Colt, and Dr. Boyce had all come to watch. Boyce was helping Spock collect data at the control panel beside his science station; the other three were gripping the handrail already. Good. I hoped they wouldn't need the support, but it was better to be prepared.

I leaned forward and grasped the armrests of my chair. "Take us in."

We slid into the moon's shadow as quietly as a cat stalking a mouse. The planet's immense ring system spread out in front of us, sparkling with gold and silver highlights in the sunlight. Spock immediately started scanning for life-forms and mapping their genetic code, while Boyce busied himself with determining each organism's role in the food chain. The rest of us held our breath, waiting for the first sign of discovery. Every ping and bleep from the ship's instruments seemed magnified, spooky, though we all knew sound was the one thing that couldn't betray us in vacuum.

"The rings are full of little photosynthesizers," Boyce said. "Looks like plankton or something similar. Hydroplankton? They use solar energy to collect deuterium and compress it in little bubble tanks about a millimeter across. I see titans scooping them up by the millions. There's bigger butterfly-like things, too, that look like they concentrate carbon into their wings. It looks like titans eat those as well."

"Do you see anything eating *titans?*" I asked. "That's what we want to find. Something that'll limit their population."

"I'm looking for parasites or signs of disease," he replied. "No luck so far. This really is a simple ecosystem."

"Something's got to be keeping them under control," I said.

"Something obviously is," Boyce said, "but I haven't found it yet. Give me time; we just got here."

Our radar jamming seemed to be working. There were seven or eight titans feeding in the rings less than a thousand kilometers from us, but they didn't seem to notice us at all. And in the shadow of the tiny moon, even our white hull reflected only the soft glow of the rings and the banded orange planet beyond.

I should have known we wouldn't be the only ones to think of that trick. I was just beginning to relax when Tyler said, "That's strange. This moon has a moon of its own."

I looked over his shoulder at the navigation display, where he had zoomed in on a bumpy asteroid only a few dozen kilometers away. It was about three hundred meters across, and its surface was heavily cratered and zigzagged with cracks. It looked like it must have once been hit hard enough to nearly shatter it. Not surprising this close to a planetary ring system, especially one with life in it; there must have been tons of debris flying around just waiting to smack into something.

"Anything living on it?" I asked.

"Let me check," said Boyce. He retrained his sensors on the asteroid, said, "Several small life-forms on the surface. Something else underneath . . . let me see." He frowned. "Hmm. That can't be right. Spock, let me borrow the deep-penetration array for a second."

"Certainly," Spock replied. "What have you found?"

"It reads like one big life-form inside, but that can't be. There's no opening for it to come and go."

"How big?" I asked, the hair standing up on my neck.

"Bigger than a titan," he said, "but it's got to be a false reading. Just a second."

We never got that second. We didn't need to; the answer became obvious when the asteroid split apart into dozens of thin shards of rock and a creature straight out of a nightmare came flying toward us.

It looked a lot like a juvenile titan, only scaled up. Its dozen tentacles were each as thick as the support columns for our warp engines. Its mouth was the size of a hangar bay. It wasn't designed for filtering hydroplankton, either. It was all fangs, multiple rows of them for ripping big chunks out of its prey. It didn't have a fusion drive; it came at us like a magnet to steel, accelerating fast.

Chapter Twenty-three

"PIZZA!" Pike said suddenly. Hompaq jerked backward in surprise, then growled.

"Pizza?" she asked. "What is pizza?"

"He meant to say 'phaser,'" said Nowan. "Didn't you? Only your incredible phasers could save you from such a beast."

"No, no," Pike said, laughing. "I meant pizza. It's food. Bread with meat and cheese and stuff on it. Great for filling an empty stomach—and for sharing with friends. I just realized I've missed dinner, and so have you, I'd bet. How about we share a pizza? That is, if this place serves food."

"Cap has a replicator," Hompaq said.

Pike had never heard of a replicator, but he took that as affirmative. The name was suggestive enough.

Nowan shrugged. "I know not what this 'pizza' is like, but I eat bread and meat and cheese. 'Stuff,' on the other hand, sounds ominous. What sort of 'stuff' do you propose?"

"Oh, you can put all kinds of things on pizza. Olives, green peppers, mushrooms, anchovies, haggis . . ."

"Anchovies?" Nowan made a face. "Not the little fish?"

"Yeah, that's right. Cured in salt."

"I would prefer not. I have eaten my fill of salted fish for quite some time."

Pike nodded. "I suppose you probably have."

Hompaq said, "I have heard of mushrooms. They are a fungus, are they not?" She also had a disgusted look on her face.

"Well, yeah," said Pike. "But they're not slimy or anything."

"Klingons do not eat fungus."

"All right, then, what do you eat?"

"With bread and cheese? Gagh would be good."

Now it was Pike's turn to make a face. "Gag? I already don't like it. What is it?"

"Serpent worms. Best when served live, but they can also be stewed, for those with *delicate* stomachs." She sneered at Pike as she said that.

"Hey, don't delicate me," he said. "I can eat mushrooms. But I'll pass on the gag, thank you."

"Haggis sounds equally unpleasant," said Nowan.

"What is it?" Hompaq asked. "The name, at least, is close to gagh."

"It's ground-up heart and liver and lungs mixed with oatmeal and boiled in a sheep's stomach."

"That sounds acceptable," she said.

Nowan paled and shook his head. "No, not for me. Sorry."

Pike sighed. "You know, pizza has been around for at least three hundred years, and it's always this way when more than one person tries to order one. Let's try it by process of elimination: Who doesn't like sausage?"

Neither Hompaq or Nowan spoke.

"North American Protectorate bacon?"

"What is that?" Hompaq asked.

"Sliced pig."

"Ah. Pigs are much like our targs. Acceptable."

"Good. Olives?"

"Cap keeps them for martinis. Salty but acceptable."

"Green pepper?"

"I prefer my peppers hot. Humans have no peppers worthy of the name, but jalapeños are adequate."

"Uh, let's skip the peppers. Pineapple?"

Neither of them complained.

Pike nodded. "Let's not press our luck. That ought to be enough. Just a minute." He stood up and walked over to the bar. On the way he realized he hadn't asked about tomato sauce, but he decided not to go down that path. Pizza without tomato sauce was no better than a sandwich.

Cap was waiting at the end of the bar. Before Pike could tell him what he wanted, Cap said, "New York, Chicago, or Italian style?"

"Uh . . . New York," said Pike.

"Just a sec." Cap walked halfway down the length of the bar to a silvery alcove in the back wall, said, "Pizza, New York style, large, with sausage, NAP bacon, green olive, pineapple, standard cheeses." He waited a moment, just long enough to scratch his head, then reached in and lifted out a steaming pizza on a round wooden board. "Here you go." He set it in front of Pike, laid a handful of bar napkins beside it, and said, "Paramecium cheese?"

"Uh . . . no thanks," said Pike. He looked down at the pizza, then over at the slot in the wall. "Replicator" was a good name for it.

He wondered where the template had come from. The pizza certainly smelled fresh. Had chefs competed for the chance to create the perfect one from which all further replicas were made? Then at just the right moment, when all the flavors were blended and the dough cooked just so, it would be scanned into a transporter buffer and stored as an information pattern. Signal degradation from the data compression necessary to store the pattern would be too great to re-create actual living cells, but the proteins would be okay.

"Amazing," he said out loud. Starfleet could do this now, with existing technology.

"No, pizza," said Cap.

Pike nodded and picked it up, along with the napkins, and carried it back to his table.

"Dig in," he said. He sat down and pulled off a slice, stringy with melted cheese. He blew on it to cool it, then took a bite. *Mmmm.* Good as the real thing.

Hompaq tried a slice, her expression dubious for an entirely different reason, but after the first bite she nodded and said, *"Mot bah!"*

Nowan wrapped his slice in a napkin so he wouldn't get his hands oily, and when he bit he was careful not to let cheese dangle from his mouth. Victorian manners, Pike assumed. Nowan waited until he had swallowed before he said, "Yes, quite good. And quite welcome. It has been a long time since my last meal."

"Eat up, then," Pike said. "I get the impression there's a lot more where this came from."

He devoured his slice, then another, before leaning back and wiping his mouth with his napkin. "All right, that's better. Now, where was I?"

"About to face the same fate as this pizza," Hompaq said.

"Oh, yes. The kraken. It was coming fast . . ."

Chapter Twenty-four

"SHIELDS!" I ordered, and a moment later, "Evasive action!" but we didn't have time for either strategy to do any good. We had demonstrated around Devernia that our shields wouldn't prevent a head-on collision with something that big, and a ship the size of the *Enterprise* can't move instantly. The impulse engines had just powered up when the creature struck.

The hull shuddered under the blow, made doubly hard by our forward acceleration. Everyone on the bridge hung on until the inertial dampers could compensate for it, but the monster didn't sit still. It swarmed over the ship like a giant squid, hanging on with its tentacles and biting at anything that looked vulnerable. Its extra mass threw us off balance, making us spin around in a dizzying spiral until I ordered Number One to try full reverse.

Again we lurched nearly out of our chairs—those of us who had them. Everyone else went tumbling. The dampers were calibrated for a mass of 190,000 tons, not twice that, so they actually yanked the crew backward faster than the ship with its passenger could move. The creature, of course, hung on with all twelve tentacles, hardly budging until I ordered, "Full stop!"

Colt and our passengers picked themselves up off the floor. We could hear the creature slide across the hull, scraping ominously just overhead, but we couldn't see it. All our sensors pointed away from the ship, not toward it. The best we could do was infer its position by the sensors that showed scaly gray hide or total darkness, but that seemed to be the entire top half of the saucer section.

"Dabisch, launch a signal buoy," I said. Buoys exited the ship from near the middle of the saucer, and they were designed to penetrate an asteroid's surface so they could cling tight and serve as a navigation warning. One of those ought to give the monster a bellyache.

It definitely got its attention. We heard the thump of launch, then the screech of tentacles and heavy banging as the creature thrashed in pain. Then the overhead sensors cleared.

"Where did it go?" I asked. "Are we free?"

"Negative," said Spock. "It has moved to the starboard warp nacelle."

That we could see. "Give me visual," I said, and a moment later the viewscreen lit up with the view aft from the top of the saucer. The hull curved away like a gentle hillside, but the warp engines peered up over it like two enormous eyes—one of which wore a patch. A *big,* writhing, multilegged patch that seemed bent on ripping the entire engine loose from its mount. If the structural integrity fields hadn't been operating it probably could have, but it wasn't dealing with simple metallic strength. The integrity fields kept the engines from ripping loose during the extreme accelerations of warp drive, but they weren't designed for random motion any more than the inertial dampers were. If we let that thing tug at the engine long enough, it would break the support pylon. And if it did that we were as good as dead, because there was no way we would survive long enough in this system to reattach it and get away.

The phasers were purposefully designed so they couldn't fire on our own ship. The only way we could hit the creature now would be to go out with phaser rifles and shoot at it by hand, but I had already seen how effective they were against titans and I had no reason to expect them to be any more useful against this.

The ship continued to shake as the creature yanked at the engine. "Can we go into warp with it clinging to the nacelle like that?" asked Colt. Half of her hair had fallen out of its ponytail and she hung on with both hands to the railing to keep from being thrown to the floor again.

"Negative," Spock replied. "The stress would rip the ship apart."

"How about if we just let the engine build up a subspace field?" I asked. "Don't actually engage the flight controls. Maybe the magnetic effect will damage it somehow."

Spock didn't immediately object, so I said, "Try it, Number One."

She worked the controls and I watched the swirling lines of the subspace field intensity monitor above Spock's station shift to their familiar cruising pattern. But the viewscreen showed the creature stubbornly clinging on, apparently none the worse for the energy pouring through its body.

A piece of the asteroid it had used for camouflage drifted past, tumbling end over end. It was thin and sharp-edged from where it had been broken off the main mass. If only we could put an impulse engine on *that,* I thought, and steer it into the monster on our ship.

"Wait a minute," I said. The asteroid fragment didn't need an impulse engine; *we* had that. And we had a bigger target to work with, too. "Forward view," I said. The screen flickered, then showed us the moon in whose shadow we were hiding, and off to the side, the remains of the asteroid. As I had thought, the greatest part of its mass was still concentrated in one chunk. The titan-eater sheared off thin pieces to cover itself with, keeping the main mass to use over and over again. Well, we could use it too.

"Mr. Tyler," I said, "set a course for that asteroid. Offset its radius, plus forty-five meters to port, twenty meters down from ship's centerline." That was how far out the warp engine stood. Any captain who's ever taken his ship into space dock knows those figures by heart. And so does his pilot. "Number One, follow that course exactly. To the *centimeter*. And don't forget to compensate for the extra mass."

She gulped. "Aye, sir."

"Course set," Tyler said.

"Ahead half impulse power."

The ship lurched and the asteroid veered downward in the viewscreen, but Number One brought us back onto Tyler's trajectory and we watched the rocky surface approach. "Shields down," I ordered, suddenly realizing they were still up. I didn't want anything to slow the asteroid's impact by even a single erg.

It grew larger and larger, nearly filling the viewscreen with its deeply scarred surface. We could see tooth marks and fracture lines from where the creature had ripped pieces loose. It seemed as if it would smash straight into us, and I thought for sure that Tyler or Number One had miscalculated.

"Brace for impact!" I yelled.

Someone behind me shouted "Aaah!" and we all winced, but just as it seemed we would crash headlong into the stony surface, it started to slide upward. That was actually us gliding past it, just far enough away to miss it but close enough to scrape off paint. And close enough, I hoped, to scrape off unwanted passengers.

We were moving at a couple of hundred kilometers per second by then; the impact jarred us worse than anything we had yet felt. I wound up draped over the helm controls between Tyler and Number One. When I struggled back to my chair I saw Colt and Perri and Lanned folded over the railing, struggling to get their feet under them again. Spock, unperturbable as ever, picked himself up off the floor and dusted himself off before sitting back down on his stool. Dabisch had turned his long-backed chair around and ridden it out in comfort. Now he flipped the viewscreen to the aft view again and we saw the monster struggling with the asteroid, which seemed to have crushed a couple of tentacles when it struck.

"Let's go!" I said. "Warp speed, anywhere but here."

Number One engaged the engines, but a harsh alarm sounded and she instantly slapped the Abort button. "Field asymmetry is beyond safe limits," she said. "It must have damaged the engine."

"It's coming back!" Perri shouted.

"Full impulse power," I ordered. "Keep some distance."

Number One flew us toward the moon, trying to stay in its shadow, but the beast flung itself loose from the asteroid and pursued us.

"Ready phasers," I said. "Full power. Number One, bring us about." We whirled around, the effect entirely visual now that the inertial dampers had only our normal mass to work with, and Tyler fired a full spread from the phaser banks. The beams converged on the monster and its scaly hide sparkled with energy discharge, but they had no effect other than that.

I considered using a photon torpedo, but then we would probably have to fight a dozen titans that were alerted to the battle as well. "Forward again," I said. "Spock, can we get any more power out of those phasers?"

"Power is not the problem," he replied. "Penetration is. Like the titans, this creature's armor is opaque to all but Q-band radiation."

"Can we modulate the phasers to emit Q-band?" I asked.

"I believe so."

"Then do it. And fast. We don't have much time."

While he worked I pressed the intercom switch. "Engineering, see what you can do about that warp field asymmetry."

Burnie didn't sound happy. "We're trying, Captain, but it's a real mess out there. The Jefferies tubes have lost their seal at the junction so I've had to send a crew out in pressure suits. We don't even know what's wrong yet, much less how to fix it."

"You've got to do something," I said. "We can't stick around here much longer."

"Phasers are ready," Spock said.

"Number One, bring us around. Mr. Tyler, fire at will."

The creature was considerably closer now; he hit it with full power and this time the effect was instantaneous. Two of its immense tentacles blew free, whirling around like bolas. Tyler fired again and another arm twitched and jerked away like a separate beast.

One last shot and the creature's body erupted in a shower of debris, accompanied by a bright flash of light. We had apparently hit its magnetic field generator.

"Captain," Colt said. "The titans have seen us."

I hit the intercom again. "Burnie, do something *now.*"

"The best I can do is lower the efficiency of the port engine," he said. "That'll balance the subspace field, but we won't be able to do better than warp one point five."

"Warp one and a half is better than eaten alive," I said. "Do it." I looked up at Number One. "You heard the man. Get us out of here as soon as Burnie adjusts the port engine."

It took him nearly a minute, during which we watched the titans draw closer. I thanked fate that our radar jammer still worked. As it was they were only investigating a bright flash, not a foreign spaceship in their midst.

One of them came close enough to spot us visually, though, and Tyler had to fire on it as well. The explosion was just as spectacular—and just as bloody—as the Devernian nuclear bombs.

That only brought more of them in. Space was starting to get pretty thick with large bodies.

"Burnie," I said, hitting the intercom button. "Do your stuff."

"It's ready," he replied, just as another titan saw us and accelerated on its magnetic fields straight for us. It flipped over and fired its plasma jet, but before it could initiate its laser Number One engaged the engines and we leaped into warp.

Of course we weren't out of the woods yet. The titans could do warp one point five, too, and they were definitely unhappy with us. Flashes of light were a curiosity; ships traveling at warp speed were evidently the enemy.

"What have they got against starships?" I asked.

"Maybe they're guard dogs," Colt replied. Number One turned away from her control board long enough to give her one of her patented withering looks, but Colt shrugged it off and said, "Well, that's how they act. Sniffing around peaceful as can be until they see an intruder, and then *bam!*"

"Yes," Spock said, "there are similarities in their behavior. If the analogy holds true, then as soon as we are out of their territory they should lose interest in us."

"And if it doesn't?" Number One asked.

"Then we will either have to stand and fight, or continue running until they exhaust their fuel supply."

"Fifteen light-years?" I asked. "That's a lot of running at warp two."

Spock said, "That was a theoretical calculation. I may have been in error by as much as seven percent."

That was comforting. Maybe we would only have to run fourteen light-years instead.

Or maybe Colt was right and we just needed to make it

out of the solar system. We crossed the heliopause, the invisible boundary where solar wind stops pushing away interstellar dust, and plunged on into deep space. Most of the titans kept following us, but a couple of the stragglers turned back. I held my breath, waiting to see if any more would, and eventually a couple more turned away, then more and more after that until there was only one titan on our tail.

"There's always one showoff, isn't there?" I asked. "Number One, take us out of warp and bring us about on my mark. Mr. Tyler, phasers at quarter power. Shoot to injure if possible, but if it gets too close, go to full power."

"Yes, sir."

I waited a moment longer, hoping the titan would tire of the chase on its own, but when it was only a few seconds away I sighed and said, "Mark."

Number One brought us back into normal space and whirled us around so fast the viewscreen actually showed a brief image of the ship rushing toward us. Right behind it came the titan. Tyler fired and struck it head-on with the phaser banks and it lurched to the side, but it kept coming so he hit it again and this time it curved away. He gave it a third shot broadside just to make sure, and that sent it completely around the way it had come, its tentacles tucked tightly up against its body.

"Guard dogs," I said. "What do you know. Good guess, Yeoman."

"Thank you, sir."

Number One didn't look up from her helm controls. "Any other life-forms nearby?" I asked.

"Negative," said Spock.

"Did you check for mysterious hollow asteroids, too?"

"I did."

I nodded. "All right, then, let's rest up here until Burnie gets the engines up to specs again. In the meantime, let's take stock of what we've just seen. Are these big things what keeps the titan population in check, or is it more complicated than that? And what do we do about it either way?"

Lanned said, "If they're the answer to our problem, I think I prefer the problem."

"I agree," said Perri. "I don't want them anywhere close to Aronnia, either."

"I think it's a moot point," I told him. "There's no way we could take something that size back with us. And even if we could somehow manage it, it would take dozens of them to even make a dent in the titan population."

The bridge grew quiet for a moment as we all pondered the situation. We could hear the electronic bleeps and pings of instrumentation and the hum of life-support machinery keeping us comfortable inside our metal cocoon, but we were all thinking about what lived on the other side of the walls. If this was what we had come here to find, then we were on a fool's errand.

"What do we call them?" Yeoman Colt asked. "Gargantuans?"

That pretty well summed up what we were all thinking. The problem we faced, the voyage we had undertaken, the creatures we had encountered along the way—all seemed overwhelming. Especially now that it was clear the titans weren't the largest nor the fiercest monsters we were liable to face.

"How about krakens?" suggested Dr. Boyce. "It's an old name for a mythological sea monster."

"I wish these *were* mythological," I told him. "With surprises like this waiting for us it's going to be damned difficult to learn anything useful."

Spock said, "On the contrary, Captain. We have already learned a great deal of useful information. It is true that none of it offers an immediate answer to the Devernians' problem, but we *are* learning how the ecosystem functions."

"By nearly becoming part of the food chain," I said. "I

don't think we can take much more of that." I leaned back in my chair and said, "No, we need to figure out a better way of gathering information. We need to find out what eats krakens, and what eats whatever eats krakens, without attracting any more attention to ourselves."

"Maybe that's our problem," Colt said.

"Maybe what is?" I asked.

"Maybe we're too conspicuous. If it's really true that the titans see us as a threat, maybe the trick isn't to hide from them so much as it is to look like less of a threat."

"And how do you propose to do that? Paint the ship to look like a titan?"

She swallowed. "No, sir. I was remembering what Lanned said, that the titans didn't attack the Devernian spaceships until they started shooting at them. Maybe it was because the ships were too small to trigger their defense mechanism. I was thinking maybe we need to be smaller."

Dr. Boyce snorted. "Smaller? How do you plan to do that? Separate the saucer and go in without the warp drive? That would be suicide."

"No," she said. "Even the saucer would probably be too big. If the titans are guard dogs, we need to be mice. I was thinking of going back in a shuttlecraft."

"A shuttlecraft?" Boyce said. "That's insane. You'd be eaten alive."

I agreed with him at first, but after I had a moment to think about it I started to change my mind. "Maybe not," I said. "The Devernian ships—the non-living ones—aren't much bigger than a shuttle, and they held their own even under attack. They could outmaneuver the titans, for one thing. That's been our biggest liability in the *Enterprise;* we can't dodge fast enough when they come after us."

Boyce stood up from his science station and came over to the handrail around my command chair. "You're seriously considering this?" he asked. "The shuttles have no warp drive to get you out of trouble. Their phasers have maybe a tenth the power of our main batteries. Even if we tech them around to emit Q-band, that'll probably just be enough to annoy a titan. And as for a kraken, well, that'd probably just get his attention."

"We won't even try to get their attention," I told him. "That's the whole point."

"The easiest way to not get their attention is to stay the hell out of their way."

"But that won't accomplish what we came here for. We've got to go back somehow, and this is the best idea I've heard yet." I looked at the people on the bridge, wondering who I should take with me on the mission. Spock, certainly. Dr. Boyce as well, despite his objections. Perri and Lanned, to acknowledge their involvement in all this if nothing else. And Colt? It was her idea, but was that enough reason to let her endanger her life?

She looked at me with undisguised eagerness, and I remembered our discussion in the conference room a few days ago. This was the sort of thing she'd come into space for. That wasn't a good enough reason by itself, either, but she was observant and quick-thinking, both useful qualities on a mission into hostile territory.

I glanced over at Number One. Equally capable, much more calm and reasoning, with more experience and better understanding of the ship's systems. Which made her absolutely invaluable on board the *Enterprise* while I was gone. Only a fool would take all his senior officers on a dangerous mission and leave nobody experienced to mind the ship.

I briefly considered sending her to command the mission and staying here myself. That would be the most prudent course of action, the sort of thing Starfleet Command would recommend. From their point of view, the *Enterprise* and I were indispensable; I was not to risk either of us unnecessarily. But I had a pretty low opinion of the kind of captain who would send someone into a danger he wouldn't face himself, and despite their policy

I suspected Command did, too. No, if anyone was going, I would lead them.

I pressed the intercom switch on the arm of my chair. "Engineering," I said. "Have someone prepare a shuttle-craft for in-system reconnaisance. Load it with full-spectrum scanning equipment, and recalibrate the phasers for peak output in Q-band." I let up on the button and said to the bridge crew, "All right, we'll try this once more, this time the sleek and silent way."

Chapter Twenty-five

In the bar, Nowan shook his head and said, "I can't fault you for courage, but there's a fine line between courage and foolhardiness. Taking a dinghy into a pod of whales is a good way to get yourself smashed to smithereens."

"I thought whales didn't mind small boats," Pike replied. "Unless they're carrying harpooners, of course."

"Oh, aye, they don't mind 'em, not in either sense of the word. If you have the bad luck to be in their way, they'll never even know you're there."

"Ah." Pike picked at the remains of the pizza. "We had a little more room to maneuver. And we didn't go straight for the biggest concentration of titans. We wanted a broader overview of the ecosystem. And we had collected quite a bit of data already. I let Spock and Boyce go over it while we prepared the shuttle, and they figured out where the gaps in their knowledge were so we were able to target our mission a little more accurately than we had the first time. We didn't just waltz in there and hope for the best."

Hompaq was toying with a napkin, tearing it into little pieces and smiling in a distracted sort of way. Pike thought she hadn't been paying attention, but now she said, "You were—what is the human term? You were sweet on her, weren't you?"

"Who?" Pike asked.

"Don't 'who' me. Your yeoman. You took her with you everywhere you went."

"That's what a yeoman is for," Pike said. "Besides their clerical duties, they're the captain's personal assistant in practically everything, and she was highly qualified for her job."

She grinned. "I'll bet she was. It must have really rankled to see her and those two aliens consorting with one another."

Pike shook his head. "It wasn't like that."

"It should have been," said Hompaq. "On a Klingon ship, sleeping with the captain is an honor. If you truly cared for her you would have let the rest of the crew know she was your chosen mate."

Pike blushed. "That's not the way we do things in Starfleet."

"Your loss. So where is she now?"

"Science officer on board the *Bozeman.*"

She laughed. "You knew that pretty quickly."

"I approved her transfer," he replied. "I'm fleet captain now, in case you don't remember that from your history books."

"Oh, I remember," she said. "Science officer? That's quite a jump in responsibility in such a short time. One would almost suspect she pulled a few strings to get there. A few heartstrings, maybe?"

Pike leaned toward her and said softly, "Don't insult either of us by that insinuation. She got where she is today by hard work and intelligence. And ambition. When the *Enterprise* went into spacedock for refitting she didn't want to stick around for two years waiting for it to fly again, so she transferred out. And up. I was happy to give her a recommendation, but that's the extent of my influence."

"Of course." Hompaq tore a few more pieces off her napkin, adding them to the loose pile in front of her. Without looking up, she said, "You want a little piece of friendly advice?"

He considered it for a moment, ready to turn her down, but at last he shrugged and said, "Sure. What?"

"Transfer her back."

He felt a little shiver run up his spine. "Why? Does something happen to the *Bozeman*?"

"Not that I know of," she said. "Nor to her, either. But that's not what I'm talking about. I'm talking about *you*. For your sake, bring her back."

Pike rolled his eyes. "I'm hardly a pining schoolboy," he told her. "Even if I *did* harbor some personal affection for her—which I'm not admitting I do—I'm not about to cut short her career just to bring her close to me again. It wouldn't work anyway. Can you imagine how she'd feel about that?"

"Can you imagine how you're going to feel when—"

"Hompaq." The voice wasn't all that loud, but it cut through the conversation in the bar like a sonic stunner. Everyone turned to look at the bartender, who stood at the near end of the bar, a glass in one hand and a towel in the other. "Don't go there," he said.

"But he's—"

"Come here."

Her aura of bravado drained away, and she stood up without protest and walked over to the bar. They whispered back and forth for a minute, during which Pike could only catch the phrases "delta radiation" and "out of the picture anyway."

Nowan cleared his throat and said, "I suspect you must feel a little like the condemned man awaiting clemency. She clearly knows something about you."

"She certainly seems to," said Pike. "I've got to wonder, though, if she's just yanking my chain again."

"The bartender seems concerned enough to reprimand her."

"Yeah." Pike listened nervously for more clues, but Cap and Hompaq had reduced their volume. "It makes me kind of twitchy knowing they know my future," he said.

"Likewise," said Nowan.

Pike laughed. "Nobody knows *your* future. Unless you'd care to give me more of a name than 'Nowan.'"

The seaman smiled enigmatically and shook his head. "No, Captain. 'Nowan' is sufficient. As our bartender is almost certainly telling Hompaq, we are not here to upset history. The less you know about me, the better, I believe."

Pike nodded, chastened. "You're right, of course."

Hompaq and the bartender finished their argument—a rather one-sided argument, it looked like—and she came back to their table. "Just in case you were wondering, you live happily ever after," she said as she sat down again.

"That's a comfort."

"It wasn't intended to be."

Across the bar, the cat-woman stood up and led one of the human men at her table toward the stairs at the back. They were giggling as they passed Pike's table, but when Hompaq growled deep in her throat the cat-woman hissed at her and bared her fangs. Pike tensed, waiting for Hompaq to leap up and start a hand-to-hand fight, but she stayed in her chair. Too many run-ins with the bartender already tonight; she evidently didn't want to get kicked out just yet.

"There's certainly no love lost between you two, is there?" Pike asked when the cat-woman and her companion had gone up the stairs.

Hompaq snorted. "Long story. And you were still in the midst of yours."

"So I was," Pike said, just as eager as she was to leave the last few minutes behind. "Let's see, we were getting ready to head back into the titans' home system in a shuttlecraft. . . ."

Chapter Twenty-six

WE TOOK THE *Kepler,* our newest shuttle. It was already set up for planetary reconnaissance, so it required less refitting than the other shuttles, which mostly served as landing craft when the transporters couldn't handle a planet's ionosphere or when the target area was shielded. The *Kepler* had room for six, but not much more than that. I sat in the pilot's chair while Spock took the copilot's position, but he concentrated on the sensors while I flew. Colt and Boyce sat in the back, monitoring the additional scanning equipment that the engineering crew had added to the hull. Perri and Lanned sat in the middle where they could look over Spock's and my shoulders or at Colt's and Boyce's monitors, whichever seemed most interesting at the time.

It would have taken us hours to fly back into the system under impulse power, so we waited until Burnie had gotten the *Enterprise*'s warp engines back up to specs, then let it ferry us into position using the same trick we had used the first time. We went back to the same planet, but we picked a different moon to hide behind, and the moment the ship dropped out of warp we launched the shuttle, flying out of the moon's shadow toward a lone titan feeding in the rings. If they weren't going to tolerate our presence, we wanted to know it while the *Enterprise* could still pick us up and get us out of there.

We waited nervously for the titan to notice us, but if it did it gave no sign. I piloted the shuttle right up to its starboard flank while Spock, Dr. Boyce, and Colt directed scanners at everything around us. Perri and Lanned and I watched through the windshield for trouble, peering down into the jumble of dust particles, ice flakes, rocks, and occasional boulders that stretched away toward infinity before us, but long minutes ticked past without any sign of aggression.

"Any evidence of krakens?" I asked.

"One," Spock replied, "but it is four point three thousand kilometers distant."

"How about hidden ones? Would you be able to spot one covered in rock?"

"Now that we know what to look for, I believe so. But I find only the one I mentioned within sensor range."

"How about other predators?"

"None in evidence," he said.

Boyce added, "Boy, you were right about how basic this ecosystem is. I get two different types of hydroplankton, the butterfly things, one species of salmon-sized filter feeder, and then the titans and krakens. Nothing in between."

"That doesn't explain what keeps the population in check," Lanned said. "There must be something else."

"If there is, it doesn't live in the rings," Boyce said. "Not this part of 'em anyway."

"Should we go elsewhere?" I asked.

"Why don't we do an overflight?" he said. "One complete circuit around the rings. That would tell us a lot."

It was easier said than done. The rings and everything

in them were already in orbit around the gas giant, so for us to move relative to them meant that we had to *leave* orbit and hold our position under power while the rings moved beneath us. Fortunately the planet's gravity wasn't so strong that we needed full thrust to do it, but I would have to keep my attention on piloting.

"Pike to *Enterprise*," I said, keying the in-dash communicator. "We're commencing a sweep of the ring system. Take the ship to safety and wait for our pickup signal."

"Yes, sir," said Number One. "Request permission to try scanning the inner planets while we wait. The titan population dwindles closer to the sun, and that would actually put us closer to you than if we left the system completely."

She was right. "Good thinking, Number One," I said. "Permission granted. Pike out."

The shuttle seemed to grow even smaller then. We were alone now, with just one thin metal wall between us and the unknown quantities outside. Yet our tiny refuge hummed with reassuring efficiency. The air recirculator hissed softly, pulling the excess moisture and carbon dioxide out of our exhalations, and the monitors bleeped and chimed musically as they relayed their information to us. The control panel added its own sounds as the navigation array warned us of debris within our path. Clothing rustled as people shifted position, and Perri cleared his throat a few times.

"Commencing sweep," I said, taking the shuttle straight out from the rings. I wanted to get up above the ring plane a few hundred kilometers before we started moving alongside it. That would give us a better vantage from which to scan for life-forms, and it would also reduce our chances of hitting something. Most planetary rings were only a kilometer or two thick, but I didn't want to take chances here. With all these titans knocking things around, there could be debris ten times as far away as usual.

A gas giant's ring system is a big place. We drifted along above it for hours, a tiny dust mote above an immense river. Occasionally Spock would say, "I read a denser concentration of hydroplankton," or Boyce would say, "There's a subspecies of filter-fish here," and when we passed near a kraken or a moon they would grow busy for a few minutes scanning that, but as time passed it became clear there was little new to discover.

At one point we saw a kraken eating a titan, ripping it apart and devouring its internal organs. The titan was freshly killed; the ends of its tentacles were still twitching.

"I guess that settles that," I said. "Krakens eat titans."

"Obviously," said Spock.

My behind had started to grow tired from sitting on it for too long. "So what we've got here," I said, "is little plankton gizmos and butterfly things that concentrate nutrients for the filter-fish, and the titans who eat both, and the krakens who eat filter-fish and titans. That seems awfully basic. What are we missing?"

"Nothing, as far as I can tell," said Spock. "However, by definition, if we were missing something I would not be aware of it."

"What I'm wondering," said Colt, "is why the filter-fish? The titans and krakens would do fine without them, wouldn't they?"

"Not necessarily," said Boyce. "Ecosystems with only one path through the food chain are dynamically unstable. A minor fluctuation in any part of the chain sends ripples all through it."

"How so?" asked Perri.

Boyce leaned back from his monitors and rubbed his eyes. "Imagine what would happen if there was only one kind of plankton, or just the titans to eat it. If the plankton died back for some reason, so would the titans. And then the krakens. Without the titans feeding on it the plankton would probably bloom again, and the titan population would boom pretty soon after, which would lower the plankton population just about the time the kraken population was rising in response to the increased number of titans, so the titans would starve *and* be hunted down to nothing, and the cycle would keep repeating itself under positive feedback until something died out completely. But with two types of plankton and with butterflies and filter-fish in the mix, there's a second food source for everything, which serves to buffer the system and prevent feedback loops from developing."

"Is that what we're missing at home then? These little filter-fish?"

"Maybe," said Boyce. "But you're missing the plankton, too, for that matter. Your titans feed directly on gas-giant atmospheres, even when there's no plankton there. That's probably the adaptation that let them colonize other star systems, but it plays hell with their natural control mechanisms."

"What if we introduced the plankton *and* the filter-fish?" asked Lanned. "It seems counterintuitive to feed them when we want to reduce their population, but if that is what it takes . . ."

"You'd probably have to introduce krakens too," said Boyce. "And that would still leave them laying their eggs on Devernia."

I dodged a meter-wide rock that the navigation array tagged as being on a collision course, then said, "So where do the titans in this system lay their eggs?"

Spock said, "Our early scans of the inner planets showed little activity there. However, I have spotted sixty-two immature titans in the rings. They must have come from nearby. It is possible that these titans lay their eggs on the moons."

"What do the hatchlings eat, then?" I asked.

"There are hydroplankton subspecies in the moons' atmospheres and in the surface ices," he replied. "There are also land-dwelling variants of filter-fish. Plus the moons contain direct deposits of deuterium-oxide ice, which the parents can seek out with their radar when they are ready to lay their eggs. When the young have absorbed enough nutrients there to lift off into the rings, they could eat spaceborne butterflies and filter-fish until they were large enough to scoop up hydroplankton directly."

"That's *it?*" I asked. "That's the complete ecosystem?"

"Substantially," said Boyce. "We could still find a few surprises, but what we've seen here is theoretically enough."

"So what does that mean for Devernia?" Lanned asked. "Suppose we seed our gas-giant atmospheres and their rings and their moons with this hydroplankton, and release butterflies and filter-fish to feed on that. Suppose we even import krakens to feed on the titans. Even so, how do we train the titans to breed on the moons instead of Devernia?"

"Good question," said Boyce. "They've got five hundred years of experience breeding on planets. More than that, actually, since they've probably bred on them halfway from here to there. That's a lot of conditioning to overcome."

We drifted along over the rings, each lost in our own thoughts for a while. How could we retrain an entire population of titans to breed somewhere else? Providing them with the alternative site wouldn't be enough; they would just use both. We would somehow have to make Devernia not worth the effort, but if killing them with nuclear bombs hadn't discouraged them I didn't see what would.

Back on Devernia, after we had witnessed the first eggfall, Yeoman Colt had suggested fencing the titans out with phaser satellites. Spock had pointed out how impossible that was, but I couldn't help thinking we had missed something else that would make it feasible. We knew how to make the phasers more efficient now; that would help, but it hadn't been the efficiency Spock had objected to. It was the sheer number of satellites it would take to provide complete coverage.

What we needed was a way to make the titans not want to go near Devernia in the first place.

"What about jamming?" I asked.

"Jamming?" asked Spock.

"Yeah. I was thinking of Colt's fence idea. That won't work, but what if we put up a few jamming satellites? Keep the titans from getting a radar signature from Devernia."

Boyce laughed. "You can't mask a *planet*. Titans have eyes as well as radar."

"But it's the radar that tells them there's deuterium on the surface," I said. "We could jam *that*, couldn't we? Without the deuterium signature, would they still lay their eggs there?"

"I don't know," said Boyce. "Spock?"

"I do not know either." Spock turned to the copilot's control board. "But there is an easy way to test the theory."

"How?" I asked.

"Mask the deuterium signature around one of the small moons that they lay eggs on here, then watch and see what happens."

That wasn't the answer I was looking for. "It could take weeks to prove that the titans are avoiding it."

"It could. On the other hand, if we find an obvious hatching ground it could take a day or less."

"And how are we going to find an obvious hatching ground?"

"By searching for immature titans. If we find a concentration of them near a moon, that would be strong evidence that the moon is where they originated. We can then scan any adult titans in the area for mature eggs in their oviducts and observe their behavior."

That sounded reasonable enough. If they moved away and laid their eggs on another moon, that would be pretty good evidence. "How many satellites will we need?" I asked.

"Two should be sufficient for the test. One in high

orbit on either side will provide coverage of the entire moon."

"And we just happen to have two jamming devices on board," I pointed out. One was hooked up to our main deflector to help hide the shuttle from curious titans if that became necessary, and we had a spare in case the first one was damaged. "Good enough. Let's try it."

It didn't take long to find a suitable moon. There were over a dozen to choose from, starting with the hundred-kilometer snowball nearest the rings. When I flew us close to it we discovered its icy surface crawling with the planetbound versions of filter-fish, and we could see circular craters dotting the ice like dimples on a golf ball. The resemblance was uncanny, for the craters were all the same size. That couldn't happen from impacts; meteor craters would be completely random.

"Blast craters?" I asked when I saw them.

"Affirmative," said Spock. "I presume they are made when the young titans fire their fusion engines to leave the surface."

I looked from the cratered landscape to Lanned, who peered over my shoulder. "Oh yes," he said, seeing the expression on my face. "Our planet is bigger than this moon, and it takes a great deal of thrust to break free of its gravity. Imagine what a city looks like after one has lifted off from within it."

I could easily envision the destruction a fusion flame strong enough to carry a titan would wreak on a city, even one made of stone buildings. "If any of this pays off," I told him, "they'll be taking off from one of your system's moons from now on. Spock, any evidence of krakens?"

"One, Captain," Spock said. "It is hidden in an asteroid much like the first one we encountered, drifting well below us in a twenty-kilometer orbit."

"Keep an eye on it," I told him. "The moment it breaks cover, we're out of here. In the meantime, let's set up our jamming signal and see what happens."

While I piloted the shuttle up to the synchronous-orbit level above the moon's surface, Spock got up from his seat and worked his way back through the shuttle's other passengers to the cargo lockers in the rear, where he removed the backup jamming device. It was a squat rectangular box about the size of a suitcase with a detector/emitter dish on top. The programmable electronics inside had been set to return an antiphase signal to nullify any signal it received, effectively canceling out meaningful reflections. It was old technology; people had been using similar devices for centuries to block everything from police radar to orbital surveillance satellites. I had no doubt it would work against the titans' simple deuterium-location system, but whether that would discourage them was the big question.

Spock set the jammer for automatic operation, then put it in the airlock and closed the inner door. He pressed the button that opened the outer door, and with a thump of breathing air it tumbled free of the shuttle. It stabilized itself with internal forcefields and began echoing signals.

"So much for this half of the moon," I said. "Taking us around to the other." I piloted us over the pole and down to synchronous orbit on the far side, where we parked the shuttle and I activated the jammer mounted on the outer hull.

Then we settled back to wait.

Six people in a shuttlecraft is about two too many even when they're all occupied. Six people just sitting there waiting for something to happen could be the legal definition of a crowd. Spock and Boyce continued to scan the moon below us and surrounding space for lifeforms, but the rest of us had little to do besides sit in our chairs and talk about what we had seen so far. When that grew old we broke out our rations and ate a meal; then Perri and Lanned, whose bodies had not yet adapted to twenty-four-hour days, took a nap.

Colt and I played a game of three-dimensional chess

on the fold-up board from the emergency survival kit, while Spock eyed our progress and tried his best not to kibitz when we made dumb moves. Neither of us was exactly a master at the game, but we were at least evenly matched, except that I kept getting distracted by the faint but unmistakable smell of garlic on her breath. I didn't even want to know what that signified, but I couldn't help wondering. She was either using it as an excuse to keep Perri and Lanned at a safe distance or she was using it as an alien aphrodisiac, and the more I thought about it the more preoccupied I became.

We traded half a dozen pieces before Colt eventually trapped my king on one of the upper platforms and began systematically wiping out my defenses, keeping one move ahead of me until I finally conceded defeat.

"Good game, Yeoman," I told her, helping fold up the board again. "Any progress yet?" I asked Spock.

"Sixteen titans have approached the moon, sent questing signals out, and turned away when they received no deuterium signature," he replied. "Of those sixteen, six carried eggs. Those six have since moved on, and two at the extreme limit of our sensor range have lain their eggs on other moons."

"So it seems to be working," I said.

He shook his head slightly. "Two eggs deposited elsewhere is hardly a significant trend. However, we have experienced no laying behavior here since we activated the jammers, so our theory has yet to be disproved, either."

"Yes, quite," I said, thinking, *Ask a Vulcan a question . . .*

Dr. Boyce spoke up. "The kraken's asteroid has come around to our side again." Its close orbit had taken it twice around already.

"Is it still in hiding?" I asked.

"I'm checking. Looks like it—no, wait a minute." He increased the sensitivity of his scanner. "I'm getting life-form readings, but it's not the kraken. Looks like . . . eggs?"

Spock looked at his monitor. "I concur. The kraken has deposited a clutch of nine eggs."

"Why'd it leave them?" I asked. "And where'd it go?"

"Unknown," said Spock. "It does not register on our sensors. It is either on the far side of the moon, or it has left for cislunar space while it was shielded from view."

"Leaving its eggs behind," Boyce said. "It snuck them in under our radar net."

"It was already inside our orbit," Spock pointed out. "And leaving eggs behind seems to be the nature of all life here. Even the filter-fish follow the same pattern."

I looked out at the tiny asteroid with its cargo of eggs, and a crazy notion blossomed in my mind. "How long before the eggs hatch?" I asked.

"Difficult to determine," said Spock. "They are shielded from our sensors by thirty meters of rock. However, comparing what metabolic readings I can get with those taken of titan eggs, I estimate at least a week. Perhaps two."

Maybe two weeks. Not a whole lot of time, but maybe enough. "I think it's time we summed up our observations, gentlemen," I said. "Do we or do we not have enough evidence to support our theory about setting up a stable ecosystem?"

Boyce looked at me with a puzzled expression. "Spock just told you it's too soon to tell for sure."

"I don't want for sure. I want probability. Does it look like it will work? And more importantly, how much of the ecosystem do we need to take back with us to *make* it work?"

"Why are you in such an all-fired hurry all of a sudden?" He grinned. "There's a bathroom in back, you know."

I laughed. "That's not it. I'm just thinking that if we're going to transport krakens back to the Devernian system, there's an opportunity right below us we're not likely to find again."

I swear Boyce's hair turned even whiter when I said that.

"You can't be serious," he said. "You want to steal eggs from a kraken's nest?"

"If krakens are important to the ecosystem, I do."

"They are undoubtedly important," said Spock. "We have witnessed nothing else that preys on titans."

"Then put on your pressure suits, boys and girls," I said. "We're going to raid the henhouse."

Chapter Twenty-seven

"YOU DIDN'T," said Nowan.

"We did," Pike replied, grinning proudly.

"Without even knowing where the parent had gone?"

"We made a quick orbit around the moon first and made sure it wasn't lurking close by. We didn't find any sign of it, so we figured it must have gone away. So we parked the shuttle near the asteroid and went in with jet packs." He laughed. "Of course, six of us suiting up in that cramped little shuttle was a comedy in a closet, but we managed it. It went considerably easier after I turned off the gravity."

"You took your entire crew?" Hompaq asked, just as Nowan said in the same astonished tone of voice, "You turned off the gravity?"

"No," Pike said. "I left Dr. Boyce with the shuttle, but I wanted him suited up in case we needed him in a hurry. And yes, I turned off the gravity. It gave us a lot more room to maneuver in. Five of us would duck down and the sixth would float lengthwise in the cabin while we dressed them for space. Of course Perri didn't like that much, since he'd never experienced free fall before, but he took to it pretty quickly. And Colt turned out to be a regular gymnast. She didn't need any help getting her suit on, although Perri and Lanned both helped her anyway."

Hompaq snorted. "While you stood by and gallantly held her helmet."

"Hey, who's telling this story, anyway?"

"If I was telling it, you'd have killed the gravity hours earlier and enjoyed yourselves."

Pike rolled his eyes. "You're incorrigible."

"Damned near insatiable, too," Hompaq admitted, leering at him.

Nowan laughed nervously, then scooted his chair back. "Time to refill our beverages," he said, picking up the two brandy snifters and the Warnog mug and carrying them to the bar. While the bartender refilled them, he came back for the pizza board and the napkins and set them on the end of the bar. Pike watched him take a pen from the mug full of them and look at the nib, then draw on a napkin with it. The nineteenth-century man couldn't hide his astonishment at seeing a ballpoint; he drew a few more lines with it, then pocketed the pen and the unused napkins.

Hompaq had been watching Pike instead. "Really, Captain," she said, "you should get out more. Beat your chest and battle some enemies. Or make savage love with exotic strangers."

"I should, should I?" he asked, eyeing her dubiously from under narrowed eyebrows. "And what makes you say that, Miss Alien Psychiatrist?"

She scratched an itch in an area that most women would have considered private, then said, "The way you tell your tale, and the way you looked when you came in here. When you walked through that door you looked like someone whose whole life had dried up and blown away, but you've shed ten years in the last hour."

He had managed to forget why he'd gone on his walk

this evening, but at her words the full load of frustration and self-doubt returned like a stifling cloud of oxygen-poor air. His days as a space explorer were long past, and despite the temporary rush he felt in reliving them, no amount of bar-story nostalgia could bring them back.

"That was interesting," Hompaq said.

"What?"

"You can switch it on and off like a light."

"Can I." It wasn't a question.

Nowan came back with their drinks, carefully set them in front of their respective owners, and sat down.

"Is it just me," he asked, "or has a chill blown through here in the last few moments?"

"We were discussing whether Captain Pike here should get out more," Hompaq said. "I think we both voted yes."

"Ah," said Nowan. He, too, lost a little of the gleam in his eye, and Pike remembered how he had looked at first. And acted. A Victorian gentleman who had renounced everything, including his manners. He had gotten them back, but Pike had just witnessed how temporary these bar changes could be.

Temporary or not, he wasn't ready to give it up just yet. Nor was Nowan. The seaman held up his glass and said, "To getting out more." They drank, then he added, "I believe you were about to get out of your shuttle to go raid a kraken's nest. How, pray tell, did that expedition fare?"

"Well enough, at first," Pike replied, glad for the respite. "Once we got out of the shuttle." He took another sip of brandy, reluctant now to go on, but both Hompaq and Nowan were waiting. He took a moment to gather his thoughts, trying to recapture the moment, then set his glass down. "As I said, I left Dr. Boyce there to guard our transportation and to warn us if the kraken returned, and the rest of us jumped to the surface of the asteroid. It was so small there was hardly any gravity to draw us down, so we had to move carefully." Pike smiled, remembering. "It was Perri's first time in a spacesuit, so he was pretty clumsy. And I think he was probably terrified, too, but he never let on. Except we could hear him panting so hard over the radio that Colt reached over to his chest controls and turned down the oxygen level in his air so he wouldn't hyperventilate."

"Why didn't you just leave him behind?" Hompaq asked. "He sounds like a liability."

"I wanted the manpower," Pike replied. "Those eggs were big, and we needed at least two of them. And I wanted the extra phaser in case there were any surprises on the asteroid. The eggs were down inside it, in a cavern the kraken had hollowed out a couple dozen meters below the surface. Our sensors couldn't detect anything in there besides eggs, but I'd been surprised before."

As Pike talked, Nowan took out the pen he had gotten from the bar and began to doodle on the napkins. He was a good artist, and quick. With a few bold strokes of the pen he had rendered a titan with its streamlined body, immense mouth in front, and betentacled fins at the rear. And the kraken, shorter but bigger around, with much larger tentacles. Both rushing toward a tiny box with stick figures floating haphazardly around it.

"You're getting ahead of me," Pike told him.

"What? Oh." Nowan blushed. "Just trying out this pen. It's amazing." He traced the wrinkles in his hand with it, then added a few extra curves and circles for eyes and it suddenly became the face of a wizened old man.

"You're not half bad with that," Pike said.

"Thank you. But I interrupt your story. Please continue." He set the pen down and leaned back in his chair to listen.

Pike shrugged. "No problem. So anyway, the five of us in spacesuits pushed off for the mouth of the cave where the eggs were. . . ."

Chapter Twenty-eight

I'D ISSUED EVERYONE a phaser rifle this time. Perri and Lanned had long since put aside their differences, and even though the phasers had been modified for peak output in Q-band I wanted as much firepower as I could get in case of trouble. I showed both men how to shoot and warned them not to unless it was absolutely necessary; then we used our jet packs to move off across the asteroid's scarred surface toward the kraken's nest.

We looked like a procession of snowmen. Our suits were white and bulky, and even with constant-volume joints they resisted movement, so we tended to move our whole bodies when we turned or bent down to look at something. I heard plastic creak as I moved, and the gentle hiss of air through the recirculator reminded me that there was hard vacuum about an inch away from my nose. The helmet had a generous faceplate so I could see to either side without turning my head, but its opaque back still made me feel like something was following me.

There was no dust on the surface, just bare rock. It was dark gray, almost black except when we shone our headlamps directly at it and it sparkled with pinpoints of reflected light. We couldn't walk on it—there wasn't enough gravity to hold our feet down—but we drifted along with our legs pointed that way out of habit. Except for Lanned, who moved headfirst like a torpedo, pulling himself along with his hands. He probably had the most experience with zero-g of any of us, I realized, since his primitive fighter craft had no provision for gravity.

Spock had his tricorder out and was scanning the surface for life-forms. The horizon was only a few dozen meters away and a tricorder couldn't go through very much rock, so I wasn't sure how much good it would do, but it was better than nothing.

"See anything?" I asked him.

"I detect no significant life-forms."

"Here's the opening," Lanned said, bringing himself to a stop at the lip of the cavern. He stuck his legs upward for the rest of us to stop ourselves with, but Perri missed and drifted out over the cave mouth.

"Ahh!" he cried out, swinging his arms wildly for balance, but Lanned snagged his left boot and pulled him back.

I thought about linking everyone together with our safety lines, but that would cut down on our mobility. Perri would be okay in the cave, I figured. There wouldn't be that much room for him to drift before he bumped into a wall.

We peered down into it, our headlights making little circles of brightness on the rock. It was a rough-hewn tube about three meters wide, but instead of running straight down to the egg chamber it curved, so we could only see a few meters into it. It looked empty.

"We're going in," I said for Boyce's benefit.

"I see you," he replied from his vantage a hundred yards overhead. "Be careful."

I pulled myself over the lip and fired my jet pack downward, going in feet first. The rest of us followed one at a time, Lanned bringing up the rear and helping

Perri. The rock walls closed in on us, and after we'd negotiated the first turn and couldn't see the stars behind us anymore I felt a twinge of claustrophobia, but I fought it off and continued on. We wouldn't be in here long.

"Anything, Spock?" I asked.

"I can detect the eggs," he replied. "Anything smaller would be beyond the sensitivity of a handheld tricorder through this much rock."

"Smaller I'm not worried about," I said. "I just don't want to surprise a kraken sitting on the nest."

My own shadow preceded me, cast by the others' headlamps as I led the way deeper into the asteroid. I shifted my phaser from hand to hand so I could push off from whichever side of the tunnel I was close to, and I peered around each bend as cautiously as I could, but anything in there had to know we were coming.

It flashed toward us without warning. Spock barely had time to say "Captain, I read—" when two silvery forms burst out of the darkness and came straight for us.

I shouted and got off a quick shot at one of them, but I was way too slow. Nobody else even tried, for which I was thankful. The radio filled with our shouts of alarm as the two creatures bore down on us, then zoomed past without slowing. I never even got a good look at them; all I could see were two bodies about the size of house cats streaking outward, never touching the walls of the cave. Evidently they had the same magnetic propulsion capability that the titans and the kraken did.

Boyce's signal cut in and out, but I heard him say, "What the . . . that? Are . . . right in there?"

"We're fine," I said when I got control of my voice again. "Filter-fish?" I asked Spock.

"Affirmative," he replied.

"I'm glad there's plumbing in these suits," Perri said.

Lanned laughed, and Colt said, "Me too."

"Cut the chatter," I told them. "Let's go."

I led them deeper into the cavern, and after two more turns we found the egg chamber. It was spherical, maybe five meters across. The eggs were coffin-sized and stacked against the back wall, their gray and scaly surfaces almost indistinguishable from the rock. With nine of them and five of us the place felt crowded. I wondered how a kraken could fit in here, and decided it couldn't. Not with its wide body and thick, scaly hide. It must push the eggs down here with its tentacles.

"How close to hatching are they?" I asked Spock, who was waving his tricorder over them.

"Fascinating," he replied.

"That's not a number," I told him. "Will they make it back to Devernia without hatching?"

"I believe so," he said. "The embryos have barely begun to differentiate yet. But what development I do see shows clear evidence of genetic engineering."

"What kind of evidence?" I asked.

He continued to scan as he talked. "The nervous system is essentially a trinary computer, not yet running but already programmed. Even in its simple form I cannot decipher the program without help from the ship's computer, but I can identify sections that clearly represent pattern-recognition subroutines. They are almost certainly a catalog of images. I suspect these will turn out to be a list of objects to either attack or defend in adult life."

Its brain was a *computer?* "Do the titans have this same kind of system?" I asked.

"Undoubtedly. I did not recognize it as such because I was unable to observe such early embryonic stages in their development, and therefore did not detect the simple underlying program that directed their actions, but from what I did see of the later forms, they are built in substantially the same fashion."

Guard dogs indeed, I thought. Ones that came pretrained. "Could the program be modified?" I asked.

"It probably could," he replied. "In this pristine form it would be relatively easy to alter the code. Once it was running it would be more difficult. I suspect the creatures were designed this way to give their creators an opportunity to modify their programming before releasing them into the wild."

"You're right," I said, "it's fascinating. And maybe even useful if we can figure out how to tap into their programs to make them less aggressive toward starships. But for now we're in the middle of a nest made by one that hasn't been reprogrammed, and every minute we stay here we're pushing our luck that much further. Come on, let's grab a couple of eggs and go."

"We will need three," Spock said.

"Three? There's three sexes?"

Spock shook his head, a gesture that was barely visible outside his pressure suit. "They do not reproduce sexually, at least not as we understand it, but there are three distinct types. We should have a specimen of each."

"Okay, then, three. Which ones?"

He ran the tricorder over the eggs. "The top three will do," he said after a moment.

I let go of my phaser rifle and tugged the first one free. It pulled slowly loose from the others, and I pushed it over to Colt and Perri. I shoved the next one toward Lanned, and I took the last one myself.

A burst of static washed over the radio and I heard Boyce trying to say something, but the signal couldn't penetrate that much rock. "We're coming out," I said, just in case the shuttle radio could pick up our signal better than we could his.

We had just made it to the first bend when Colt shouted "Look out!" and shoved Perri back toward the rest of us. Reaction sent her forward straight into the tentacle that snaked down the tunnel toward us.

It was as big around as a tree trunk, but flexible enough to wrap around her waist the moment it touched her. The only thing that saved her was the egg she was pushing; it bumped into the tentacle and the creature paused to loop itself around that, too. By then all four of us had opened fire on it, aiming for the spot just ahead of where it held her. The tentacle twitched and Colt screamed in pain, but a moment later our phasers blew the end of it free and it loosened its grip on her.

The ragged ends oozed blue-green blood which spattered on our white spacesuits and smeared our visors, but we kept firing at the end that was still attached to the kraken until it vanished back up the tunnel.

I pushed myself over to Colt, who was bent over and clutching her left side. "Are you all right?" I asked, knowing already that she wasn't. I could hear her breathing hard over the radio, and there was an ominous bubbling sound to it.

"I think it—broke some ribs," she said.

There was nothing we could do for that here. We'd have to get her out of her suit and let Dr. Boyce go over her with a protoplaser . . . provided *he* was okay.

Her spacesuit had taken a beating, too. It had deep gouges on the chest and arms where the kraken's scaly hide had slid around it. I checked the pressure gauge. The external readout on her chest control unit read 1.02 atmospheres. That meant the suit wasn't leaking, but I wondered why the pressure was high. I watched it for a moment, and it clicked to 1.03. The internal sensor had been damaged.

We were only thirty or forty meters from safety, provided the kraken had left the shuttle alone. Colt would make it that far without overpressurizing.

"Let's get out of here while we can," I said. "Come on." I pushed the kraken egg into the tunnel ahead of me, then gently helped Colt along behind it. We all advanced with our phaser rifles ready, but the kraken didn't poke its tentacles down the hole again.

We saw why when we got to the surface. Dr. Boyce had taken the shuttle out of harm's way and tried to warn us by radio when the kraken approached, but when we didn't respond and he saw it going for the cave he had returned to shoot at it with the phasers and scare it away. Trouble was, it wasn't scaring. It moved like a ghost, bobbing and weaving through space on its magnetic drive while it lashed out at the shuttle with its tentacles. We had removed the last couple meters of one, and Boyce had blown another one off at the base, but that still left it ten good ones to fight with.

Boyce was doing a good job of piloting. The shuttle darted around the kraken on its impulse engines, and whenever he got a second to reach the phaser controls he would fire at the creature's head, but he had his hands full just staying out of its way.

"Open fire!" I said, and all five of us—even Colt—raised our phaser rifles and shot at the kraken.

"Hey, the cavalry's here!" Boyce said. "Boy am I glad to see you. I was afraid you'd been smashed to pulp down there."

"It almost got Colt," I told him. "She's got—look out!"

The kraken had whirled around to face the new sting in its side, and when it saw us at the edge of the cave with three of its eggs floating into space in front of us, it rushed toward us. We scattered like ejecta from an explosion, firing our jet packs at maximum thrust in six different directions. I spun myself around and kept firing at it with my phaser, hoping to draw it away from the others, but they all had the same idea.

The kraken had its own ideas as well. Boyce had followed it in, firing steadily at its backside, but the kraken hit the asteroid, flexed its tentacles, and sprang back at him with surprising speed.

"Reverse thrust!" I yelled at him, but it was way too late. The kraken struck the shuttle a direct body blow, then it wrapped its tentacles around it and started to squeeze.

Boyce fired the phasers again point-blank. There was a big explosion and two tentacles flew away, but the blast must have taken out the phaser emitter as well because he didn't fire again.

We shot at it from below, still aiming for the thing's

head, but it was hard to reach anything vital through the writhing tentacles.

The kraken squeezed hard and the shuttle's windshield blew out in a howl of breathing air. "Boyce, get out of there!" I shouted.

"Just a minute," he said. The shuttle lurched forward under full thrust, slamming hard into the kraken, but the tentacles didn't release their hold on it. Our phasers were having no better effect. The kraken tightened its tentacles again, and we could see the body of the shuttle constrict like an hourglass.

"Jump, dammit!" I shouted.

"Yeah, that looks like a very good idea," he said. He didn't bother with the airlock; he just leaped out through the hole where the windshield had been. He brushed one of the tentacles on his way out and it curled around to snare him, but he fired his jet pack and shot upward, then curved back behind the shuttle and out of the tentacles' reach.

"Hold your fire," I said. "We're not hurting that thing a bit from here. We're just wasting energy."

Our phaser beams winked out, and we watched the kraken crush the shuttle. It was still facing away from it, but we watched it twist around, pulling its head in through the knot of tentacles and rotating them around until it could get its mouth into position.

It took the entire shuttle in one gulp. I watched its massive jaws come together and grind sideways, eerily silent in the vacuum of space, but I knew what it was doing to the shuttle inside that armored maw. Then, suddenly, I realized what was about to happen.

"Take cover!" I shouted. We were too far apart for anyone to help anyone else; I just jetted for the cave entrance and hoped the others could make it as well. Perri and Lanned joined me there, but Colt and Spock and the doctor took off around the curve of the asteroid, putting its entire bulk between them and the kraken.

I hit the first curve in the tunnel feet first and actually

ran around the corner, the centripetal force holding my feet to the floor. I used my hands and my boots to bring myself to a stop, and I helped Perri and Lanned do the same. We waited for a few seconds, breathing hard, while I wondered if I had misjudged the situation, but just as I was about to go peek around the corner there was a bright flash and a chunk of blue-gray flesh smacked wetly into the exposed face of the tunnel.

"Fuel tanks?" Lanned asked.

"Fuel or air," I said. "Either one was under a lot of pressure."

We crawled back out of the tunnel. There was no sign of the shuttle, and of the kraken I could only see tentacles whipping around in pinwheels as they receded into space.

Boyce and Spock and Colt came back over the horizon. I noticed that Boyce was helping Colt, who held her arms close to her chest. "Now what?" asked Boyce.

"Did you manage to get out a distress call?" I asked.

He snorted. "Things were a little busy there."

"I imagine they were. Well, let's try it now." I switched from the suit intercom frequency to the general hail frequency. "Pike to *Enterprise*. Come in, *Enterprise*."

No response. Of course there wouldn't be; we were on the dark side of the asteroid, and Number One had taken the ship into the inner system.

I kicked off from the surface and dodged kraken debris until I made it into the sunlight. We were quite a ways from the star, but it was still bright enough to cast shadows. I called on the general hail frequency again, "Pike to *Enterprise*. Come in *Enterprise*."

Still no reply. I switched back to the intercom frequency. "Let's all try it," I said. "Maybe our combined signal will reach."

So we all jumped free and radioed for help, but that had no better effect.

"They'll come investigate pretty soon when they don't hear from us, won't they?" asked Perri.

"I'm sure they will," I said, "but Colt's got broken ribs and a busted pressure sensor in her suit. We don't have long."

"Add a punctured lung to that," Boyce said. "She needs help as quick as we can get it."

Spock was holding his tricorder up to his faceplate and pointing it out toward the gas giant. "The explosion seems to have attracted the attention of the titans," he said.

Of course it had, I thought. Things hadn't been bad enough yet. "How many?" I asked.

"Fifteen."

"The *Enterprise* couldn't pick us up even if they knew we were in trouble," I said. "Not with them just waiting for the ship to pop out of warp."

I looked down at the cavern mouth. If we hadn't had an injured crew member we could have hidden in there until the titans went away and the *Enterprise* could come get us. We didn't have that kind of time, though. We had to get completely away from here, and we had to do it *now*.

Out in the rings, which we saw edge-on from our vantage point, fifteen tiny points of light grew brighter. The titans were coming fast.

"Wait a second," I said. "Perri, how do you actually control a titan once you've saddled it up?"

"Saddled?" he asked.

"Harnessed. Put your pressure dome on it. How do you make it go where you want it to?"

"We run electrical current through its skin at sensitive spots along the tail fins and nose. Um . . . why do you ask?" His tone of voice made it clear he was hoping for a different answer than what he thought it would be.

I had to disappoint him. "Because I think we've got just one chance to get Colt to safety in time."

"By riding a *titan?*" asked Boyce. "That's suicide."

"Are you willing to let her die while we hide out and wait for rescue?"

Colt said, "Captain, I'm not hurt that—" but she coughed and we could all hear the gurgling of blood in her lungs. It took her quite a while to stop coughing, during which the rest of us floated helplessly, unable to do anything for her.

I didn't wait for her to protest any more. "Come on," I said. "The krakens have already shown us how to sneak up on a titan. Let's use those eggs for cover and set ourselves adrift before they get here."

We used our jet packs to chase down the eggs, which were tumbling end over end from the explosion. Spock and Lanned and I brought them together and all six of us crowded into as tight a ball as we could, using our safety lines to tie ourselves to the eggs and holding them like a shield between us and the advancing titans. We jetted away from the explosion site, then waited to see what the titans would do when they got there.

The first ones shot through the debris field with their mouths closed, letting the hunks of kraken meat bounce off them as they looked for danger, but when they found nothing threatening they moved back through and began feeding. The later ones caught up with them and they began pushing one another around, fighting for the choicest pieces. Some of them bit into pieces of the shuttle and spit them back out, only to have others try the same thing. They looked a little like fish in an aquarium right after you've dropped the food in, but I kept reminding myself that these fish were nearly as large as the *Enterprise*.

One of the titans kept getting pushed aside, and I noticed that it was drifting farther out of the group—the *fleet*, as Lanned called it. It ate a few tiny bits of shredded kraken when it came upon them, but mostly it just drifted motionless with its nose pointed toward the others, looking for all the world like somebody's younger brother who's been left out of all the fun.

"That's our baby," I said, pointing at it. "Let's see if we can sneak up on it from behind."

"We . . . really don't . . . have to . . ." Colt said.

"Save your breath, Yeoman," I told her. "Let's go."

We fired our jet packs and moved closer, keeping the rocky surface of the eggs between us and the titan. Just as we had almost reached its broad tail fins it saw something it wanted and surged away, but a moment later it was knocked back by a more aggressive companion. One of its fins sailed past just a few meters beneath our bellies; then the rough hide slid by, growing closer and closer as we worked our way up the thickening body.

I pulled out a long loop of line from my safety tether's belt reel, and just as the eggs bumped into the creature's skin I reached out and ran it around one of the dinner-plate-sized scales. The skin twitched, nearly throwing us off, but I tugged us back down and the others each looped a line around a scale.

I peeked out from under our cover. We were on the top of a gently curving hillside. The huge fin behind us stuck up like a ten-story building, its three tentacles reaching forward to scratch an itch they couldn't quite reach. I shivered, thinking how lucky we had been not to hit the fin.

I saw the bulge of an eye socket up ahead, watched it swivel around, but it couldn't move far enough to let the creature see us, either. Another ripple ran along its hide, but we rode it out easily. If that was the best it could do then we were set.

"So, Mr. Perri, where do we zap it to make it go?" I asked.

Chapter Twenty-nine

"AHAB," SAID NOWAN.

"Gesundheit," Pike said automatically.

"No, no, *Ahab*. Melville's character. Though I suppose it's a stretch to hope a book that was already ten years old and obscure in my time would still be read in yours."

Pike laughed. "You mean *Moby Dick*? Sure we still read it. It's assigned in school alongside *Fear of Flying* and *The Shining*. It's been a long time since I studied it, but didn't Ahab come to a bad end?"

"You might say. Dragged to his death in the sea by the whale he'd chased half his life."

"Yeah, that's right. I hope you don't think I'm going to end my story that way."

Nowan shook his head. "I rather doubt that, since you're here to tell it. I was just caught by the similarity to Ahab in his moment of desperation, entangled with his nemesis even after it destroyed his ship."

Hompaq yawned and stretched, a motion that drew the attention of both men at the table. "I do not know this Ahab," she said, "but I know that human books

221

contain much silliness and soul-searching when action would better suit them."

"Act first, think later?" Pike asked her.

"Act first, then act again while your opponent lies unconscious," she replied.

"Uh-huh." Pike edged away theatrically.

She laughed, then reached out and slapped him on the back. "Relax, Captain. You would enjoy my way of rendering *you* unconscious."

Klingons certainly weren't subtle, that much was certain. Pike wasn't sure exactly what she had in mind, but he got the general drift of it, and while he was flattered that she thought him heroic enough to consort with, he wasn't sure if he was willing to risk broken bones in order to prove anything more to her.

But oh, how tempting it was.

Nowan was squirming in his chair like a five-year-old at a museum. Victorian ladies apparently didn't talk about such things in public. Or even in private, if the history books were to be believed. Pike took pity on him and said, "Anyway, the titan dragged us through plenty of space, but it didn't drag us to our deaths. We found death aplenty on board it, though."

"What?" he asked. "I was sure you had gotten away unscathed. Save for your yeoman's injury, of course."

"We thought so too," said Pike. "And for the first million kilometers or so we did, but we had a couple hundred times that far to go, and an asteroid belt full of more titans and krakens to get through."

"Not again!" cried Nowan.

"That's what we said, too, when the first one came after us." Pike leaned forward in his chair. "Especially when we realized we'd picked a slow titan."

Chapter Thirty

IT TURNED OUT the way to goose a titan was to hit it on the trailing edge of its tail fins. There was no way I would let my crew get close to the tentacles that reached forward from there, so we had to make do with shooting from high on the flanks with our phasers set on "stun." And then we had to hang on for dear life, because a titan's first response to being hit in the privates is to twitch a whole lot harder than it had when we tied ourselves down to it.

I heard Colt cry out the first time it happened, but the titan hadn't gone anywhere so I ordered everyone to fire again. It was just Spock and Perri and Lanned and myself with phaser rifles; Dr. Boyce stayed with Colt to do what he could for her, which at the moment meant holding her hand and occasionally venting her suit when its air pressure built up to the danger level.

Our second volley got it moving, but slowly, so we fired again and this time it really took off. It wasn't pointed toward the inner reaches of the solar system, though, so I had Perri fire at the outermost fin and that turned it inward. It took some fine-tuning, but we eventually had it aimed straight at the star and then we poured on the fire until it was booming along at thousands of kilometers per second. There was no way to tell by eye how fast we were going, of course, but Spock could triangulate on the planets with his tricorder and calculate it out.

"At this rate we will reach the primary in four hours, thirteen and a half minutes," he said.

"Boyce?" I asked. "Will that do?"

"Maybe," he said. "If she doesn't run out of air first. I'm having to blow off a couple liters a minute just to keep her suit from overfilling."

"Let me see," I said. I tugged myself down to the mottled gray titan hide by my safety line and pulled myself over to Colt, who had curled into a loose fetal position beside the kraken eggs, which Boyce had tied down as well. I bent down to look at her suit's chest controls, trying to see if I could override the internal pressure sensor somehow, but those things were designed to be idiotproof. The linkage was completely internal, and short of opening her suit to vacuum and adjusting the sensor by hand there was nothing I could do.

Her air supply was down to sixty percent. It had only been fifteen or twenty minutes since her injury. She wouldn't make it at this rate.

I looked at her face, pasty white and sweaty. She had always looked like a little girl to me; now she looked even younger. I felt like five times a fool for bringing her out here. Adventure, pah! What kind of adventure was it to drown in your own blood while tied to the back of an alien monster a hundred light-years from home? And I was the man who had led her there.

Her eyes fluttered open and she looked up at me. It was all I could do to keep from turning away.

"Don't try to talk," I said. "You're going to be all right. We're on our way to the *Enterprise* now."

She nodded slightly. She knew I was lying to her, knew she was going to die.

Her pressure gauge read 1.3 atmospheres. Boyce let off more air, but stopped at 1.2. "The suit's safe at that," he said. "I've upped the oxygen content, too. With all the blood she's losing and that lung filling up, she needs all she can get."

"Good," I said. "Keep her going. We'll share our air supply if necessary."

"How?" he asked. "We've got no hoses, no couplings, nothing. I don't even have my damned emergency kit."

"We'll think of something," I told him. "You let me worry about that; you just keep her alive."

"Yes, *sir!*" he said sarcastically. From anybody else I'd have reprimanded him on the spot for insubordination, but I felt like I deserved worse.

I stood up and pushed off toward Perri. "How do you get them to go into warp?" I asked.

"You don't want to try that," he replied.

"I do. How do we do it?"

"Captain," he said. "One-half of all attempts end in failure. This is with *trained* pilots, and tame titans."

"That's for interstellar flights," I replied. "I'm just talking about going for five minutes or so until we're in radio range."

He turned around and looked at the star, a hard, bright dot not much bigger than Venus or Jupiter seen from Earth.

"We haven't got a choice," I said.

He sighed. "Very well. We must stimulate the warp engine directly."

The warp engine was in one of the two bulges right at the very tip of the tail. Down around the curve of the creature's tapering flank. "We can't reach it from here," I said.

"No, we can't," he replied. "One of us will have to go down among the fins and shoot at it from there."

"How do you stop it once it's going?" I asked.

"You stop shocking it—or in this case stop shooting it—and then you pray," he replied.

"Great," I muttered. "All right, you guys make damn sure it stays aimed for the inner system. If it veers off course at warp speed, we're all in deep trouble." I turned away and pulled myself down toward one of the fins, looping my safety line around half a dozen scales as I went along.

"Captain, no!" Colt said. She could hear everything we said over the suit intercoms.

"I'll be fine," I told her. "Don't worry. Spock, you calculate how far we've gone, and tell me when we need to stop."

"Very well, Captain," he said. I could tell he didn't think much of the idea, either, but he was officer enough not to question my order.

I looked down toward the tentacles, all reaching for me. The titan couldn't see me back here, but it could feel the tug on its scales. That's what I was counting on. I kicked off toward the back, then tucked my feet up so I wouldn't touch anything and unreeled safety line as I drifted toward the creature's tail. My line kept a steady pull on the scales up ahead.

It was a long glide. At one point I got disoriented and felt like I was falling down an infinite cliff, but I kept myself from grabbing the line and halting my progress. I passed between two fins, just below the questing tentacles, and on toward the back.

I didn't stop until I was well out of reach behind the titan. From that vantage it was easy to see which bump was the fusion engine and which one was the warp drive. I pulled myself forward a ways until I was out of the blast cone if it lit the engine, eyeing the tentacles to make sure I wasn't in their reach either, then said, "Everybody brace yourselves. Here we go," and fired my phaser at the warp engine.

The tentacles all whipped around toward the back.

One of them grazed my tether and snapped me forward, but I stopped myself with my jet pack and fired again at the warp engine.

The *Enterprise*'s engines are set way in back of the living quarters for a reason. The intense subspace distortion right next to the field generators can turn a person inside out if they're too close. It can scramble your brain and short out every nerve in your body. The titan's engine wasn't nearly as powerful, and I was probably twenty meters away from it so I didn't get the full effect, but I saw plenty of crazy images when the titan finally decided to engage it. The stars seemed to bulge in front of us and narrow down behind us, and bright streaks of intense white light rushed toward me. I knew then how Zefram Cochrane must have felt in his unshielded ship when he made humanity's first warp-drive trip across the solar system.

I let out a little more line, continuing to fire the phaser one-handed while I put some distance between me and the engine. I didn't want to get *too* far away—if I fell out of the warp field entirely I would be left behind in interplanetary space—but I figured another dozen meters or so would be safe enough.

Then the titan, in full panic, fired its fusion drive as well, and a moment later the magnetic squeeze effect turned it into a laser. A two-meter-wide, blood-red death ray, beside which I bobbed on the end of my tether, my boots maybe one foot's width from the edge of the beam.

My heart froze, then lurched back into action.

I quit firing my phaser and scrambled hand-over-hand up the line again. The titan continued on under warp drive for a few more seconds, then dropped back into normal space. I looked outward and saw hundreds of scintillating points of light in all directions.

"Asteroid belt?" I asked.

"Affirmative, Captain," Spock replied.

"Let's see if we're close enough to reach the *Enterprise* now," I said. "Hold on." I switched over to the hailing frequency and called, "Pike to *Enterprise,* come in *Enterprise.*"

After a few seconds I heard Dabisch's voice, buried in static. *"ssss . . . that you? Say again . . . ssss."*

"Dabisch, this is Pike! We're in the asteroid belt. Come get us!"

"sssssteroid belt? How'd you sssss?"

"Long story. We need pickup *now.* Do you copy?"

"Give us *sssss.* We'll *sssssss.* "

"Drop whatever you're doing and come *now.* Immediate pickup. Do you copy?"

There was a moment with no carrier at all, then, *"ssss on the ground. sssss abandon sssss?"*

Dammit. Number One had sent someone down to the surface of one of the planets. "Negative, negative," I said. I wasn't going to endanger one group to rescue another. "Do not leave anyone behind. Pick up your ground party first, but hurry!"

"Undersss. We'll be there as *ssss* possible."

"Good. Pike out." I switched back to intercom mode, leaving the receiver set to pick up anything on either channel. "I got through," I reported. "They've got to recall a team on the ground first, but they'll be coming as soon as they do that."

"Good," said Boyce. "Her condition's deteriorating."

I pulled myself up the line to where he and Colt had tied themselves to the titan's scaly hide. We were in free fall again, so it was relatively easy to reel in line as I went. "Hang in there, Yeoman," I said. "Help's on the way."

"G-glad to . . . hear that," she whispered.

"Unfortunately, more titans are also on the way," Spock said.

I looked out at the asteroid field. Sure enough, the specks of light were now distinct bodies, approaching fast. "Let's hope they just want to check out the new-comer," I said.

That seemed to be the case at first. When the other titans arrived they drifted up alongside ours, their immense bodies sliding past slowly like starships in spacedock, but suddenly one of them turned away and sprayed hot exhaust plasma at us. The brunt of it hit farther up, toward the creature's head, but there was enough scatter to set off my suit alarm.

I whirled around and fired at the fins to prod our ride into action, but there was no need. Our titan didn't like the welcome any more than we did. It surged away, but the others chased it, one of them roaring past and firing its fusion engine again. This time the exhaust plume lased, and the fiery beam streaked along the creature's flank only a dozen meters from us, throwing out gouts of vaporized flesh. It raked across one of the fins and sliced it off as cleanly as a knife before winking out.

The titan shuddered and the radio filled with voices as everyone shouted at once. I prepared to leap for the back and zap the warp engine, but there was no need for that, either. The titan did the job itself. Space folded up on us again and we streaked away from our attackers.

It didn't last long. I felt a nauseating sensation in the pit of my stomach, like intense gravity waves passing through me, then we dropped back into normal space.

"The titan's subspace field generator has burned out," Spock said.

We were still in the asteroid field, but the titans who had chased us were long gone. Apparently whatever had set them off wasn't worth going into hyperspace for.

"Let's hope the *Enterprise* gets here before we're discovered again," I said.

The titan was shuddering like a ground car on a bumpy road. Dark blood bubbled into space from the severed fin. I didn't think it was going to survive its wounds.

"I wonder what set them off?" Lanned asked. "I've never seen titans attack one another before."

"I thought it was us they were shooting at," I replied.

Perri said, "I don't think that was it. The ones back home don't seem to even notice the life-support modules we put on them."

"They did seem to be targeting the titan itself," Spock replied.

Boyce straightened up and jetted over to Spock. "Let me see that tricorder for a minute."

Spock handed it over and Boyce crouched down to the titan's skin with it, then moved down to the gaping wound and scanned that for a moment. "Well I'll be damned," he said. "This thing's sick. There's some kind of disease organism all through its tissues."

Sick? I hadn't imagined that something this huge could get sick, but I supposed it had to be possible. I said, "The others must have sensed it somehow, and were trying to drive it off before it infected them."

"That'd be my guess," Boyce said. "Spock, have you got a sample vial?"

"I do." Spock jetted down to where the doctor was and helped him collect a sample of the sticky, bubbling blood.

Our brief jump into warp had taken us to a less densely populated area of the asteroid belt, but I could still see specks of light moving around out there. It wouldn't take long before the local titans discovered us and came to finish the job.

I switched to the hailing frequency again. "Pike to *Enterprise*. What is your status?"

Static, then, "Landing party *ssss* on board. Proceeding to *ssss*."

"Pour on the coals," I said. "The natives are hostile."

"Say again?" Dabisch replied.

"Just get out here!" I ordered.

"We're coming."

Over the intercom I said, "Get ready for pickup." We

all crowded together near Colt, holding on to one another in a rough hexagon. Boyce let her stay on her side so she would be lying down when gravity returned.

I looked out toward the other titans and saw them coming. "Any time now," I said, then switched frequencies.

"*Enterprise?*" I called. "Are you in range yet?"

"We're entering the asteroid belt, but we can't locate the shuttle," Dabisch said. His voice came through loud and clear now.

"We lost that," I told him. "We're on the back of a titan. Home in on my signal."

"On the back of—affirmative." I heard him relaying our situation to Number One, and a moment later he said, "We've spotted you."

I saw at least six blimp-shaped bodies drawing nearer. "So have the titans," I said. "Hurry."

A moment later the *Enterprise* hove into view. It stood at about a seventy-degree angle off our port side, its underside glistening bright white in the sunlight. I just had time to say "There she—" before the transporter locked on to us and I finished my sentence on the receiving platform.

"—is. Get Colt to sickbay immediately. Bridge, stay on station." While Perri, Lanned, Boyce, and Spock all lifted Colt as gently as they could and rushed her across the hall, I twisted off my helmet and said to the transporter chief, "We left three kraken eggs on that titan; beam them aboard too." I wasn't about to leave empty-handed, not after all we'd been through.

"Kraken eggs?" he asked, but he was already scanning for them. "Ah, found them. Transporting."

The eggs materialized on the platform, standing erect like people until the containment field released them and they fell over with three loud bangs.

"All right," I said into my helmet, which Dabisch was presumably still listening to. "They're on board. Get us out of here."

The ship lurched sideways as a titan struck us, but a

second blow never came. I went to the intercom panel on the wall and hit the bridge button. "Damage report?"

"Minor hull damage to deck five, starboard side," Dabisch reported. "We are now fleeing at warp six."

"Good. Bring us to a stop once we've reached safety. We're not quite done here yet."

I switched the intercom over to security and ordered a team to take the kraken eggs and put them in a cargo hold under a tight forcefield; then I peeled out of my spacesuit, leaving it piled on the floor, and crossed over to sickbay. Colt lay on her back on an exam table, unconscious, her suit in shreds beneath her where Boyce had cut it away. He stood beside her, still suited except for his helmet, and ran some whirring gadget back and forth above her chest.

Perri and Lanned stood by the side of her bed, also still in their suits, not quite getting in the way while Boyce worked. Spock had apparently headed for the bridge already.

"Is she all right?" I asked.

"As all right as you can be with a punctured lung," Boyce replied, "but she'll be okay in a day or two."

Perri was looking down at her face. It's always hard to read aliens' expressions, but I thought the simple lust I'd seen in him before had become a bit more complicated now. He looked up and saw me watching him. "She saved my life," he said softly.

"Yes, she probably did," I told him. "She probably saved us all."

There was little else anyone could say. I left them in the sickbay and took the turbolift to the bridge, where I found Spock and Number One already comparing notes.

"Welcome back, Captain," said Number One.

"It's good to be back," I told her, settling down in my familiar command chair again. "It sounds like you found something on one of the inner planets that was worth a closer look. What was it?"

She sat down at the helm controls. "We discovered ruins on the second planet that date back over a million years. There's not much left, but what we found looked like a bunch of tombs."

"Tombs? As in dead bodies?"

"That's what it looked like. They were full of big buglike exoskeletons. It's like the whole population just filed into these things and lay down in a heap. But the kicker was what we found on the *out*side."

"What?"

She pushed a stray wisp of hair into place. "More guard dogs. Long dead from some disease, but their skeletons were all over the place. About twice the size of a person and shaped almost exactly like an immature titan. I found enough organic residue for a gene scan and the code is pretty close. Definitely the same basic plan. But it's not anything like the bugs' code."

I rubbed my stubble-encrusted chin. We knew the krakens were genetically engineered, and by implication the titans as well. And probably these things outside the tombs, too. Dead bugs, guard dogs on the ground, and guard whales in orbit. "Somebody really didn't want people disturbing their graves," I said.

"That's the way I read it," she said. "Whatever happened, though, it was a long, *long* time ago."

"We'll leave it for the archaeologists to puzzle out," I said, then I laughed. "If they want to try. I've had my fill of this place. Mr. Spock, I assume we need to gather a few filter-fish and some hydroplankton before we go?"

"We do," he replied. "Fortunately, that can be done with the transporters from a safe distance."

"See to it," I said. I turned to Number One. "The moment we get the specimens, take us back to Devernia, warp eight."

"Warp eight, sir?" she asked. "We can't sustain that for the entire trip."

"Run at that speed for as long as we can," I told her. "We've got eggs in the cargo hold I'd just as soon didn't hatch there."

She nodded. "Understood."

I went back downship to clean up, but I had just gotten to my quarters when the intercom whistled and Dr. Boyce said, "Captain, have you got a minute?"

"I—sure. Be right there."

I hurried down to deck seven, afraid something unforeseen had happened to Colt, but she was sleeping peacefully on a diagnostic bed, the overhead monitors all reading normal. Perri and Lanned and Dr. Boyce were in the lab across the hall from the intensive-care room. "Take a look at this," Boyce said when I stepped inside. He pointed at a desktop monitor on which a microscopic organism of some sort crawled along with tiny cilia.

"This is one of the species of hydroplankton," he said. "Now look at this." He pressed a switch and the image blinked over to a similar picture.

I couldn't tell much difference, and said so.

"This," he said, "is the bug I got from that sick titan's blood. It's a mutated plankton. Mutated to eat *titans*. It's really slow, but I did a comparative scan of the genetic code and found where the changes are. It would be child's play to tweak it a little further and make it work faster."

I looked at the tiny bug on the screen. It was little more than a mouth and a collection of little bubbles for storing and metabolizing food. "You could create a titan plague?" I asked.

"I think so."

I looked over at Perri and Lanned. Lanned's eyes were bright, and he was smiling wide. Perri looked considerably less pleased.

"We don't need to do that," he said. "We have already figured out how to control them naturally."

"This is natural," Lanned said. "As natural as the titans, at any rate. And it would certainly control them."

"Exterminate them, you mean! This is no better than your previous policy of reckless slaughter."

I looked from one to the other, then back to the monitor. What were we trying to protect, anyway? All these creatures were apparently the result of some paranoid alien race's dying wish for isolation. Maybe it would be simplest to wipe them out. We could spread the disease among the various populations of titans all the way back to Devernia and prevent them from causing any more damage.

I heard Yeoman Colt's soft breathing from the intensive care room, thought about what had happened to her and what had happened to so many Devernians over the centuries. What would they say?

I knew what I had to say. "Make the enhanced organism," I told Boyce. Perri started to protest, but I cut him off. "I don't know yet whether we'll use it or not, but I want that option. *You* want that option, believe me. After what we've seen on the way out here, I think everyone would sleep better at night knowing there's a fast way to control these monsters."

Perri had no response to that, but Lanned nodded and said, "I agree, Captain. I, at least, will sleep better. Let the doctor make this disease, and let us go home and decide then whether or not to use it."

"I've already given the order," I told him. "We're headed back as soon as Spock finishes collecting specimens."

I saw the satisfaction those words brought to both him and Perri. After all they had been through, they were going home again, each bringing their own brand of solution to the problem that had sent us out here.

Chapter Thirty-one

"You couldn't!" exclaimed Nowan. He slapped his hand on the table for emphasis. "The entire species, wiped out in a heartbeat? Tell me you didn't do it!"

Pike held out his hands, palms up. "I don't know," he said. "It was pretty tempting. They were artificial, after all, and they had already gotten loose and destroyed dozens of solar systems. They could still destroy Devernia if our plan to import their natural ecosystem didn't work. And releasing krakens into inhabited space didn't seem like as good an idea as I'd originally thought. Not after fighting one hand-to-hand."

"It seems like a fine idea to me," Hompaq said. "Klingons would give much to know the location of these creatures. If they still exist, that is."

"Oh, they exist," Pike said. "Nowan's right. We couldn't just sow the plague among them and watch them die off. They might have had artificial origins, but they had been around for a million years already. Longer than the human race. I couldn't kill that off with a wave of my hand." He shook his head, remembering. "We

236

tested the enhanced disease organism on a couple of titans to make sure it would work, then we dropped their bodies into the sun and took the disease back to Starfleet Headquarters for safekeeping. Lanned wasn't happy with me, but I didn't care. Beggars can't be choosers, after all."

"Hah," said Hompaq. "You talk a fine rationale, but I know why you saved them. Admit it: You did it for the adventure. You're a better man than you think, Captain Pike."

"For the adventure? That's ridicu—" He stopped, his eyes narrowed. "Well, okay, maybe that was part of it, but—"

"A sufficient part. No Klingon could survive what you did and then slay the beasts in such an ignoble fashion. And neither could you. You left them alive for others to pit themselves against." Hompaq took a drink of her Warnog.

"I—no, really that wasn't . . . I mean, maybe a little, but—"

Nowan said, "I think she has the right of it, Captain. Remember why you and your yeoman, at least, were there in the first place."

Pike scowled. "If she'd died, I'd have spread the plague through every star system in the sector."

Hompaq nearly sprayed Warnog on him. She managed to swallow it instead, then said, "Hah! You don't care for her, no, not at all."

"Look, she was a crew member," Pike said impatiently. "I cared about her the same as I cared about anyone else."

"As you wish," said Hompaq. "So what did you do when you got back to Devernia? Distribute the krakens and plankton and so forth?"

"Yes," said Pike. "I was afraid the kraken population would boom because of all the food available to them, but Spock spent his time on the trip back studying the embryos and he discovered that they were already programmed to limit themselves to a fraction of the number of titans. A hundredth of a percent or so, which meant when the titan population stabilized there would only be a hundred or so krakens in the entire planetary system. Lanned decided he could live with that. And Perri figured the Aronnians would probably want to import the entire ecosystem to their own gas-giant planets so they wouldn't have to depend on the migration from Devernia anymore."

"Did it work?" Nowan asked.

"Last I heard it was starting to. It'll take a while to know for sure. There's still a sample of the mutated hydroplankton in the Starfleet gene lab just in case it doesn't, but we haven't gotten a distress call from either planet yet."

"And the Aronnians are still riding their magnificent beasts from star to star?" asked Hompaq.

"As far as I know. It's been a few years." As Pike said that, he felt a blanket of melancholy descend on him again, and at that moment he made a decision. To hell with his groundside job; he was going back into space. It had been so long since he'd flown anything that he had lost his proficiency rating, so he would have to requalify for pilot's status, much less a captain's chair, but even a trainer would be more fun than flying a desk. He could pull a few strings, get himself assigned to one of the class-J ships Starfleet used to train cadets. From there it would be relatively easy to get his own ship again.

Nowan seemed a bit lost in reverie, too. He had been drawing something else on a napkin while Pike finished his story; now he was looking at it and rubbing his chin, but he raised his head when he realized Pike and Hompaq were looking at him.

"Sorry. I was just thinking what it must be like for you. Exploring strange new worlds. Going where no man has gone before." He looked toward the door. "Eighteen sixty-one awaits me out there, doesn't it?"

"If that's when you came from," said Hompaq.

"Is there no way to leave with one of you instead?"

" 'Fraid not. But the Captain's Table will always be here whenever you need it."

He nodded. "That is some comfort, I suppose."

Pike was looking at the napkin. He reached out and turned it around so the drawing was right side up for him. He had thought at first that it was another drawing of a titan, but now he saw that it was more like a fish. The nose came to a sharp point, and the top of its head had some kind of bony ridge sticking out of it—rather like Hompaq, Pike realized. The fish's midsection had a round oval like her cleavage-baring outfit, as well. It had a more aquatic-looking dorsal fin and tail, however, except that the tail was cut out and a tiny figure eight stood in the gap.

Then the entire picture seemed to morph in his mind as he realized that the figure eight was a propeller. The open waist was a large porthole, and if the tiny dots above and below it were normal-sized ones then the entire vessel was large indeed. The dorsal fin was actually a conning tower, and the bony forehead was a massive spur, jagged-edged for ripping the bottoms out of boats.

"Not as grand as your *Enterprise*," said Nowan, "but it's a start. If I must stay in my own era, there is at least one domain left to explore." His expression grew darker. "And a few warships left to avenge myself against."

Pike looked at it with his mouth agape. "It's . . . it's the *Nautilus*."

"It's nothing but a gleam in a bitter man's eye, at this point," said Nowan. "But that's not a bad name." He retrieved his napkin, drained his brandy, and pushed back his chair. "On another night I would tell you a tale of my own to match yours, but my mind is filled to bursting with strange notions and strong drink, and I feel the need for solitude. Besides, if Hompaq is to be believed—and she undoubtedly is," he added hastily when she bared her teeth at him, "then we will have other opportunities." He stood up and extended his hand.

Pike shook it, still somewhat stunned. "You—I—" he stammered, but Nowan had already turned to Hompaq. She held out her hand to clasp arms in the Klingon fashion, but he lifted her fingers to his lips and kissed them instead. "I do, milady," he said, then Pike realized he was speaking French.

He turned toward the door, but before he left he stopped at the piano and pressed a few keys down at the low end. Pike recognized the first few notes of Bach's *Toccata and Fugue in D Minor*.

"Fitting music to exit by," he said.

"It sounds better on a pipe organ," said Nowan. He nodded to Pike and went to the door. When he opened it, the clop-clop of horses' hooves could be heard for a moment before it closed again behind him.

The other patrons in the bar had watched him leave, then turned back to their own concerns. Pike looked over at Hompaq. "Do you know who that was?" he asked.

She shrugged. "He called himself Nowan. Beyond that, I have no idea."

Pike looked over at the door again. Could it be? He took a deep breath, trying to clear his mind. He'd drunk a lot of Saurian brandy tonight. But *that* much?

"Whoever he is," he said at last, "I bet in a few years he'll have tales to tell that'll make mine seem tame."

He heard a squeal of high-pitched laughter and a thump from upstairs as a door opened momentarily, then slammed. Had that been the cat-woman? It had sounded more like a wild animal.

"What's up there?" he asked.

Hompaq laughed softly. "You want to find out?"

She was looking at him with the frankly appraising eyes of a predator sizing up its prey. "I, uh, well," he stammered, feeling himself growing warm. He had a pretty good idea what would be up there for the two of them.

"Come on," she said. "Where's your sense of adventure?"

She held out her hand. Pike took it, and when she stood up he found himself following her.

"You sure know which buttons to push, don't you?" he said.

She grinned at him as they took their first step upward. "Not yet, I don't, but you'll be amazed how fast I learn."

The gecko awoke when a dollop of beer landed on his nose.

Waking—sleeping. He recognized little difference between the two states. One involved snuggling his belly tight against whatever heat source was available and soaking up as much warmth as possible for as long as possible; the other involved doing the same thing with his eyes open.

So he opened his eyes.

The fireplace stones still hummed with residual heat, even though the flames responsible for that warmth had died to ash hours ago. Feet in more styles than his olfactory-oriented brain had ever conceived of clumped back and forth on the wood planks beyond the hearth, and the unpleasantly tepid splash of beer dripping off his wedge-shaped nose raised him up on his front legs in a defiant bob of protest. It was the last casual indignity from these huge and raucous mammals. His sensitive belly receptors had already begun to complain that the stones beneath him were cooling, and he'd found only one careless spider to eat during his last perambulation along the baseboards. Even the beautiful, fierce princesses who'd whispered sweet promises and tickled his throat had long since lost interest and wandered away. It was time to shake the kinks out of his newly regrown tail and head home.

Little five-toed feet stepped delicately onto wood planking so old and well trod it had taken on the color and softness of amber. What mammals felt as a warmness in wood was really little more than a lack of cold; his sensitive belly recognized room temperature for what it was, and identified no delineation between the air above him and the floor below. He padded methodical S-curves into the chaos of shoes and bare feet, feeling like he was flying through his own single-temperature world.

It took a few steps to get his rhythm—the regrown tail followed behind without the sinuous undulations of his long-lost original. That had been a beautiful tail, fat and long and supple all the way down to its brown-banded tip. He'd regrown—and relost—its replacement so many times by now, he could no longer remember when or how it first happened. All he retained now was a patch of lizard memory, like skin that never shed, which sometimes reminded his dreams how it had been to shake his tail for a harem of pretty admirers.

He knew the path to the door by rote, where to speed up, when to swerve. Toes larger than his head brushed past close enough to bite, but he'd long ago given up hissing at them. They never heard, or didn't notice, and his splinter-sized brain didn't come with the luxury of paying attention to more than one thing at a time. He kept his tiny bright eyes fixed on his goal, waiting for the moment light cracked around its edges, then kicked his little legs until they slipped on the floorboards in his hurry to dash out before the door swung closed.

The advantage of a regrown tail was that it didn't hurt when it was bitten, or stepped on, or slammed in a closing door. He realized he'd been caught only because his feet skidded back and forth in place on the metal deck outside without taking him anywhere. By then, it was too late. Whatever primitive mechanism in his primitive biology identified a pinned tail as life-threat-

ening had already cinched closed the blood vessels
running past the base of his spine. With a little hop, he
detached himself from the bulb of trapped flesh and
scampered off with new lightness. Tails came and tails
went. There was no room for regret in a lizard mind.
He'd almost forgotten the weighty burden by the time he
made the first corridor junction and turned by instinct in
the direction of his home.

He recognized the smell of home by the metallic
cleanness of its air, recognized the light's burnt-cayenne
tint when he skittered past windows and transparent
aluminum doors. The dusty musk of his native sand
made his toes tingle with excitement. A rise in temperature, slow and pervasive, hurried him along, and the feel
of warm, moist earth beneath his toes welcomed him
back to his quiet little kingdom.

A long walk for little legs. An eternity of travel to a
little lizard mind. He found his favorite rock, the tallest
and roundest of the slate mountains erratically clutter-
ing his home. Well placed at the foot of a long, unobstructed length of window, it drank in the warmth of the
sun all day, then offered it back into the nighttime with
such sweet jealousy that it could make a lizard happy
until sunrise. He liked the view from here, well above the
sandy ground and even most of the low-lying plants. He
especially loved the diamond scatter of stars that filled
the window like spots on a female's long back. If a lizard
could conceive of gazing into forever, he might have
understood. If a lizard could appreciate the awe of
standing so close to the edge of the infinite, he might
have named the swirl of pleasure that curled through
him at the sight. Instead, he let instinct take him as high
up on the rock as he could climb, not realizing when he
passed from warm rock to warm trouser leg until a gentle
voice greeted softly, "Well, hello there, little guy. What
happened to your poor tail?"

The hands which lifted him were even warmer than

his accustomed rock, and he felt no fear when he looked up into the friendly golden face smiling down at him. Snuggling his belly into the human's palm, he dropped his eyes to half-mast and enjoyed the mammalian heat as he tipped his chin up toward the stars.

The human chuckled. "Looks like I'm not the only one who likes this view." He lifted the somnolent lizard even with his red-jacketed shoulder and rotated his hand to offer a better vantage. "That's my ship there, the *Excelsior.*" He pointed to one of the shining motes outside the window, and smiled again. "I'd offer to give you the captain's tour, but you're probably not the adventurous type."

The lizard blinked placidly up at the timeless sea of stars, but didn't reply.

Transparent aluminum spun a delicate membrane between the spindly green of transplanted Martian foliage and the blue-black Martian sky. As he watched one of the shipyard's many crew transports crawl patiently starward along a sparkling length of duranium filament, it occurred to James Kirk that man-made atmospheres were always the most fragile. Mars's chilly surface, although no longer the frigid wasteland of just a few centuries before, still clung to the planet only through the heroic efforts of her tenants. Outside the tame habitat of interlinked domes and tunnels, carefully tended flora lifted from Earth's highest mountains and harshest tundras braved Mars's seasonal extremes, while the excess carbon dioxide from captured comets and a few million adventurous humans preserved just enough liquid water on the surface to reward the plants with the occasional rainshower. The end result was a certain defiant beauty—spidery junipers and upright bracken reaching toward the teal spark of a homeworld their ancestors had left generations ago.

Not unlike humanity. Granted, humans pampered themselves with heaters, oxygen co-generators, and pressurized suits and homes. But they still survived where nothing larger than a dust mote had survived before them, and Kirk liked the view they'd created.

Utopia Planitia's shipyards stretched from the skirt of the colony's main dome to beyond the horizon, arcing magically upward in the guise of shuttle-bees and crew elevators. The twinkling strings of force and fiber bound the orbiting ships only temporarily. Some nearly finished, others bare skeletons of the great leviathans they would become, they'd all turn outward soon enough. Darkened engine rooms would thunder with the pulse of great dilithium hearts, and the blood and muscle organs in the chests of her eager crew would leap up in answer, until what finally ignited her sleeping warp core was that combined symphony of animal and mineral, creature and machine. It was a song that kept an officer's heart beating long after no other passion could. *Old captains never die . . .*

Kirk stepped off the moving walkway in the northmost Agridome, the one dedicated to the sparse rock gardens and dark succulents of a Terran gulf environment whose name Kirk no longer remembered. It wasn't crowded the way so many of the lux-enhanced Agridomes always were. Everyone wanted to watch the crews ship out while surrounded by bright Colombian parrots or Hawaiian orchids, as though they'd never really dared to leave Earth at all. But here the lack of tall plant life offered an unobstructed view through the sides and top of the dome, and the foliage reflected the reddish moonslight in silver washes, as though leaves and stems were spun from raw pewter. Kirk remembered coming here as a freshly minted ensign the night before he rode a crowded elevator up to his first assignment on board the *U.S.S. Farragut.* He'd stayed here until dawn, trying to count the multitude of stars he could see in the single patch of sky surrounding the ship that was to be his home, his life, his family for the next five years. That was more than forty years ago, but it felt like only yesterday.

He could still hear the reverent hush of the leaves against his trousers as he picked a path through the foliage, and he still remembered the cool surface of the rock that served as his perch at the foot of the dome's widest panel. Best seat in the house.

He found the man he was looking for seated in exactly the same spot, shoulders square, head high, hands folded neatly in his lap. Beyond him and a thousand miles above, the brilliant glow of a refurbished starship dwarfed the dimmer signatures drifting around her.

Kirk smiled, and paused what he hoped was a respectful distance away. "Quite a view, isn't it?"

The younger captain rose, turning with an alert smoothness born of courtesy rather than surprise. That was something Kirk would always associate with Hikaru Sulu—the politeness which came to him apparently as naturally as breathing, with no taint of impatience or condescension. That, and an endless capacity for brilliance.

Sulu mirrored Kirk's smile, looking only a little embarrassed as he stole one last look at the magnificent ship hanging over his shoulder. "All the way into forever." He kept one hand cradled close to his waist, and extended the other as he stepped away from his now vacated stone seat. "Admiral."

His grip was firm and even, as befitted a man of his position. Kirk returned the warm handshake in kind. "Captain."

"I didn't realize you were in-system," Sulu told him. "If I'd known, I would have stopped by to give my regards." It might have just been politeness, but Kirk could tell from his former helmsman's voice that the sentiment was sincere.

"Just passing through on my way to finalize the Khitomer negotiations," Kirk assured him. "I heard at the commodore's office that you were laid over to take on your new executive officer." A movement from the vicinity of Sulu's cupped hand caught Kirk's attention, and he found himself suddenly eye-to-eye with the small, spotted lizard who had clambered up onto Sulu's thumb for a better view. "He's shorter than I remember."

Sulu glanced fondly down at his stubby-tailed companion, tickling it under the curve of its bemused little smile until it blinked. "Actually, we're not scheduled to rendezvous for another two hours. This is just one of the friendly locals." Or as local as any living thing on Mars. Its anteriorly bilateral eyes and five-toed little feet hinted at a Terran origin, but it was the nearly identical gold-and-brown speckled relatives Kirk could now see lounging among the thick-leafed shrubs that gave its ancestry away. The Martian Parks Service didn't like mixing one planet's flora with another planet's fauna. Therefore, Terran landscaping equaled Terran lizards.

Each chubby little eublepharid had staked out its own rock or branch or hummock, blunt little noses lifted skyward, hind feet splayed out behind them as though they were laconically bodysurfing on their own bliss. Kirk envied their abandon.

"Anything on your agenda for those next two hours?" he asked Sulu.

The younger captain shrugged one shoulder, startling his small passenger into an aborted scrabble partway up his wrist. It paused there, as though forgetting where it meant to go, and Kirk noticed that unlike its lounging neighbors, this lizard's tail looked recently broken and rehealed. Its curiosity and boldness must have gotten it in trouble recently. "I've got nothing in particular to do," Sulu admitted. "Just some long-overdue relaxation while I have the chance." Kirk wondered if he'd been watching the meditating lizards instead of his own starship after all. "Did you have something in mind?"

"Some*place.*" Kirk caught the politely questioning cock of Sulu's head, and smiled. "The perfect spot for overdue relaxation, as a matter of fact."

"Sounds good." Sulu glanced down as the lizard squirmed determinedly under the cuff of his uniform jacket. Before he could stop it, all that was left was a sausage-shaped bulge and an exposed nubbin where its brown-banded tail should have been. "Are they friendly toward nonhumanoids?"

"I've never known that to be a problem before," Kirk assured him. "And I'm sure that in the lizard world, that little guy was the captain of its very own rock somewhere. He'll be welcome in the Captain's Table."

He led a willing Sulu back out of the Agridomes and down the stately, curving avenues that led eventually to the spaceport and the feet of those rising elevators. The door to the bar was where Kirk remembered it, looking as always like the entrance to a supply cabinet rather than to the cozy tavern he knew lay within. Plain, nearly flush with the Martian stone of this ill-lit subterranean passageway, it was set apart from the other more ostentatious establishments on either side by nothing except a neatly painted sign just to the right of a hand-operated doorknob: THE CAPTAIN'S TABLE.

Sulu cocked his head with a thoughtful wrinkling of his brow, and Kirk knew he was trying to remember why he'd never noticed the little entrance before. "This must be new," the younger captain decided at last. He still held his arm balanced across his midsection in deference to the small passenger up his sleeve.

Kirk hid his smile by stepping forward to take hold of the door. "I found it the first year I commanded the *Enterprise,* but some other captains I know claim it's been here for dozens of years before that."

Sulu gave a little grunt of surprise, then moved back to let the door swing wide. "Sounds like the Federation's best-kept secret."

A gentle swell of warmth, and sound, and scent rolled over them like a familiar blanket. "More like the galaxy's most exclusive club." And, just as a dozen times before, Kirk found himself inside without specifically remembering stepping through the doorway.

The Captain's Table had never been a large establishment, and that didn't appear to have changed over the years. A brief, narrow entry hall spilled them abruptly into the bar's jumble of tables and chairs, and Kirk found himself veering sideways to avoid tripping over the tall alien seated directly in his path. Slitted eyes shifted almost imperceptibly within an almost featureless skull; one long, taloned finger dipped into a fluted glass half-full of viscous red liquid. It was a dance they'd performed the first time Kirk came into the Captain's Table thirty years ago, not to mention every other time he'd stumbled onto the place on Argelius, Rukbat, or Vega. He stopped himself from laughing, not sure the lizardine patron would appreciate his humor, and instead nodded a terse apology before turning to join Sulu in search of their own table.

"Jimmee!"

It seemed everyone was here tonight.

Kirk spun around just in time to catch Prrghh at the height of her leap. It wasn't one of her more spectacular jumps—Kirk would never forget watching her pounce from the second-floor banister to land on her feet amid a particularly rousing discussion—but she still contacted him almost chest-high and entwined legs and arms around his torso in lithe, feline abandon. Kirk felt himself blush with pleasure more than embarrassment when she stroked her own sleekly furred cheek against his. Acutely aware of all the other eyes in the bar, he resisted an impulse to wind his hands in her long primrose mane.

"James!" The bartender's roar collided with the low ceiling and ricocheted all over the room. "How in hell are you? Long time gone, boy-o!"

At least seven years, Kirk admitted to himself. But not a damned thing about the place had changed. Not so much as a dust mote.

"Don' bee *fex*, Cap!" Prrghh squirmed around in

Kirk's arms to look back over her shoulder, a position that would certainly have dislocated the spine of any anthropoid species. "Jimmee allas heerr!"

"Everyone is always here," a gruff voice behind them snarled. "Especially tonight." The female Klingon pushed past Kirk as though she had somewhere to go, then stopped abruptly and crouched to thrust her nose into Prrghh's pretty face. "If you're staying, sit down. If not, get out of the way and take your *mris* with you."

Prrghh's hiss was dry but rich with hatred. Kirk turned them away from the Klingon, already knowing where things could lead once Prrghh's ruff had gotten up. "Why don't we find a seat, then?" he suggested smoothly. The Klingon grunted, but made no move to follow.

Kirk swung Prrghh to the floor as though he were twenty years younger or she twenty kilograms lighter. He let her fold her hand inside his, though, basketing his fingers with lightly extended claws. Her palm felt soft and familiar despite the years that had passed since it had last been fitted into his. Beside him, he noticed Sulu's failed efforts to hide a knowing grin by pretending to check on the lizard now peering curiously from beneath his cuff. Kirk wondered briefly what sorts of tales the younger captain might tell out of school, considering his former commander's reputation. This time the heat in Kirk's cheeks had a little bit more to do with embarrassment.

It might have been a Saturday night, the place was so packed with bodies and voices and laughing. But, then, Kirk's memory said that it *always* looked like Saturday night, no matter what the day or time. Never too crowded to find a seat, thank God, but always just threatening to burst at the seams and overflow into the rest of the world. Kirk snagged Sulu by the hem of his jacket when the captain started toward the bar along the long end of the crowded room.

"A seat," Sulu said by way of explanation, lifting his

lizard-filled hands to indicate his objective. Kirk glanced where the captain pointed and shook his head. The empty seat in question—several of them, in fact—surrounded a grossly fat Caxtonian freighter pilot who appeared to have congealed around a tankard of milky brown fluid.

"He's Caxtonian," Kirk said. "By this time of night—"

Prrggh wrinkled her delicate nose. "—hee stinkk feersly!" Her long, supple tail snaked up between the men to twitch their attention toward the foot of the stairs. "Thees othur qhuman dances for you."

The captain Prrghh pointed out looked human enough, at least. Salt-and-pepper beard, with hair a matching color that hung just a little longer than the current civilian standard. Kirk liked the well-worn look of his leather jacket, with its rainbow shoulder patch and anomalously fleece-trimmed collar. He was lean and wiry, with an earnest smile and tired but friendly eyes. Two other seats at his table were already filled by a rapier-thin dandy with his black hair pulled back into a neat queue, and a broad bear of a man with a wild white beard and a curl of pipe smoke covering most of his head. When their leather-jacketed comrade waved again, Kirk acknowledged his gesture by slipping between a knot of standing patrons to blaze a path to the table.

"Gentlemen. Welcome to the Captain's Table." The salt-and-pepper human took Kirk's hand in a firm, somewhat eager shake. "Humans?" he asked, with just the slightest bit of hopefulness in his tone.

Kirk glanced at the freighter designation stenciled beneath the ship name on the leather jacket's patch, and recognized the wearer for a fellow captain. Of course. "The genuine article." He stole a chair from the table next door and offered it to Prrghh as Sulu conscientiously offered the freighter captain his left hand for shaking to avoid disturbing the reptilian passenger sprawled happily across his right palm.

The freighter captain pumped Sulu's hand without seeming to notice either the deviation from convention or the little passenger. "I'm sure pleased to see you," he grinned. "We were feeling a bit outnumbered tonight." He tipped a cordial nod to Prrghh as she slipped into her seat. "No offense, Captain. I just sometimes get real tired of aliens."

Her ears came up and green eyes narrowed on the other captain's lean face. Kirk recognized the expression—she liked a challenge. "Purrhaps you haf not met the ryght ailyens."

The freighter captain lifted an eyebrow, and Kirk suspected he enjoyed his share of challenges, too. "Perhaps not," he admitted with a smile. "Maybe you can educate me."

". . . a surprisingly trusting lot, all points considered." The black-haired dandy tipped the tankard in his hand and squinted down its throat to verify it was empty. He hadn't interrupted his story for Kirk and Sulu's arrival, and didn't interrupt it now as he waved the tankard over his head to catch a server's attention. "They brought us neatly upside, lashed our hulls together, and came aboard with every thought of liberating our hold of its treasures. Alas, our only cargo was a crew of well-armed men and the good old Union Jack. By the time we'd taken our due, that was one Jolly Roger which never flew again."

"A clever story." The white-haired captain bit down on his meerschaum pipe and nodded wisely. "You're a cunning man, Captain, using that pirate crew's own expectations against them."

"The best judge of a pirate is one of his own," the Englishman admitted. His tankard still waggled above one shoulder. "My duties may seal me now to the queen, but I'm loath to believe that any man who never ran with pirates can ever be their match."

Kirk straightened in his seat, stung by the remark. "Oh, I don't know about that."

The table's patrons turned to him almost as a unit, and he found himself momentarily startled by the frank challenge in their stares.

"Do you mean to disavow my own experience?" There was steel in the dark-haired Englishman's voice despite his friendly countenance.

The white-haired bear lifted one big hand in an obvious gesture of placation. "Easy, my friend. He sounds like a man with experience of his own."

"Some." Kirk settled back as a wiry serving boy scampered up to their table with a tray full of drinks. He gave the others first pick from the offerings since he knew whatever he wanted would be still left when they were done. "Pirates were never my primary business, but I've run across my share." He wrapped his hands around the mug of warm rum the boy placed in front of him, well familiar with the price every captain had to pay for the first round of drinks after his arrival. "Let me tell you about a time when I rescued the victims of some pirates, only to find out they weren't exactly what I'd expected. . . ."

I told myself it wasn't resentment. I didn't have the right to resent him. He hadn't killed my helmsman; he'd never placed my ship and crew in danger; he hadn't forced my chief medical officer to retire. He hadn't even murdered my best friend. He had never been anything but responsible, conscientious, and reliable. In these last few weeks, he'd stepped into a position made vacant by my own actions—not because he wanted it, or because he hoped to prove anything to anybody, just because it was necessary. He was that kind of officer; service without complaint. Duty called, and he answered.

Still, I hadn't quite figured out how to separate him from everything that had come before. So while he stood there in the gym doorway, waiting for my answer with his damned, impenetrable patience, my first instinct was to tell him to go to hell. Instead, I asked in the mildest tone I could muster, "Mr. Spock, can't this wait until later?"

I must not have sounded as patient as I'd hoped. He lifted one eyebrow a few micrometers, and peered at me with the same keen interest he probably applied to alien mathematics problems. Subtle emotions often had that effect on him, I'd noticed. As though he couldn't decide what informational value to assign such a random variable, and it annoyed him to settle for an imperfect interpretation.

Except, of course, annoyance was a human emotion.

"Regulations stipulate that a starship's captain and executive officer shall meet once every seven days to coordinate duties and exchange pertinent crew and mission information." He didn't fidget. He just folded his hands around the datapad at his waist and settled in as though there was no place else he needed to be. "Our last such meeting was eleven days ago."

I turned back to my interrupted workout, leaving him to recognize the implied dismissal. "Then a few more hours won't make any difference." I aimed a high sweep-kick at the sparring drone, and earned a flash of approving lights for smashing into the upper right quadrant target.

Spock was silent for what seemed a long time, watching me with his usual cool fascination, no doubt, as I did my best to sweat out my personal demons at the expense of a supposedly indestructible robot.

In the end, they both managed to outlast me. I stopped before I started to stumble, but not before I was forced to suck in air by the lungful, or before I raised dark welts on the edges of both hands. I still secretly believed that if I could push myself just a little further, a little longer, I'd finally beat out the last of my uncertainty and guilt. But I'd entertained this secret belief for at least three weeks now, and hadn't yet found the magic distance. I refused to fall down in front of my new executive officer while I still struggled to find it.

He gave me what was probably a carefully calculated amount of time to catch my breath, then said to my still-turned back, "May I remind the captain that when he is not eating, sleeping, or engaging in some necessary physical activity, he is on duty. As senior science officer, my duty shift is concurrent with the captain's. As acting executive officer, my second duty shift coincides with when the captain is off-duty. Logic therefore suggests that rather than disrupt the necessary human sleep function, the most efficient time period during which to conduct our required conferencing would be during the one hour fifteen minute interval between the termination of my secondary duty shift and the beginning of your regular tour." He paused as though giving my slower human mind a moment to process his argument, then added blandly, "Which is now."

I swiped a hand over my eyes to flick away the worst of the sweat, and heaved an extra-deep breath to even out my panting. "Is this your way of telling me you're working a few too many hours, Mr. Spock?"

Both eyebrows were nearly to his hairline; I could almost feel the lightning flicker of his thoughts behind those dark Vulcan eyes. "No, Captain." As deadly serious as if I'd asked him to contemplate the course of Klingon politics over the next hundred years. "My current schedule allows ample time for research, personal hygiene, and the intake of food. Since Vulcans are not limited by the same stringent sleep requirements as humans, I find the hours between my shifts more than sufficient for meditation and physical renewal."

I tried not to sigh out loud. My entire Starfleet career would be a success if I could teach even one Vulcan to have a sense of humor. "What would you like to discuss, Mr. Spock?" I asked wearily.

Where anyone else—anyone human—would have promptly flipped up the padd to consult its readout, Spock announced, apparently from memory, "According to the first officer's log, there are currently eight hundred fifty-four individual crew evaluations which are late or incomplete."

I paused in scooping up my towel to frown at him. "There are only four hundred and thirty crew on board the *Enterprise.*"

Spock acknowledged my point with a microscopic tilt of his head. "Four hundred twenty-four evaluations are still outstanding from the quarter ending stardate 1013.4. The other four hundred thirty were due at the end of the most recent quarter, which ended on stardate 1298.9."

And Gary—perpetually behind when it came to such mundane administrative duties—died before he had the chance to turn in even one from the most recent batch. I tried to disguise a fresh swell of frustration by scrubbing at my face and scalp with the towel. "Since last quarter, Lieutenant Lee Kelso was killed in the line of duty. Dr. Elizabeth Dehner—killed in the line of duty. Lieutenant Commander Gary Mitchell—" I hid a bitter scowl by turning and banning the sparring drone back to its storage locker. "—killed." The word still tasted like cold gunmetal in my mouth. "I've ordered the lateral transfer of Lieutenant Hikaru Sulu and Ensign David Bailey from astrosciences to cover the vacant bridge positions, and have accepted Lieutenant Commander Spock's application for temporary assignment as ship's first officer." Snatching up my tunic and boots with a brusqueness that surprised even me, I came to a stop just shy of touching Spock, knowing full well what a discomforting situation that tended to make for Vulcans. "On a brighter note, Chief Medical Officer Mark Piper has retired to a safe, well-paying civilian position at Johns Hopkins University on Earth, and his replacement, Leonard McCoy, seems to be adapting nicely." That last was half a lie, since I hadn't actually spoken to my old friend since the day McCoy first came aboard. I hadn't managed to say much even then, thanks to the doctor's colorful tirade against the ship's transporter. I hadn't remembered him being quite so technophobic, and found myself wondering if this was going to be a problem. "Why don't you put all that in Gary's files and call them done?"

Spock said nothing as I pushed past him on my way to the shower room, merely stepping neatly to one side to avoid any unseemly physical contact. These were the kinds of little skills he must practice daily, I realized. Memorized patterns of behavior, movement, and response based on the thousands—perhaps millions—of social interactions he'd endured with a species whose conduct must seem positively arcane to him. I doubted he even understood much of the social data he mentally collected about his crewmates—he simply made note of what interactions produced what results, and adjusted his model accordingly. If there was a difference between that and how a soulless machine would make use of the same information, at that particular moment I couldn't see what it was.

He followed me into the shower room at what was no doubt a carefully calculated distance. Why did his patient silences always make me feel so guilty about whatever random bitterness popped into my head? Probably just another side effect of his conversational style. I made a note to read up on Vulcan social customs, naively believing that I might find some understanding in their workings.

"The completion of Commander Mitchell's reports should pose no undo difficulty. I calculate that, by committing only forty-two point three percent of my on-duty time, I can deliver the reports to you within sixty-eight hours."

I hoped he didn't expect me to vet them quite so quickly. Eating and sleeping aside, I still had too much shoring up to do with the ship's new crew assignments to catch up on nearly nine hundred reports over the next three days.

"I must confess, however . . ."

Reluctance? I paused with the water crashing over my head to stare at him.

He all but rushed on before I could say a word. "I find the guidelines as laid out by Starfleet . . . baffling."

That admission of near-weakness surprised me more than almost anything else he could have said. I turned off the water and leaned out to study him. "How so?"

If he were human, I almost think he might have blushed. Not in embarrassment, but in the stone-faced frustration young children sometimes display when confronted with an impenetrable question they secretly suspect is a joke at their expense. I wondered if Vulcan children ever teased each other, or if the Vulcan Science Academy practiced hazing.

"The precise goal of such record keeping in the format specified is unclear," he said, quite formally, yet somehow without actually meeting my eyes. "There are no statistical data to be compiled, no discreet procedures to be followed. The desired end result is entirely inadequately conveyed."

I felt a strange warmth when I realized what he was saying. Sympathy, almost. "The desired end result is insight." He looked at me, and I smiled gently, explaining, "It's the first officer's job to be liaison to the crew. As captain, I depend on your observations—your instincts and feelings about the crew's state of mind."

Any emotion I might have imagined in his features evaporated with the infinitesimal straightening of his shoulders. "I am Vulcan. I have no instincts or feelings, only logic."

But the crew is human, I wanted to tell him, *just bubbling over with emotion.* Who in God's name had ever thought a Vulcan could serve as a human crew's XO?

The chirrup of my communicator saved us from pursuing a discussion neither of us was sure how to follow. I ducked out of the shower, careless of the water I dripped as I scooped up the communicator and flipped back the grid. "Kirk here. Go ahead."

The communications officer's honey-rich voice seemed strangely out of place in the conflicting Vulcan-human landscape of our interrupted conversation. "Sir, sensors have detected a disabled ship two point two million kilometers to our starboard. There's some shipboard functions, but they don't respond to our hails."

A real problem. Not overdue reports, Vulcan emotional illiteracy, or misplaced captain's angst. A way to avoid feelings of helplessness by directing all my energy toward something I could change. "Plot a course to intercept, and scan the ship for survivors. I'm on my way to the bridge." I was already shaking my tunic free from the rest of my clothing by the time I snapped the communicator shut and tossed it to the bench. "I'm afraid you're on your own with those reports, Mr. Spock." I flashed him a grin over the collar of my shirt, one that was probably as reassuring as it was strictly sincere. "Just do the best you can."

The bridge felt alien and strangely too quite when the turbolift deposited us on its margins. I missed Gary's laughter. It had been omnipresent—sometimes irritatingly so—and I found myself missing the sudden guilty hush that meant Gary had been sharing some particularly bawdy story with the rest of the crew before my arrival. I missed his liar's smile, and his all-too-innocent "Captain on the bridge" to announce my arrival.

Instead, the smoothly deep voice of my new helmsman made the call, and nobody abruptly ceased what they were doing or ducked their heads to hide a sudden onset of blushing. Decorum reigned, and I felt like I'd stumbled onto some other captain's vessel.

Still, I made that first step beyond the turbolift's doors without any outward sign of hesitation, briskly taking the steps down to my chair as Spock rounded behind me to head for his own station at the science console. "Mr. Sulu, report."

The helmsman—*my* helmsman, I reminded myself firmly—half turned in his seat, one hand still hovering possessively over his controls. "Sensors detect life on the vessel, but still no response to our hails. Their power exchange is in bad shape—the distress call might be on automatic."

Meaning the crew either couldn't use ship's systems to respond, or were too badly injured to make the attempt. I drummed my fingers on the arm of my command chair, thinking. On the viewscreen, the flat, elongated vessel drifted lazily clockwise, passing into a long silhouette, presenting us her nose, wafting lengthwise again. Her engines had been burned down to nubs, and the characteristic shatter of disruptor fire carved jagged stripes down her sides. It looked like at least half the ship was in vacuum, and the other half looked too dark to be getting anywhere near normal power. If there was anything or anyone still alive on board, they wouldn't stay that way forever.

"Spock, do we have any idea what kind of ship that is?"

He was silent for a moment. I gave him that—I'd figured out early on that he didn't like giving answers until he'd looked at all the data.

"Sixty-three percent of the identifiable ship's components strongly resemble an Orion Suga-class transport," Spock said at last, still scanning the computer's library screens. "Eleven point six percent are from an Orion-manufactured slaving facility. Four point two percent still bear the registration codes for a Klingon unmanned science probe. The remaining twenty-two point two percent resemble nothing currently on record."

I rubbed thoughtfully at my chin. "Could they be Orions?" I asked after adding up those bits and pieces. "Or maybe Orion allies?"

"Starfleet has reported no recent Orion pirating activity in this sector." While it wasn't exactly an answer to my question, it still led me a few steps closer to something that was. Spock swiveled in his own chair to lift an eyebrow at the screen. "To my knowledge, the Orions have no allies."

Which told you everything you needed to know about the Orions. Still . . . "Just because we don't know about any allies doesn't mean there are none." I resisted an urge to toss Spock a puckish grin he wouldn't appreciate. "After all, even the Devil had friends."

He tipped his head in grave acknowledgment of my point, and I felt for one startled moment as though he were teasing me. *He's a Vulcan, not Gary Mitchell. Vulcans don't tease.* I turned forward again to hide my chagrin, and tapped my chair intercom with the side of my hand. "Bridge to transporter room."

"Transporter room. Scott here."

It worried me sometimes that my chief engineer spent so much time with the transporter. I tried to reassure myself that it was a fascinating piece of equipment, with all manner of systems to explore. But sometimes I just couldn't shake the suspicion that there was more to Scott's constant tending than mere affection. Probably not something I should mention around Dr. McCoy. "Scotty, can you get a fix on the life-forms inside that alien vessel?"

"Fifteen to twenty of them," he reported, managing to sound pleased with himself and a little frustrated all at the same time. "Maybe as much as twenty-four—the numbers are hopping all over the place."

"See if you can isolate them with a wide-angle beam." I muted the channel and glanced aside at Spock. "What sort of environment does that ship hold?"

He opened his mouth, took a small breath as though to say something, then seemed to change his mind at the last minute. Without having to reconsult his equipment, he informed me, "Slightly higher in oxygen and nitrogen than Earth normal, and at a slightly greater atmospheric pressure. Fluctuations in their gravitational equipment average at just a little less than one Earth gravity." Then he continued on without pausing, saying what I suspected had been the first thing to cross his mind. "May I infer from your questions that you intend to bring any survivors on board?"

"Indeed you may." I sent an automated request to security for a small reception committee, and a similar request to sickbay for an emergency medical team. "I've never ignored another ship's distress signal, and I don't intend to start now."

Spock stood smoothly as I jumped up from my chair, his own quiet way of announcing that he was following me down to the transporter room. "And if the captain who initiated this distress call is an Orion ally, as you speculate?"

I looked up at the viewscreen, quickly refreshing my image of its crumpled superstructure and ruptured sides. "Then they still need rescuing." We certainly couldn't tow them anywhere—I doubted their ship would stand up to the grasp of the tractor beam, much less to having its tumble forcibly stilled and its whole mass accelerated along a single vector. Besides, towing wouldn't take care of their wounded. I wouldn't put any captain in the position of being helplessly dragged along while his crew died around him. Not if I could help it.

"Don't worry, Mr. Spock," I continued as I circled my command chair and took the stairs to the second level in a single step. "We can isolate our guests in rec hall three until arrangements are made to drop them off with whatever allies they're willing to claim." The turbolift doors whisked aside for me, and I slipped inside with one hand on the sensor to hold them open as Spock caught up. "No one's going to get free run of the ship just because we're giving them a ride."

He stepped in neatly beside me, pivoting to face the front of the lift with a precision that seemed to be just a part of his movement, not something he planned. "Worry is a human emotion," he stated, as though correcting me on some particularly salient fact.

I stepped back from the doors and let them flash closed on us, taking up my own place on the opposite side of the turbolift. "Of course it is," I said, rather flatly. I kept my eyes trained on the deck indicator to avoid having to look at him. "How could I have forgotten?"

**Continued in
STAR TREK
The Captain's Table
Book One
War Dragons
by L. A. Graf**

Christopher Pike
by
Michael Jan Friedman

Christopher Pike grew up in the Mojave region on Earth, a part of North America that had been uninhabitable desert only two hundred years earlier. However, by the time of Pike's birth in the early part of the twenty-third century, the Mojave had been converted into a paradise of glittering cities and wide belts of lush, green parkland.

It was here that the young Pike learned to ride horses—particularly his beloved Tango—and to enjoy the wide-open spaces, passions which remained with him throughout his life. It was here as well that Pike first glimpsed the stars in the crisp night sky and knew he wanted to devote his life to their exploration.

Even before he took command of the *U.S.S. Enterprise,* in 2250, Pike was known throughout Starfleet as a bright, dedicated, and compassionate individual—prime command material. Never one to crack a joke, he took his duties and responsibilities as captain quite seriously.

According to his critics, he may have taken his responsibilities too seriously on occasion. For instance, when the *Enterprise* was involved in a violent conflict on Rigel VII and three crew members were killed, Pike blamed the incident on his own carelessness in not anticipating hostilities on the part of the Rigelians—even though his colleagues on the ship assured him there was nothing else he could have done.

In 2254, Pike and the *Enterprise* were en route to the Vega colony when they received a distress call from the *S.S. Columbia*—a spacegoing vessel that had disappeared near the Talos star group some eighteen years earlier. His investigation led to the discovery of the *Columbia*'s crash site on planet Talos IV and, subsequently, contact with the planet's indigenous inhabitants—a race of technically advanced humanoids.

The Talosians captured Pike and attempted to detain him with their ability to create realistic illusions. Their aim was to mate him with a human female in their possession in order to breed a line of captive humans. However, Pike managed to outwit the Talosians and win his freedom. His behavior convinced them that humans are unsuitable for captivity.

Nonetheless, the human female whom Pike encountered—Vina, the lone survivor of the *S.S. Columbia* crash—opted to remain with the Talosians. Apparently, she had been badly disfigured in the crash and had come to prefer illusion to reality.

Pike left Vina there, though he felt a strong emotional attachment to her. Soon after, Starfleet Command imposed General Order 7 on Talos IV, prohibiting Federation contact with that planet on pain of death.

Pike went on to conduct two complete five-year missions of exploration, the second ending in 2261. He relinquished command of the *Enterprise* to James Kirk in 2263, at which time Pike was promoted to fleet captain.

For three years, Pike proved a capable and creative administrator. Then, in 2266, he suffered severe radiation injuries in an attempt to save lives during an accident aboard a class-J training ship.

Wheelchair-bound as a result of delta-ray exposure, Pike found life difficult, to say the least. Always a very active individual, his disability drove him to the edge of despondence.

Finally, with the help of the Vulcan Spock, who had served on the *Enterprise* under Pike, the fleet captain managed to return to Talos IV despite General Order 7. Once there, he took the Talosians up on an offer they had made to him twelve years earlier—an offer to use their power of illusion to give him a life unfettered by his physical reality.

Though little is known of Pike's life after that, Starfleet chroniclers have speculated that he lived out his natural life in Vina's company, as happy and fulfilled as any human could be.

Though Pike himself left Starfleet, his accomplishments went on to inspire a great many of the fleet's finest officers. One of them was the aforementioned Spock of Vulcan, who later served under James Kirk, Pike's successor as captain of the *Enterprise*.

Pike City, a town on the Federation planet Cestus III, was named for the sometimes grim, always unpretentious, and yet stirringly adventuresome Captain Christopher Pike.

Look for STAR TREK Fiction from Pocket Books

Star Trek®: The Original Series

Star Trek: The Next Generation®

Star Trek: Deep Space Nine®

Star Trek®: Voyager™

Flashback • Diane Carey
Mosaic • Jeri Taylor
The Black Shore • Greg Cox

#1 *Caretaker* • L. A. Graf
#2 *The Escape* • Dean W. Smith & Kristine K. Rusch
#3 *Ragnarok* • Nathan Archer
#4 *Violations* • Susan Wright
#5 *Incident at Arbuk* • John Greggory Betancourt
#6 *The Murdered Sun* • Christie Golden
#7 *Ghost of a Chance* • Mark A. Garland & Charles G. McGraw
#8 *Cybersong* • S. N. Lewitt
#9 *Invasion #4: The Final Fury* • Dafydd ab Hugh
#10 *Bless the Beasts* • Karen Haber
#11 *The Garden* • Melissa Scott
#12 *Chrysalis* • David Niall Wilson
#13 *The Black Shore* • Greg Cox
#14 *Marooned* • Christie Golden
#15 *Echoes* • Dean W. Smith & Kristine K. Rusch
#16 *Seven of Nine* • Christie Golden

Star Trek®: New Frontier

#1 *House of Cards* • Peter David
#2 *Into the Void* • Peter David
#3 *The Two-Front War* • Peter David
#4 *End Game* • Peter David
#5 *Martyr* • Peter David
#6 *Fire on High* • Peter David

Star Trek®: Day of Honor

Book One: *Ancient Blood* • Diane Carey
Book Two: *Armageddon Sky* • L. A. Graf
Book Three: *Her Klingon Soul* • Michael Jan Friedman
Book Four: *Treaty's Law* • Dean W. Smith & Kristine K. Rusch

Star Trek®: The Captain's Table

1252.01